THE CHRISTIANIST

By Gregory Derasmo

CHAPTER ONE

I.

I feel that I must introduce myself even to you who knows every part of me. You who surely marks every pain and triumph of my life, and perhaps even wrote them long before I endured them, in some pious book at the top of a foreign tower.

Still, since we have never spoken before, I am the infamous bastard son of the late Emperor Septimius Severus, and half brother to the more recently late Emperor Lucius Severus Augustus.

You, of course, are the father of all, the creator of the mess, the king of the here and the beyond, and the wherever else you please.

In early memories, I prayed for the god Juno to kill other children who mocked my bastardhood. I prayed to Venus to put the girls I had fallen in love with into a deep sleep so I could do as I pleased with their bodies.

(Here I pause, my patient master, to remind myself that this prayer is also a confession. To that end I will omit no depravity or sin, of which you are undoubtedly already aware.)

As a boy I'd lay many sleepless nights, making demands of the idol gods in my head. I'd order the Venti down from the skies of Briton. With crushing winds they'd push the nasty rebels into the frigid northern seas, to turn blue and drown. This would swiftly end my father's campaigns there and return my beloved brother, Lucius.

To call these kiddy wishes prayers, would be vulgarity.

Later, in my teen years, when Lucius became Emperor, and every pleasure in Rome was mine, I thought certainly not of prayer. Not even as the vaguest of concepts. I was focused mainly in those days with pretty nubile flesh, and how to find my way up against it, and in between it. And that I could afford without divine assistance.

After my trip to Syria, and bloody conversion by dagger (oh, Lord, I know you were watching me on that day) and during my subsequent exile on the Spanish coast, I knew you were there, but still I did not pray to you. Not because of some fog of disbelief, quite the contrary, I was brimming with clarity of faith. Nor did I refrain because I lacked the words. I had many for you, indeed. And though I no longer had a tongue to speak, my mind was as eloquent as ever.

What kept me from calling on you for conference in these latter days, was my utter lack of worthiness. I do not claim worth now, far from it. Yet, with death short hours away, and the fallen Lucifer coming to collect his broken tool that is my cursed soul, I thought it was time you and I had a little chat.

My Lord, I feel the air from your sigh of discomfort. I feel you shifting in your armchair made of clouds. You are growing weary of introductions and formalities, and you'd like the story to begin.

II.

I owe my birth not to my mother, and not to the impostor who would come to call herself so, but to a soothsaying whore and the superstitious nature of the times.

As one never remembers their own birth, and certainly not the events surrounding it, this first story I will recount is one that was conveyed to me by another. I present it to you now, oh great judge of all, in the hopes that you would grace me with a thunderclap at every falsehood, so I may know which details of my origin are lies.

III.

When I was born my father was not yet wearing the purple, and had been assigned by the current Emperor, Commodus, the legions of Pannonia to oversee and discipline.

He brought with him his wife, Julia Domna, their toddling son, Lucius, a cohort of hand picked praetorian guards, and a cadre of maids, slaves, and whores. One of the more popular whores claimed herself a mystic and sometimes the recipient of visions of the future. It was one of these visions that would spare my life.

Or so says an imperial palace cook who was a member of my step mother's entourage on this eastern journey. Julia Domna was a fastidious eater, avoiding all meat, save for uniquely prepared small winged creatures, and was known to survive mainly on a diet of grapes. The fruit, and its fermented cousin. This left my step mother perpetually drunk, hungry, and in need of her most beloved palace cook, Calpurnia, who knew just how to spice and grill a quail to her mistress's desire.

Calpurnia was one of your heavier creatures, Lord. When she finally succumbed to her gluttony and died in bed one winter morning, it took six full bodied slaves to carry her to the public burial pit on esquiline hill. Two of these slaves complained for a whole week of neck and shoulder pain, and were heard to comment that Calpurnia's polenta was "never any good, anyhow". I disagreed, but I like watery polenta.

(I wonder, how do you prefer your morning polenta, dear god? Have you, like us, a stomach that needs filling at the dawn of each day?)

It was while mindlessly stirring one of her many cauldrons in her spacious kitchen that fat Calpurnia told me about my real mother and how I came to be the special type of bastard I was.

IV.

My bedroom was on the southern side of the palace, across the central courtyard from the royal suites. I slept alone in a comfortable loft above the kitchen and the more elite servant's quarters.

This was my step mother's idea, a maneuver to reinforce that I may have been my father's offspring, but I was not his son, and his family was not my family.

Some mornings the smell of frying pig fat and boiling polenta would wake me and I would join Calpurnia downstairs to watch her prepare the slaves breakfast. I was quiet as a young boy, and people took my shyness for intent listening, and would often spill private stories into my half caring ears.

Once, when I was twelve and on a hunting expedition with my father and brothers, a country plebeian who was paid to carry my quiver began to tell me of his sexual conquests. Innocent at first, just winks and innuendos, he eventually became comfortable with this shy little boy who seemed content to just listen approvingly and not say a word. Over the course of the hunt he would come to tell me, as if commenting on the weather, how he had stolen a pretty little girl off a barley farm a village over. She was half my age but with the same brown eyes and wavy black hair. He was keeping her shackled in his carpentry hut, "for fun and games" as he put it, but now his wife was returning from visiting her sickly mother and he would have to get rid of the girl. "Oh well", he looked to the brightening sky, "looks like the clouds are passing".

(I regret not marking this vile country pleb's name for you to smite, Lord. At the time my only thoughts were that this boring man had a big mouth, and none of his domestic scenario was any of my business. I now know how wrong I was, and that nameless abducted girl with my brown eyes has become yet another ghost to haunt my cluttered mind.)

Calpurnia had no great sins of her own to confess, but kept a thorough account of the ones belonging to those around her.

V.

Calpurnia would stir the polenta. She would know I was there, sitting on a foot stool behind her, but she would not turn, and would never say good morning.

"Be useful and fetch the cream." And I'd quietly hop off my stool and get her the fresh cream from a dim, cold corner. The servants, and some of the bolder slaves, treated me not as a master, but as a vermin. I was a special treat for them, really. I was a spoiled child of the imperial cloth, yet I was unprotected, exposed and vulnerable to their whims. Everyone in the palace knew that running afoul of the bastard boy would never mean reprisal from the house mistress, as it so viciously did for one of my brothers, who were her true sons.

Gardeners, tormented by my younger brother Geta's degrading teases, would like to trip me as I walked by, and curse at me, shaking an angry fist. "All the gold in Italy won't make you more than the clumsy bastard you are!"

I would cry, and run to my dear older brother Lucius, who would kiss my cheek and sometimes order his private guards to crush the servants hands or feet with boulders. Or if Lucius had ridden into the city, or was studying with a tutor, I would hide in the kitchen, on my stool, listening to Calpurnia, and waiting for some bits of crispy pork like a mutt.

3

"The motherly arms of Julia Domna are the downiest wings of luck a helpless bastard like you ever fell face first into." Calpurnia was fond of her mistress and of saying so.

I never understood why I was given the title bastard. I always wanted to scream that my father was alive, and had claimed me. I lived in my father's house, I ate his food. The world saw me as a bastard, because this was how Julia Domna saw me. On Earth, in Rome, to the pagans who know you not, oh my Lord, there are fewer gazes more influential than that of my step mother.

"Your mother watches out for you. Even knowing where you come from, still she watches. Her heart is too large, that's why. Julia Domna has endless compassion. You sacrifice a goat, Julia Domna will kill a dozen."

This was too tempting for the quiet six year old bastard who knew nothing of where he came from. I spoke up, "Where? Where do I come from?"

Calpurnia scoffed and spit into the thickening polenta, something she did with every batch, and said warded off rebellious spirits in the slaves.

"You came from the sand."

VI.

I sometimes trick myself into thinking I remember the telling of Calpurnia's story exactly as she told it that one and only time. This couldn't be true, as it has been fifteen years since I heard the story, and many details must have been lost. My constant examination of the remaining ones have undoubtedly left them altered. Much like a rider will never experience the true speed of his horse unencumbered by a man on its back, one can never remember something without the added weight of his own perceptions. Why, in your infinite wisdom dear Lord, did you not equip your creation with a perfect and unbiased memory? Seems rather a mistake if you ask me.

Regardless, I am convinced that some of her words, the ones that wounded me and would remain as scars, I remember exactly as Calpurnia spoke them:

"You are made of the sand from where you come from. In the east, where the sand is born, so too emerged your mother. A sand whore, was she."

My mother (Made of sand apparently. Wet sand? That would hold shape better than dry.) had been from either Syria, or farther east, perhaps Persia. Was she actually made of sand? I was six, and at the time I had to at least consider the possibility. Was I made of sand? It didn't seem likely. I had cut and scraped myself before, and I bled red like all the others, but what was deeper?

"She came with a horde of her kind. A mass of rosy cheeks on dirty faces, traveling north, pillaging the good Roman men of their seed."

I imagined my mother with her animal sisters, feral and covered in dusty orange sand, hair burnt from the sun, moving across the outer lands of the eastern territories. They'd arrive in Roman military encampments and entertain the men with exotic dances, only to steal their cocks once they were drunk on lust and in a trance. The sand whores would then flea to the woods, to fuck the stolen cocks, howling at the moon. And there was my mother among her pack. And Lord, forgive my mother her howls.

"The Emperor, noble defender and father of Rome though he is, had a weakness for this whore's wildness."

If you constructed men and women of things other than flesh and bone, dear creator, and had made my mother of sand, surely you molded my father of rich, steaming soil. When I dream of my now long dead father, he is always dressed in green robes, among Punic stone columns, overgrown with olive vines. He was as much a part of your nature, dear god, as your mountains and seas. And as looming as them, and as immovable. And Lord, forgive my father his pride.

"In Panonnia, with the lovely Julia Domna there by his side, still the dog took up with the sand temptress"

My father had many passionate affairs with women, both before and during his marriage to my step mother. She was his only wife though, and he depended on her for counsel in all things. It is, as it always has been, very out of the ordinary for nobleman's wives to accompany their husbands on military endeavors, yet Septimius refused to be without his Julia, and so never was. She had been raised by a Syrian tribal leader, who lost his fortune to debts and floods, but not his political acumen, which he passed on to his daughter. Julia could speak as well as any man on the peninsula about issues of government, law, history, and her favorite topic, gnostic astrology. My step mother appealed to many parts of my father's nature, yet not consistently enough to his most natural part, and so he drank down whores like gulps of water.

"Most whores have the decency to wash a man from her after he's left. Not your mother. No. She was a thief, and wanted to steal away a prince in her womb."

I liked this part best, dear god. I know you did as well, for in my ear you turned the sound coming from the fat cooks mouth into a softly romantic violin. So my mother had a scheme. She hatched a plot to seduce a powerful man. She wanted to create a baby that would one day be a prince, and in so doing insure her own future. Perhaps it was underhanded, conniving, and devious to an extreme degree, so what? It had worked, hadn't it? I survived. Here I was, oh my Lord, born healthy and living in the imperial palace, my mother's little prince.

"Your father's seed secured in her rotten pit, your mother stole off to the woods, so you could ripen inside her."

On evenings when my mind is clear, and I lay in a comfortable bed, in a warm room, in the home of people I trust not to murder me in my sleep, I feel a familiar type of calm. Drifting towards oblivion in these rare places, listening to nothing but the echo of a heartbeat, I always sense my true mother. Curled in blankets and the warmth of my own body, I am returned to a blink in time when my mother and I both lived in this world, together.

(I pray that my true mother is beside you now, Lord, or better yet, sitting upon your great knee. I pray that she overhears me. If she be in heaven and her cursed son doomed for hell, and we are to never meet again, I want her to know that I worship the days I spent within her and that the heartbeat I hear at night comes not from my own chest, but from her's.)

"Came the day, swollen and waddling, your sand whore mother reemerged, demanding gold and declaring her unborn son no less than the king of Rome. The gracious and merciful Lord Severus took the poor wretch in and prepared her a tiny villa, out of pity."

I await your thunderclap, my Lord...

It comes not. Yet I sense, looking up at the sky through the open window of my small room, where I am now kneeling and have been throughout my prayer, that your unease with this last remembered bit is brewing the wind. I hear the trees rustle and bend. The sky is dark and moonless. Perhaps because it is hidden behind looming storm clouds? Do you wish to herald a lie where I myself have heard the whispers of one for so long?

The logic of this last bend in Calpurnia's story seemed sound enough to me upon hearing it, yet grew impossible to my thinking mind as it aged and came to know the world and its workings. Had my mother, who very likely was a prostitute from the east, gotten herself pregnant by Septimius Severus, and arrived at his door one morning, about to give birth, she'd have been met with the bottom of the doorman's sandal on her ass. Indeed, there were and would be many other whores and many other bastard sons and daughters belonging to the great Septimius Severus, and none of them were ever afforded as much as a second glance from the Emperor, let alone a villa, no matter how tiny. I realized that for him to have even been aware of my existence, my father would have had to think something unique of my true mother.

I don't imagine he ever intended on disposing of his Julia Domna to marry the girl, but perhaps my mother came to Severus with the news of my inception, perhaps she offered to kill her child, perhaps even kill herself, if it would please and honor the man she had become so fond of. Perhaps my father, feeling something for her as well, and not being able to completely forsake the poor girl, ordered her to keep her child, and channel the devotion she felt towards him into raising their boy on her own. The boy would be her consolation for being deprived the simple joy of marriage. She would see the father's face in the boy's as she coddled him to her breast on cold nights, and the boy would be the benefactor of the mother's untapped excesses of love.

Of course, and by your will, this was not to be. Bitter plans you have, oh my Lord. Bitter plans.

"The wise Julia Domna saw how her husband had become bewitched by your sand mother. She read the stars, and they spoke to my mistress, demanding the whore's throat cut opened and her belly emptied of any coming demons."

Suddenly, Calpurnia turned from her cauldron to look at me for the only time during the telling. She pulled the heavy wooden stirring stick out of the polenta and aimed it across the kitchen at me. It was dripping with hot mush.

"You, my little royal bastard, were as good as dead before you ever saw the sun."

I shivered and broke our gaze. She returned to her cauldron. The slaves would enjoy their breakfast this morning, for in order to extend time enough to finish her tale, Calpurnia had been stirring far longer than usual, and the polenta was growing thick.

Calpurnia's story now turned into less of a yarn about a bastard's origin and more a kind of gossiping. There was another whore, not my mother, who the fat cook claimed was my true savior.

"Lycoria the whore laid down with every man I ever cared for a day in my life. That yellow toga wearing bitch had them all, and me never a one. But here I am, still alive, and her, a headless skeleton."

Lycoria put her head on the chopping block for my sake and had it lobbed off. She was a sinner of such great fame, oh my Lord, that I doubt you did not know her. You are very likely to have been drawn in solemn judgment to her celebrated stage show, in which she did no more than sit on stacked pillows, bare bosomed, making predictions for the coming harvest while pinching her nipples. Her production costs were decidedly low, and profits high. Eventually word of Lycoria's voluptuousness, and vaguely accurate warnings, came to the attention of the powerful men of the city, and soon Senators and Generals were paying high prices for personal visits and spiritual readings from the part mystic, part whore. As her popularity in bedrooms grew, so did the credibility of her visions among the upper echelons of imperial society. Even the great star reader Julia Domna was seen as an amateur when compared to this soothsaying meretrice. My father must have paid a fortune to bring Lycoria along with him to Pannonia as one of his concubina.

"The felonious Lycoria made a big scene at the mistress's dressing one morning. Screaming and carrying on in front of the entire court about dreams of peacocks and pomegranates, hurling herself on the floor and claiming possession by the goddess Juno. Lycoria had, of course, been paid by your whore mother."

And how did my whore mother pay for such a performance? With sand? Certainly not. This must have been the desperate act of my father, who was attempting to dowse the fire of his wife's blood thirsty vision, with a more peaceful divination of his own. Lycoria told all who would listen that Julia Domna's interpretation of the divine message was wrong. There was a dark power with this child, yes, but killing the thing would do nothing but loose its chaos on the world. Juno had demanded my mother's pregnancy be carried to full term. With the child's life went the fate of Rome itself. Extinguish the light in this woman's womb and extinguish the torches of Rome, unleashing the darkness.

(May I not, oh my Lord, look upon this brave Lycoria, and for the same matter my own mother, with pride and fidelity? Though both may have been sinners for profit, do I not owe to these women my every breath? Perhaps for this reason, I should curse them. Yet, did not your own son, oh my everlasting master, know a whore well enough to count her among his favorite disciples?)

"But no whore is cleverer than my mistress. A devious husband, trying to spare his lover, pays a soothsayer to conjure an omen of protection over her filled womb. Fine. Julia Domna is a patient woman, and her vengeance will wait for its emptying."

Why, Lord? Why such abandonment? If my father had cared enough to acknowledge my true mother's pregnancy, take her in as his responsibility, enlist the service of an overpriced oracle to save her from his wife's clutches, why at the last moment did he leave her unguarded? Abandoned to have her son stolen from her and to be drowned by the callused hands of house slaves.

The best midwives in Pannonia at the time would have been the ones traveling with my step mother's entourage to care for young Lucius. Perhaps my father underestimated the degree to which his servants gave their loyalty to his wife over him. Julia would be informed immediately upon the severing of the cord. She would rush into the room and take charge of the prophesied child, leaving my dazed mother with the well compensated slaves to be wrapped up along with her afterbirth in a sheet, and delivered to the chilly banks of the Danube.

"Not long after this mess, Commodus was dead and your father was Emperor. We were assembled and on the road back to Rome when the concubinas realized their yellow queen was not among them. A scout was sent back to the camp to investigate. He knew the corpse he found laying in her bed was Lycoria from the size of her famous tits, and nothing more, for she was headless."

I see my step mother, oh my Lord, mad eyed and grinning, standing in the open threshold of Lycoria's hut. Lycoria, seeing Julia Domna, seeing the madness, seeing the gladius blade at her side. Did she pass instantly from this world, oh my Lord? Or did she linger, however briefly, in that way, separated from herself, sensing nothing but a cataclysmic numbness. My step mother, though determined, was never a physically powerful woman, and it would have taken her several thrusts to complete the job. I pray that Lycoria's pain in dying was pennants enough to spare her soul its continuation in the pits of hell.

Calpurnia giggled and gurgled and crouched down below her cauldron, picking up a small iron rod to stoke the flames. Fearing that her story was finished I spoke up.

"And the prophecy? Is it true?"

"The one about you?"

"Yes."

"Bastard's always make me laugh. Of course not, you little fool. Have grand dreams of yourself, have you?"

"No. It's just... why didn't she drown me in the river? Or cut off my head?"

Calpurnia shrugged like it didn't matter, or she didn't know. "A wife needs to keep certain signs around, for the sake of her husband. Remind him daily of what he's burdened the fabric of his family with, and what sacrifices his goodly wife has made to keep the seams mended."

So there and finally, dear god, was my purpose. I was a signal to my father that he should walk the line of temperance and discretion. I was the wall that surrounded my father's heart and kept it insulated and unexpressed. Better not fall too hard for a pretty young lady, great and powerful Emperor Septimius Severus, for look at the remainder of your last folly: a sand whore with lungs full of water, a pair of rotting breasts minus the head above them, and a frail bastard boy who is a black eye of shame on your clan and good name.

Calpurnia reached into a cabinet and took out a stack of tin cups for the slave's breakfast. She clanged them out one by one on the long table between us, and began to ladle each cup full of thick polenta. It fell in heavy steaming balls from her spoon, splashing into the tin with a wet whacking sound. I could see chunks of walnuts that had not quite dissolved into the creamier barley meal. Once the cauldron was empty, Calpurnia took what was left of the cream and distributed it evenly among the now filled tin cups, forming a small white reservoir above the polenta. She then lifted a cloth from over a large chunk of parmesan sitting on the table, and shaved off a thin piece for each cup. The cheese melted quickly and the smell, oh my Lord, was rich and wonderful. I stood with my nose up against the edge of the table, staring at the cups of delicious breakfast. I smacked my lips. Surely this was the most perfect looking polenta I would ever see in my entire life.

Calpurnia quickly counted the number of tins she had prepared.

"Not enough. You can't have any."

VII.

Sleeplessness can unearth such evil thinking, oh my Lord and savior, and on restless nights in my childhood, alone in my secluded loft, I sometimes fantasized about killing my family.

The doors to the imperial suites were commonly left unbolted, and the guards would never suspect a little boy. In the dark they might even mistake me for one of my brothers, who unlike me, were allowed open access to their parent's bed chamber.

With a knife stolen from the kitchen I would creep into my brother's bedrooms and cut their throats, my hand gripping their mouths to muffle their screams. One and then the other, first the younger, Geta, then the elder, Lucius. I would pause over Lucius's dead body and I would kiss his cheeks and make sure his eyelids were shut. I would clean him of his blood, and dress him in his whitest tunic.

Even in my fantasy I feared getting too close to my father, so to kill him I would steal a speared javelin from the palace armory, and slay the Emperor at a safe distance. Once he was dead, I would procure his favorite golden gladius from where he kept it beneath his pillow, unsheathe it, and cut off the vile head of Julia Domna.

I would appear before the Senate the following morning, a boy drenched in his brother's blood, his father's sword at his waist, his step mother's head flung by its hair over his shoulder. I would demand a loyalty oath from every Senator and Nobleman in the country. The penalty for refusal would be swift death by beheading. They would have no choice but to obey my every command, for the entire imperial family was dead, and I was the only one left in Rome with royal blood in his veins. I would be king. The bastard king. Rex Severus Bastardus.

CHAPTER TWO

I.

I did not learn to read Greek until late in the grammaticus of my education, so was deprived of many of the greatest written works of man until my eleventh year. My older brother, Lucius, who had received a far more privileged schooling, and was reading Plato from age six, allowed me his old texts to peruse and study whenever I pleased. He had been leant many great old books from his tutor, the wise Erasmus Grigio, and would spend hours transcribing his favorites. He had accumulated a great collection in this way, and Lucius's suite was filled with dried out wash buckets stuffed with rolled up scrolls of papyrus.

(Oh, god, how I long, even still and more than anything, to be back there in that room. Lucius and I reading beside one another, laying with our bellies and elbows flat on the cool floor, our chins cupped in our hands, the knowledge of the ancient world laid out before us. If I were to deserve heaven, oh noble redeemer, surely it would resemble this vision.)

At fourteen, and three years my senior, Lucius was, like most boys his age, fondest of the Greek philosophers. Unlike his fellows, though, not of the popular Socrates, whom Lucius decried as a worshiper of virtue, a characteristic he did not see in himself nor the world. He was attracted more to the thinking of the ultra-hedonist Aristippus of Cyrene, who was a student of Socrates, but was rebellious and preached that the only true virtue was the ruthless pursuit of pleasure.

In my years of villainy and foolishness, oh my Lord, I found Lucius's lack of moral sentiment to be a stoic value, allowing him to clearer choose from the world what he wished to take from it. Next to my timid desires to win over people who I was sure hated me, his disdain for all things that did not please him, seemed the height of enlightenment. He was untangled, unburdened, free to explore his inner self and to be unashamed of whatever he might discover. From boyhood Lucius talked boldly of his basic trust of pleasure as a guiding principle in all things, and as you would see alongside me, oh my Lord and constant companion, these were not just words, but the formulation of plans. Plans Lucius had for how to live as a man, and eventually how to rule as a Caesar.

My understanding of Greek being fresh, the language of the philosophers was far too exquisite for my understanding, and seemed like logic averting nonsense. I later found that with my Greek skills greatly improved this opinion wouldn't change much. I was always more interested in the less poetic, more action packed, histories of war.

Thucydides's account of the Peloponnesian war was one of my favorites, and I read his description of the battle of Delium so many times as to commit parts of it to memory. A particularly juicy section detailed fratricide among Athenian hoplites. After a successful charge, the Athenians were circling the remaining contingent of their Thespian enemies, surrounding them on all sides. As the bloodbath ensued, crazed Athenians butchered their way to the center of the Thespian ranks, where they met and killed their fellow countrymen who had been slaughtering in from the other side. How embarrassing. The idea of this comic mess of blood, guts, thrusting spears, and wild confusion, delighted me to no end, oh my Lord. I think even you must see the humor in such tragic idiocy, otherwise why allow it? What is the violent farce of the battlefield if not a spectacle for your diversion?

I was reading Thucydides in Lucius's room on the night my father told me the tale of the rat in the eagle's nest.

II.

"Do you know what happened to the rat in the eagle's nest?" Asked my father.

"It was eaten?" I guessed.

III.

So lost was I in a technical description of a Boeotion military flame throwing machine, that I could almost smell burning flesh when my father's voice arrived to interrupt my study.

"Geta! Geta! Publius Geta Septimius! Where is my son?!"

The Emperor was drunk. I could hear his burping and labored breathing as he stumbled his way up the main staircase to Geta's chamber door, which was across a small threshold from Lucius's.

It was a full moon, and as was the routine, Lucius and Geta had gone with their mother to the river to receive evening colonics with freshly cut reeds. I was never jealous of being excluded from this family cleansing ritual, which Julia Domna said was essential to the health of growing boys.

My father was supposed to be in the city, meeting with Senators, and then dining with the family of his loyal prefect and consul, Fulvius. I thought I had an empty home all to myself, oh my Lord, and was distraught to suddenly be joined by the most powerful being my young presence had yet known.

"Where are you, boy?!" I heard my father stomp around Geta's bedroom, turning over his bed sheets, knocking over a chair, not finding him. He returned to the hallway that joined the brother's bedchambers, and was now heading for Lucius's door, and for me.

"Lucius! Bassianus Lucius Septimius! Are you here, boy?!"

I had but a moment to act. Soon the Emperor would be before me, I would have to speak, I would have to meet his gaze, and answer his questions, and all my body would want to do would either be to run or utterly collapse.

The white moon shined brightly through the window, but still the room was dark and I had been reading by candlelight. I could blow out the candle now, and rush across the room to the side of Lucius's bed hidden from the doorway. My father was drunk, and already having thoroughly checked Geta's empty bedroom, he would assume the brothers were out together, and would not search this room nearly as vigorously. He'd retire to his own bedchamber, pipe, and another flask of wine or two. He'd be dead asleep in no time, with hours still before the rest of the family returned. I'd sneak to the torch in the hall, relight my candle, and read some more before fleeing to my loft for the night.

I did not extinguish the flame. I decided I would stay still and in plain sight and defer all judgment to my father. To make any attempt to hide from this all seeing, all knowing creature was pointless. He would hear me breathing. He would smell me. Could he read my thoughts? It was possible. If he were to enter the room, see his bastard laying on his son's floor, reading his son's scrolls, and was raised by anger to beat me bloody with his bare fists, that would be alright by me. He would find my body as limp as a newborn calf, accepting his kicks and punches with soft gratitude. My life then was his prerogative, as now it is yours, oh my Lord, to be given when called for.

There was also the chance that instead of a beating, he would greet me with fig cakes and apricot leather he had brought back with him from the city. I had seen him surprise my brothers in this way before, with a new kite, or hobby horse, or once a pair of matching latrunculi boards, with playing pieces made of carved bone and ivory.

My father came calling for Geta, his strong little soldier, and not finding him, called for Lucius, his cunning little politician, but the boy he'd finally discover would be me, his uncertain little bastard. And perhaps, oh my Lord, I stayed to find out if I would suffice.

IV.

My father entered the room and saw me.

There he was, and there I was, and there we were, oh my Lord. It had been several years since we were alone together, the last time was when we were both terribly ill with the same fever from an unknown origin. Julia Domna took the boys into the country until we got better, and for ten days I had every meal at my father's table, just the two of us.

We were both sick with aches and waves of deep heat, and would distract one another with stories. My stories were always a retelling of Roman military defeats I had read about, but with new reversed outcomes. At the crucial moment the clouds would open and the god Mars would come down with his mighty spear to disembowel Rome's enemies and rescue her doomed patriots. My father liked these stories very much. His were always absurd trifles that would have me in a fit of laughter that would lead to long painful coughing. A sparrow who lived in the palace was stealing Calpurnia's hard biscuits leaving feces behind, or bundles of dead worms. Calpurnia would never notice the bird had tricked her until it was too late, and the story always ended with Calpurnia getting a mouth full of shit. Calpurnia would enter the room at the climax of one of my father's stories, to clear our plates, and we would become quiet and stiff as could be, only to burst out laughing when Calpurnia would inevitably ask, "How'd it taste?"

"You tell us, dear Calpurnia." And my father would wink at me, and I would laugh so hard that I thought I might die. Whatever he was, or I was, or what misery we would come to accomplish together, there was a father and a son enjoying each other, and I swear to you my dear god, it was blessed.

After doing its worst, the mysterious sickness packed up in the middle of the night and departed our bodies. At breakfast the servants were all remarking on what a miracle it was that we had both regained our health on the very same morning. The Emperor smiled at me, and said, "Is he not his father's son?"

Julia Domna returned the day after with her sons, sunburned and complaining of the sweltering country heat. When my father informed his wife of our simultaneous recovery, she said she was not surprised, since I was likely the cause of the sickness in the first place.

The fever made the ten days with my father seem all the more dreamlike. Looking back on it now, only god knows if it really happened.

Well? Did it?

V.

And so, my Lord, there we were, in my brother's room, on a moonlit night. My father and I, together again, alone.

We remained in awkward silence for a moment, my father dumbed by his wine, and me by his very presence. Big, bearded, tree trunks for limbs, his heart seemed to shine golden light through his eyes. He stood over me, his hands curled in hammer fists pressed against each hip, and he was panting. I still lay on my belly, looking up at him from the floor, like dust, like a bug, like, oh keeper of my truest nature, the rat that I am.

I could smell the wine on his breath, but more pungent was the smell of his sweat, which was flowing from every pour, pooling at his armpits, chest, and belly, and yellowing his white tunic. The tunic, oh my Lord, with the green silk sewn into the sleeves that he wore when visiting noblemen for conference or casual suppers. I had seen him drunk and soaked like this before, but there was a spirit of panic to his sweating this night, and his activated, unblinking eyes, verified to my young mind that the Emperor was in the midst of some form of controlled frenzy.

Whatever I thought I saw in my father's eyes, when he spoke his voice rose from deep within him, and emerged with an eerie calm. "Where are your brothers?"

I sat up on my butt, and crossed my legs. "It's a full moon. They've gone with mother to the river for cleansing."

"I suppose you're pleased to have been left out. No worse way to welcome a full moon than a reed up your arse."

I giggled loudly, his friendly nature caught me off guard. Perhaps it hadn't been a fever dream after all? He wiped his dripping forehead with his damp, hairy forearm, drying neither. Then he knelt before me, the historical volume between us. He bent his head oddly so he could see from upside down what it was I had been reading. I saw an opportunity to please him, and gently rotated the unfurled scroll around so that he could get a proper look. He untwisted his neck and said, "Thucydides. Wonderful stories the old man spews, hmm?"

13

"The battle descriptions are the best I've ever read."

"Me too. And I should know. I've seen battle close, and from within its thickets. Thucydide's understands chaos, and a man who understands chaos, understands battle."

I solemnly nodded as though the wisdom I was receiving was from your own divine mouth, dear god.

"Your brother Lucius doesn't care much for stories of swords crossing shields, and cutting bone, does he? More of a thinker, that one."

"Yes" I answered. "Lucius prefers philosophy."

"Prefers the side of the Greek that could care less about war. The side that wants to lay on his fat arse, scribbling nonsense all day, and getting molested by his pedagogue all night."

I had no answer for this and so offered none.

"And your younger brother, Geta, all he cares for is riding his horse, and practicing his swordplay with my praetorians."

"Yes" I answered. "Geta will make a fine soldier."

"But not a thinker. And a Caesar must be both."

I again had no answer.

The Emperor suddenly stood, and instructed me to do the same. "Let me have a look at you."

I stood before him, filled my lungs with air to puff up my chest, straightened my spine to appear as tall as possible, and curved my shoulder blades forward to give the illusion of muscle mass. I must have looked ridiculous. As my designer, you must, oh my Lord, remember my peculiar physicality at age eleven. I was short, with a plump, round head and belly to match, but my arms and legs were so skinny that I looked something like a ripe pear with four sewing needles sticking out of it.

My father took in my body with kind forgiveness. "You're young yet, still time to grow." And he patted my head, and then my cheek. I thought my skinny legs might give out beneath me.

The Emperor cleared his throat, balled his hands back into fists, and returned them to his hips. He spoke with authority, "Something has happened. An occurrence. An imperial matter that needs attention. I brought this matter to my heirs so that in their dealing with it, they might prove their mettle. Or not prove it, as it were. Finding them gone, I believe we shall put you to the test. Discover what hidden value you may contain. Or may not contain, as it were. What say you, boy?"

I wanted to throw my arms around him, hug him tightly, and tell him that I would do whatever was needed, accomplish any task set before me, if only he would hug me back.

I didn't move, I simply asked my father, "What would you like me to do?"

"Good. Follow me to the stables."

VI.

The first man I ever murdered, I did so with my bare hands. Or bare armpit, to be precise. I'm sure you remember the scene well. Nonetheless, I am compelled to confess it to you, my judge and expiator, in all of its detail, so I may perhaps finally be rid of its miserable embedment within my heart.

VII.

My father led me up the southern hill of the estate and into the dark palace stables, guiding us by torch light. At first all I could see was my father and the hay beneath his feet. Eventually the main section of the stable revealed itself, lit by hanging oil lanterns, and I could see the rows of horses.

The horses had never been as silent as they were that night. Not a kick, not a whinny. In fact, all I ever saw of them through the entire event was their back sides, tails swatting at flies, giving coy flashes of their assholes as they did. No matter what noises I would make or cause others to make, the horses remained turned away, their heads stuck through the back stable windows. I never checked to see what it was they were fixated on, but what could it have been if not your glorious full circle moon?

(Were these animals aware, oh my Lord, of what was about to occur in their stable? Did they turn their backs before I even entered so as not to witness my contemptible display?)

Among the horses were men. Six of them. Posted at the four entrances of the main stable were fully armored praetorian guards, standing at ease. They saw my father, and their postures stiffened, grips on spears tightened. My father handed off his torch to one of the guards, who doused it in a nearby water trough.

At the center of the barn was a pitiful looking young man, maybe five years older than me, with blonde hair, blue eyes, and a long flimsy neck. This neck immediately reminded me of a goose's. His thin arms and legs were shackled with irons behind his back, and he lay in the dirt, naked but for his loincloth, beaten and bloodied. His chest and belly were covered with fresh bruises. Bits of straw were sticking to the gore that was oozing from a gash above his eye where the flesh had split. His nose was so broken that you could hear the bones rattle as he suffered to breath.

The sixth man was my father's cousin, and most trusted advisor, Gaius Fulvius. At this point in his career, Fulvius was Prefect Commander of the Praetorian Guard, and viewed as a stabilizing force in my father's sometimes chaotic leadership. He was the only man in Rome who had the Emperor's ear as consistently as the scheming Julia Domna, who, for this reason, was scornfully distrustful of Fulvius. Despite my step mother's protests, my father honored Fulvius as no less than a brother, even having coins minted with his image. I did not know Fulvius well enough yet to have formed any of my own opinions of his character, but my step mother's venomous hatred of him spoke to me of his likely virtue.

15

Fulvius was reclining on a bail of hay, crunching and munching on a red apple, short fat legs crossed over one another, his small sandaled foot bobbing in the air. He always looked to me like a prematurely birthed version of Septimius, an underdeveloped half-man, my father being the completed project.

Fulvius noticed our arrival and sat up, tossing the apple core to the horses, who ignored it completely.

"Returned to the festivities, have you? Not enough revelry for one night?" Fulvius reached behind the hay bail he was sitting on and lifted a clay flask. "Or have you just grown weary of drinking your own wine?" He stood and walked towards my father with a wide conspiratorial grin that my father returned. They traded swigs of wine, and then the flask was offered to me. I drank greedily, and burped.

Fulvius laughed. "Not the pup I was expecting when you said you were off to retrieve your son."

"They're at the river with their mother. This one'll prove my point as well as the others, perhaps more mightily so."

"We'll see." And they drank some more, and this time I wasn't offered any.

While Fulvius and my father finished off the flask, joking with each other as they did, I turned my attention back to the captured young man with the pulverized face, and the neck of a goose. I noticed for the first time, what you had probably noticed since we entered the stable, oh my Lord. The pathetic gooseneck was staring at me. Not at my father, not at Fulvius, not at the guards. It had been them who had put him in this predicament, and they were the ones he had reason to fear, yet he felt I was the one worthy of his gaze. His eyeballs narrowed at mine through their bruised and swollen sockets.

(Did the gooseneck know what our destiny was? Did he know what you, in your everlasting and unknowable wisdom, had planned for the two of us in that stable? Did he stare because he knew I would be the one to murder him? Or did he stare because he saw a boy. Another boy, like him, skinny and weak. One of his own to show him compassion and mercy. Did he see me as his chance at survival, oh my Lord? Did he see me as his savior?)

"Has he spoken any more drivel?" My father asked this as we approached our prisoner.

"Not a word." Answered Fulvius. "He's too afraid to speak unless spoken too, and I haven't engaged him in any banter, I can assure you."

"Fine."

The gooseneck continued to stare. His lips quivered as if he wanted to say something, but god forgive me, I sneered, and looked away from him in disgust.

"Listen up, boy." My father was talking to me. "This very night, not an hour ago, I escaped an assassination attempt."

VIII.

The Emperor aimed a thick finger down at the gooseneck. "This pathetic wretch is the only surviving conspirator."

The gooseneck's father had been the head of a monotheistic cult. Not the correct monotheistic cult, oh one true god, but they at least had a scent of the right idea. The central commandment of their single god, who lived behind the sun apparently, was the ennoblement of every warm-blooded creature, down to the rats. To this end the members of this small cult did not feast on animal flesh, only fruits and vegetables, and they viewed the Emperor's monthly demands of animal sacrifice to be an assault on their very relationship with god.

The obligatory animal sacrifices at every full moon was my father's ingenious way of rooting out just this type of one-god behavior, which he saw as a poison to the Imperial Republic.

"Dangerous folk, these one-god plebeians, dangerous folk. Not because their god is to be feared, naturally, or even exists for that matter. It does not, because no gods exist."

I had heard the idea before. My beloved brother Lucius was, as a matter of integrity, a vocal atheist. He often talked of the poet Lucretius, who wrote of the gods as no more than tools of politicians to control the masses, but I didn't know Lucius was talking about our father. Did he?

Fulvius sighed, like a party had just abruptly ended, and he turned away from my father's solemn talk, to go retrieve another apple from the stable pantry. I couldn't tell then, and am not sure now, whether Fulvius turned because he disapproved of my father speaking in such a way to a child, or because he disagreed with his sentiment.

To make sure I marked well where he stood on the issue, my father repeated himself, "No gods exist. Not theirs, and not ours. We are our minds and our hands and what we can do with them in this world, do you understand?"

I looked down at my hands, with their weak little sausage fingers. I couldn't do much with these. "Yes." I said.

"The many-god plebeian is of no threat to us. They think divinity can be shared, you see. A little god here, a little god there. From the many-god plebeian an Emperor can depend on a degree of worship."

My father further explained how municipal soldiers had been making their rounds, collecting from the plebs their goats, lambs, and chickens to be sacrificed to the gods for the health of Emperor Septimius Severus and his family. When they arrived at the home of the cult leader and his sons, they were met with an ambush of stones from rooftops, and axes thrown from open windows. The unprepared soldiers were hacked to pieces, and their captured animals released to freedom. No doubt they were quickly recollected by the plebs who had given them up in the first place, some beginning the day down one chicken, and ending it up three goats.

The rabble of sun worshiping fanatics then took their axes on a march to the Senate. They planned to meet and kill The Emperor as he traveled through the forum to dine at the apartment of Fulvius. The cult members were outnumbered and out skilled by a terrific margin, and my father's praetorian guards made short work of them, taking not a single injury upon themselves. The fanatics were left as bloody streamers of flesh, scattered about the thoroughfare, as if a parade had passed.

The gooseneck was the only one who survived the onslaught because he was the most cowardly among the cult members and so stayed in the rear during the fighting. When his last comrade fell, he threw himself on his knees, his arms to the sky, and begged mercy. My father ordered the gooseneck be taken as prisoner, and after a short beating and interrogation, he revealed that the plot was never expected to be a success. It was designed to show Rome what a true sacrifice looked like. The cult elders had a vision of the gory affair that ended with The Emperor's white tunic being drenched in their own red blood. The only thing he was drenched in was his own sweat.

The Emperor sucked snot out of his nostrils and into his mouth and then spit at the gooseneck's face. Despite the thick spittle now across his right eyelid, he did not, oh my Lord, cease his staring at me.

IX.

"So we come to it. Here is this pathetic assassin. He is our captive, ours to do with as we please. Yours to do with as you please."

I looked up at my father. "Mine?"

Fulvius rejoined our conversation amidst slobbering bites of his new apple. "There's been a bit of a wager, my boy."

"No need for that." My father shot a look at Fulvius that seemed to hush him.

I was tipsy from the gulp of wine and all the excitement and I spoke up without fear. "What wager? Tell me."

"Fine. You shall have the whole truth, and then you shall decide."

The gooseneck, perhaps inspired by my own will to speak freely, chose this moment to speak the only word I would ever hear him utter. Soft and pleading, "Mercy."

Fulvius reached back with his half-eaten apple and then brought it crashing forward, smashing it against the goosenecks right ear. The apple exploded into pulp, flying into the barnyard air with a mist of juice. "Shut your filthy mouth!"

The gooseneck fell onto his side, rubbing his now likely deaf ear against his bony shoulder, and whimpering in pain.

(Mercy, oh my Lord. The poor whimpering boy wanted mercy. And here I am, on my knees this night, begging you for the very thing I have so often refused to others. Mercy, oh my Lord.)

"As I was saying," my father continued, "he is yours to do with as you please. I brought him here so that one of my sons could play at Caesar. The wager that was mentioned had to do with a disagreement between the noble Fulvius and I."

Fulvius and my father nodded at one another, regally.

"My dear Fulvius asked me, in a rather rhetorical manner, what was to be done with this surviving assassin? Should he be put to death on the spot? Was there value in putting the young man on trial? Punish him with a life of slave labor, so that he may live as an example to others like him? Shall the boy be flogged to death in public? Could there be another way? The Emperor can do as he pleases, why not use his saintly powers of forgiveness?"

Fulvius scoffed at this, my father winked at him.

"I answered Fulvius, that in this situation, even a child would know what needed to be done."

Fulvius concluded the story, "To which I replied, would you like to bet on that, your majesty?"

The two cousins laughed. The guards, who were audience to this morbid theater, laughed. The horses remained stoic.

"So, you've heard all the options, they are all at your disposal. You can save this man. Give the order and we'll have Calpurnia fill him with polenta, get him a good night sleep in one of your brother's beds, and in the morning, send him home to his mother and sisters."

I looked down at poor gooseneck. He heard this option and his eyes widened at mine. This was it, he knew it. There was one soul in that stable who gooseneck thought would be inclined to save him and that soul was just given the power to do so. I'm going home, he thought, I'm going home.

"Or, give the order and we'll have the guards decapitate him, burn his body on the hillside, and put the head on a pike to be displayed at the forum magnum."

Ever so slowly, so as not to be whacked with another piece of fruit, the gooseneck got up onto his butt, and then his knees. Looking at him there, on the floor, his scratched legs as skinny as my own, I thought of my earlier self, sitting in Lucius's room, reading, in peace. Now, here I was, not a half hour later, the Emperor of Rome for one moonlit night.

"The decision is yours. I will not judge it, simply carry it out as ordered. Act as your mind and hands would guide you." And with that my father took a distinct step backwards, and Fulvius followed in suit. Though they were just feet behind us, I suddenly felt completely alone with the gooseneck, who was now upright on his knees, praying to me with his eyes.

X.

Our eyes locked, the gooseneck's and mine.

The stable was silent, the horses were silent. I shifted my weight, from one foot to the other, and then back again. I never looked away from his eyes, oh my Lord, as if I was searching in them for a sign. Was there a soul in there? Was there any way to be sure? Were they just glass orbs in red meat? There were no gods. My father just said there were not. We were minds and hands. We were actions. We were spiritless.

While my mind was contemplating these cold variants, the gooseneck did something that would engage my hands, and end his time on this earth. He smiled. He smiled at me. A little smile. A kind smile. A smile that read: I needn't worry, this would all turn out fine for me. Wouldn't it?

No. It wouldn't.

The gooseneck smiled and I smacked him across his face with my open palm.

It stung him, and he lost his stupid smile. He reeled back to look at me again, my fat little paw left a red print across his cheek.

I took a half step back onto my right foot and then with as much force as I could muster, lifted my right knee up into the air beneath the gooseneck's chin. I cracked him good with my kneecap, and his whole head whipped backwards, his body toppling onto the floor behind it.

The gooseneck was spitting shattered bits of teeth out of his mouth when I knelt down on the ground behind him.

Fulvius stepped forward urgently to retrieve me, but my father put a firm hand on his chest to stop him.

I continued my work. The gooseneck could not use his bound arms or legs, and was easy prey, but for a first timer like me, it was a terrible exertion killing this young man.

I knew my hands would never be powerful enough for the job, so I rapidly searched my body for a stronger joint. Where could I clamp this twig of a neck where it was most likely to snap? Some inner instinct lead me to quickly settle on my under arm.

I picked up the young man's long head from behind him and reclined it against my chest. I hugged his neck with my left arm, tightening my shoulder as hard as I could, while simultaneously pulling my left elbow with my right arm. I could feel his gullet gripped at the very center of my arm pit. I felt him struggling to breath, I closed my arm tighter, and then I felt his breathing become stuck. His body began to shake. He tried to kick his shackled feet out from under him, he tried to punch me with his shackled hands, but his frantic movements only made him more desperate for air, and he accomplished nothing by them.

I tugged on my left arm as hard as I could, and though I nearly dislocated my shoulder, and it would be sore for weeks, I heard exactly the sound I wanted. The decisive pop of his windpipe caving in. I could have released him then and he would have still been a goner, but I held him anyway, and waited for him to die in my arms. After a few hopeless spasms, he did.

My heart was beating thunderously, but slowly, steadily. I unhooked my numb left arm from around the gooseneck's throat, and pushed the sack of dead bones off me. His eyes remained open, dear god, but he was no longer staring at me, nor at any object of his own choosing.

I looked up at my father. His mouth was wide open in shocked amusement. The same could be said for the praetorian guards, oh my Lord, who looked inclined to applause.

Fulvius broke the dead silence of the stable. "I owe you ten denarii, your majesty."

"Pay it to the boy." Said my father. "He just earned it."

They all laughed. I did not laugh. The dead boy with the neck of a goose did not laugh. The horses did not laugh. I have a mind to imagine that you, my tender Lord, wept.

Fulvius turned to me. "Where did that come from, young man?"

I did not know, so did not speak, but the Emperor answered for me.

"Is he not his father's son?"

XI.

My father and I left Fulvius and the guards to deal with the body, and we walked back to the palace alone, together.

On this walk through the dark, my father told me the story of the rat in the eagle's nest.

"Do you know what happened to the rat in the eagle's nest?"

"It was eaten?"

He laughed like I was joking, but I couldn't have been more serious. What else would have happened to the poor critter?

"Not the one I'm talking about. No, there was once upon a time a rat who found himself thriving quite nicely in the eagle's nest. The family of eagles were at first afraid of their rat brother. They wanted to gobble him up, not because he would have been so tasty, but because he was foreign to them, an outsider. But outsiders have skills insiders lack, and the father eagle knew that the rat would be helpful in the winter months."

"When they flew south?"

"No. Not this family of eagles. They had responsibilities in their home nest. These were very important eagles. The whole woodland depended on the family of eagles for leadership, for protection. When the snow came, they couldn't just up and leave behind their kingdom. No, they were forced to stay, and suffer the thick blanket of white that covered the ground beneath them. And who would be able to scurry beneath this layer of snow, to retrieve the delicious dead mice and moles for the eagle's supper? The rat, of course. And for his part, the eagles let the rat share in their nest, and its lofty view of the forest. Truly, no other rat had enjoyed such fantastic vistas of earth as the family of eagles allowed their rat."

XII.

We reached the stairway that lead up to my loft, and the promise of a long night of sleep ahead. My father patted my head one last time for the evening, so drunk at this point that he nearly fell over and had to use the very head he was patting to get his balance. I nearly fell over with him. He pulled himself together, and laughed.

"Good night, boy." And he yawned, and he turned, and he walked away without looking back.

I fell asleep the moment my head hit the pillow, oh my Lord, secure in knowing that I had finally found my place in the world. I was the wintertime-rat that would rescue my family from the cold.

CHAPTER THREE

I.

"How many people must I kill to guarantee my place in hell?"

Lucius asked this once of a bishop he was about to murder. After he put a blade in the holy man's stomach he added, "And over how many years must I do my killing?"

At the hour of this current prayer, I have been alive for twenty-seven years, and nearly three months. One might think that twenty-seven years is still a young enough age for a man to redeem his soul and make up for his past sins, but this person would be unwise in the way of things. You and I, oh my Lord, would know better. I could live for a thousand years, and I'd find myself needing a thousand more.

You have kept, I'm sure, an official tally of my years of killing, dear god. A clay tablet that you filled in with events backwards, starting with my own looming execution. If you don't have the information on hand, send one of your secretaries to heaven's hall of records, for I cannot be depended on for the exact figures.

Yet, I rejoice my Lord. For I sense between us an understanding that my years of killing are at an end, and I will not live past the coming morning. My enemies have cornered me. They are in the village, they have asked for me by name, and since I have made no effort to hide my identity, they have surely been directed to the monastery. I have told my companions to leave me undefended, and to pray for my soul.

And, Lord, shall they want to cut my head off? Shall they want to break me on a bed of stones? I say to them, good, have your justice.

The room is cold. My knees ache. All I've eaten for days are crusts of bread soaked in red wine. It's all my appetite will allow me. I may have contracted some disease when I cut my tongue off, and if the vengeful hunters don't kill me at sunrise, certainly the untreated infection will within another month or so.

Sorry, I'm getting ahead of myself, tender listener. It's better I confess my ruining before I describe my state since.

Was I ruined on that night in the stable with the gooseneck? Was it before that? A callus look I gave a beggar on the street? Was one of them working for you, oh my hidden master? A spy from your army of angels? Was there a moment in my boyhood, when I spit at the feet of some leper who, if I were to remove his tattered cloak, would unleash a concealment of feathered wings?

I think not. I was never a fixture of angelic attention, was I, oh my Lord? No, there was a lower being with its eye on me. That lamentable serpent, Lucifer.

The devil got a whiff of me. He caught the reek of my actions in the stables. The snake was impressed at how slowly my heart was beating as my victim's stopped.

"This bastard is one to watch." Hissed the devil. "This bastard is special."

II.

"My father tells me you're special." Said Lucius.

"I'm special?"

"Well... no." He corrected himself, "That's not precise, actually."

Lucius sat down beside me, on the floor in front of a map I was studying. We were in his room.

"My father tells me you have a special talent."

III.

I don't think I'm over putting it to say that at age thirteen, my older brother, Lucius, was the very beating of my heart. Each thump echoed his name inside my chest. He was taller than me, stronger than me, smarter than me, better than me in almost every way.

I realize now that the boy, and the subsequent man that I admired, was a kind of fruitless husk. A shell that never had a creature to protect. Lucius was a wall surrounding a void. He had no country within. No castle, only vast motes. Yet the greatness of the defenses, their depths and heights, implied to me a guarded treasure. I thought if I could possess this treasure then I could be more like Lucius, and more like my father's true son. A fool I was and remain, oh my Lord, for despite all my gained knowledge of his evil, when I close my eyes to sleep, it's the empty face of my villainous half-brother that I see and desire, above all else, to be reunited with.

Our destinies always seemed to me so basically and naturally entwined, that it's difficult to target what scenes from our young lives first drew me to Lucius. Had he never spoken to me, had he never looked me in the eye, I fear, dear god, that my life would have been his nonetheless. As it was, Lucius did speak to me, and he did look at my eyes, and cared what they saw in the world, and that they saw him.

Lucius was nothing like our father, neither in appearance or temperament. Young Lucius was slender and long, and taller than his father by the time he was fifteen. His skin was olive, his eyes and hair were black, his cheeks were razors. Lucius had the felineness of his mother, Julia Domna, and the two always seemed to glide in their movements, while I and my younger brother Geta, having taken after our father, stomped and slobbered like dogs.

(I wonder, oh my Lord and designer, why did you divide my family's looks in this way? Was it your deceleration of our final allegiances? Flags sewn on our faces and bodies? Were you somehow warning my father, and Geta, and even me, that these two others were the set apart ones? Are heart-ridden dogs always made fools by scheming cats?)

My father's reign was guided by his ever-shifting passions, Lucius's by his philosophies, which were set seemingly from birth, and never changed. In himself, I believe Lucius found nothing, and so he projected his vacancy onto the physical world. Septimius Severus loved what he found in himself and so loved the world, was drunk on it, enraptured by it. My brother was indifferent to life, was amused by it at best, and annoyed by it at worst. Like all your greatest monsters, oh good Lord, my brother was equally a stranger to love and hate. In many ways, this made Lucius a more effective Caesar than our father. His chilled mind gave him an edge over his political enemies, who could be prodded into self-betrayal by a coolly accurate insult or a stoic threat of shock-horror. My father relied on a volatile mixture of fear and loyalty to rule, Lucius relied on nothing but his own ruthlessness, which was dependable and everlasting.

IV.

The map I was studying that night in Lucius's room, when he came inquiring about my talents, was of the Cloaca Maxima. Of all the gifts you have bestowed on the city, oh my Lord, surely her great labyrinth of underground sewers is among the most blessed. What measurement of a civilization is more telling than its handling of waste? What would we be as a people without an effective method of banishing our shit? Germans, I suppose.

I had known the sewers were down below, and made use of them every day of my life. But in the way man takes the oddness of the sky hanging moon for granted after years spent with it, so too I overlooked the magnificence of what lay beneath our toilets, and the good Roman asses that sat upon them.

My sudden interest in the Cloaca Maxima, and its endless branches of limestone tunnels, was owed to the dimwitted twin brothers, Felix and Faustus. The kind-hearted fools, and only sons of the Royal Tax Collector, had been exploring the sewers for months when they introduced their wonders to me one afternoon at the baths of Trajan. Shortly after that I paid a slave to an Aedile at the department of sanitation to steal some maps for me. They arrived the very day Lucius approached me with his problem, and his hopes that my talents could help him solve it. With the knowledge I had just absorbed, they could, and would. The closeness of these events to one another made them feel contrived. A scheme was unfolding. Was this scheme yours, oh my Lord? No, I think not. God makes plans. Schemes are the work of the snake.

Plebeians tend to take their shits in public baths or latrines. If they shit at home they do it squatted over buckets in some smelly corner. In the poorest enclaves they throw the buckets out the windows, and let it fall where it may. In more refined neighborhoods, they carry the full bucket down the street to toss it into the local drain, which leads to the local sewer, which flows to the central line of the Cloaca Maxima, and finally to the Tiber river and out to sea.

(Why, god, does man shit? Why, god, must we eat food in the first place? If all options of creation were open to you, why didn't you invent a creature whose body is self-sustaining? Are you limited in this way, or was it out of fear? Fear that without a belly to fill and empty and fill again, mankind would become stagnant, motionless, refusing to run about on your earth, loving and killing one another, accomplishing the destinies you've chosen for us. Is hunger the engine of man?

God, do you shit?)

Noblemen do their dirty work in much the same fashion as the plebs, but slaves carry the buckets. In certain elite households of blessed families, personal baths are built and supplied with rushing water from the aqueducts by a private tunnel and drain network. The Imperial Palace was, naturally, equipped in this way, but still Julia Domna insisted we join the other children of the royal court on their weekly trips to the public bathhouses on the Oppian hill. There we would sit in the gardens and take lessons in philosophy, take shits, wash and steam our skin, then wrestle, or flirt, or argue with each other by the expansive marble pools and fountains. My step mother said it was imperative that my brothers form social bonds with the other children of the court, who would one day grow into the Clarissimi, and would assist in running their inherited empire.

As a child I wondered why Julia Domna allowed me the privilege of going along with my brothers and the other high born children on these trips to the public baths. My step mother was in charge of my education, and she made every effort to exclude me from as much of it as possible. I didn't learn to ride a horse until I was seventeen, and never received a day's training in swordplay or soldiering. I was never tutored in mathematics or the physical sciences, and have found those subjects to be nearly impossible to self-teach. I learned to read thanks mostly to Lucius, and to hunt thanks to my father. Yet, when it came to the trips to the bathhouses, Julia Domna was magnanimous.

"Yes, my dearies, go to the public baths, learn how the common leech lives so to better squash him as he scurries about your sacred feet."

It would eventually be my younger brother, Geta, just before his death, who would inform me of why my step mother was eager to see me go out into the wild city. Because of his close, comradely, relationship with all soldiers, Geta was often privileged with secret information only known among the ranks, and he used this particular revelation to try and hurt me during an argument when we were grown. The imperial guards who escorted my brothers and I on excursions into the city, had been given special orders by their mistress to turn a blind eye to my well-being. They were there to protect my brothers, the princes, not me, the bastard.

I was a little boy alone in a city of thugs and killers. If some pervert in the baths decided to snatch me up and run off to make me his bride, the guards were to allow it. If I were to challenge some sailor twice my size to a wrestling match, and was beaten within an inch of my life, they were to allow me that last inch by their own negligence. When my step mother sent me to the public baths she was sending me through a gauntlet, blindfolded.

Though I would never be hurt or kidnapped, thank you, dear god, I was often left behind at the baths, forgotten when it was time to leave. I would have to walk by myself across the city back to the palace, a journey fraught with dangers for a boy of my age, and yet, with your watchful protection, or perhaps the serpent Lucifer's, I always made it home. Once I got there, I would routinely not be recognized by the guards at the gates. They would turn me away like a beggar, sometimes they'd kick me, or spit at me. This was another instruction from Julia Domna. Another of her insidious plots to remove me from her family without culpability. How frustrated she must have been each time, after being so late in returning from the baths, I would reappear at the gates, not a scratch on me.

I would curl up against the perimeter wall for the night, and in the morning Lucius would let me in, and chastise the guard who had pretended not to know me.

"Was dark when he first showed, my young master, and he was covered in filth. Beg forgiveness."

And usually Lucius would begrudgingly award his forgiveness with a scowl that always pleased me. Once though, after a certain blue eyed guard had repeatedly turned me away as a stranger, even after Lucius had formally introduced us, he did more than scowl. He demanded the guard remove his own ear, and offer it to him as apology.

"Did you not hear me when I said this was my brother? If you aspire to be hard of hearing, we shall make you so. I'll have your ear, if you don't mind."

After Lucius convinced the young guard of his seriousness, and his willingness to bring the matter before his father, blue-eye unsheathed his sword and sliced his dangling lobe off with a splash of blood. His hand trembling, he presented the bit of dripping flesh to Lucius, who regarded it with disappointment.

"I said I wanted your ear. Not your ear lobe."

The guard looked to Lucius for mercy, and found none. He returned the blade to the side of his head and cut off the ear proper. As he did, god forgive me, I swooned with love for my brother and defender.

V.

"My father tells me you have a special talent."

Lucius's bony knee knocked into my own as he sat down beside me. This was something that I was sure he did not notice doing, and if he had, thought nothing of it. However, if my senses were made visible in the material of the world, there would have been a spark, dear god. There would have been a flame.

"A talent at what?" I asked.

"Killing." Said Lucius.

"You're the superior hunter."

"It's not a talent at killing game that my father told me of."

"I've never killed anything but."

Lucius smiled. "But for a thin necked boy." He said. "Out there in the stables. It's alright, you needn't be embarrassed. The Emperor told me of your talent with great pride."

"It was only the once. I wouldn't call an ability a talent."

"Well than, shall we hone this ability and make it such?"

"On whom?"

"Someone I know we both detest equally. That fat hog of a boy, Marcus Gallus."

27

"Marcus? But his father belongs to the Emperor."

"I know who he is. That's why my father suggested I speak with you."

Marcus Gallus was the only son of Gaius Gallus. And as you know, dear accountant of all, Gaius Gallus was the Count of the Privy Purse, and had to be consulted by the Emperor before almost any expenditure of cash. Gaius was a miser, a value that was likely the reason my father appointed him to the Privy in the first place, knowing his own nature to be frivolous when it came to coin. Still, Emperor Severus had become annoyed with his Privy Count, and his constant disapproval of lavish feasts and games, which he voiced openly to fellow Nobles. Gaius Gallus didn't have the power to say no to Septimius Severus, but he did have the ability to weigh on his reputation and his conscience. I recall, as you must dear god, how my father, behaving uncharacteristically melancholic at a garish palace party, remarked to Julia Domna that he could not enjoy the celebration after speaking with his Privy Count. Gaius Gallus had poisoned the kings thinking so that when he looked upon the cooked gooses, hired belly dancers, and pyrotechnics display, he did not see good food and merry distraction, but gold coins draining from his purse. The Emperor could replace his tightly clenched Privy Count, but Gallus was well respected in the Senate, and such an action would make The Emperor look like the irresponsible spender that he was. So, dear god, I would imagine and you would know, that my father was tickled when Lucius presented him with the idea of killing the treasured son of Gaius Gallus. The loss would likely cripple the man's motivations. His work would no doubt suffer, and for as long as the mourning would last, the flood gates would be open. And what if the boy wasn't known to be dead, just disappeared? The search would no doubt consume Gallus for years. My father would be able to rid himself of a monetary overseer, without the political embarrassment of actually doing so.

"Marcus Gallus is a miserable twat of a bully." Lucius continued, "The lovely Plautilla Fulvius, who is promised to be my wife when we are grown, was just this last week chased mercilessly around the pools of Trajan by that brute, all the while him demanding a fist of the innocent girl's hair."

"For this you'd see him killed?"

"I'd see him more than killed." Lucius smiled devilishly. "Do you remember father's story about the forest bear and the hunter?"

VI.

Do you remember it, dear god? Perhaps your eavesdropping time must be divided, and so spent with thrift. Can you possibly listen to all of mankind's trifling talk? Every conversation we have about bread, and eggs, and fish, and the weather, and who's fucking who, and where did you leave the wooden spoon? Beside the stove, you say? But I've checked there. Check again, you say? I shall. Ah, here is the wooden spoon. And all the while the king of kings sits dutifully on the roof listening to this nonsense. No, I think not. There must be many conversations of man that you miss while attending to more important business, or that you skip purposely to go for a swim when days are humid in heaven.

If you weren't there to hear my father tell this story the first time, I will retell it briefly for you now. It was not one of my favorites, though Lucius was very fond of it. It was terribly violent, lacked any real logic, and the ending was as fanciful as my father got. He must have been drunk when he thought it up. Actually, knowing the Emperor as well as you and I do, dear Lord, he must not have been drunk enough.

The story began with the gruesome slaughter of an entire royal family by a giant black bear as they vacationed in a deep wood. I'll spare you the gory details, dear god, my primary tale having enough blood and guts of its own. Suffice it to say that the black bear made a glutton of himself, eating every last bite of every last family member, even the king himself. But there was an especially beautiful princess who survived. She was off in the trees having a piss when the bear ambushed her family's camp site. The princess returned to find the bear picking flesh from its fangs with a twig, yawning and stretching after a good meal. The princess was brave, and had nobility to match her extreme beauty. She released a war cry, and charged at the digesting black bear. She may have been brave, she may have caught him off guard and satiated, but still, this is a princess taking on a black bear, you can imagine how it turned out. The humongous bear simply reached out with its huge mitt, and plucked the dainty princess up off the ground. Still having fight in her, the princess flailed her arms at the beast, socking him good on his muzzle with her balled fists. The bear used his free claw to slash the girl's shoulders, parting them to the bone, and then yanked each arm off like flower petals. The princess cried in agony, and now the black bear looked to her face for the first time. He opened his mouth to take a bite, but stopped at the last second. The princess was indeed so beautiful, that even this wild animal was stunned and enchanted. Her gorgeousness gave the bear a rush of guilty feelings for the massacre he had made. He could not understand this emotion, but he felt it, oh my Lord. The bear felt that he had done wrong. Sure, he had been a hungry bear, and all of god's creatures must devour others in order to survive. But the bear had been full by the time he finished with the princess's chubby sisters, and if his feeble mind had the ability to be honest, he would have to admit that he ate the rest of the family out of sport. The bear gazed for a long time at the crying, orphaned, armless beauty. Then the remorseful bear sighed, let the princess out of his deadly grip, and slouched away, back into the dark of the woods.

Luckily, which is how most things happen in these stories, a strong young hunter was passing through the same part of the woods where the bear had killed this family. He saw the smoke from their squelched fire, and the blood splashed all about the leaves and branches surrounding the scene. He heard the whimpering of the dying princess. The hunter took an arrow from his quiver, drew his bow, and cautiously approached the clearing. He saw the massacre, he saw a pile of shit the bear had left. He saw the princess, and though her body was brutally disfigured, he saw her beauty. The hunter knelt beside the bleeding princess, and vowed to bring her to safety, to a village, to a doctor who could treat her wounds. She may not have her arms, but she would have her beauty, and she would have her life. So taken with the princess was the hunter that he even assured her that if she should live he would marry her and take care of her until the end of his days.

But the princess said no. No, she would not be carried from this spot. No, she would not see any doctor in any village. No, she would not marry the hunter. She did want his help, though. The princess requested that the hunter leave her this instant, pursue the bear to its den, kill it, and return to her with its heart. The hunter was at first reluctant, trying to convince the girl that without quick attention she would surely die. The princess only told the hunter that without quick attention the monster that ate her family would surely escape. An immediate devotee to her beauty, the hunter wasn't reluctant for long, and before he knew it, he was following the bears paw prints deep into the forest. After some searching he found the thing, reclining against a rock slab near the cave that was his home. The hunter was surprised but pleased to find the bear so defenseless. He wouldn't dare get closer and ruin his advantage, but from his position in the thicket, the hunter thought the bear was crying. He took an arrow from his quiver, drew his bow, and shot the bear through his brain. The bear stood, growled long and mournfully, and the hunter planted another two arrows in its skull, only inches behind the first one. The bear shook its head, bellowed deeply, laid down against the rock once more, and died. The hunter unsheathed his knife and approached the bear. He cut the bear's chest down the middle of his rib cage and carefully removed its enormous purple heart.

The triumphant hunter returned to the princess, carrying the bear's heart in a rucksack over his shoulder, and then came the part of the story I liked the least. Upon seeing the heart, the princess entered a sort of vengeful fit, jumping to her feet, and dancing armlessly in celebration of the bear's death. The hunter, worried, begged the princess to save her energy, for she had lost buckets of blood and they had a long journey ahead. The princess laughed at this, and made another request of the hunter. That he should take his knife, cut the heart into bite sized pieces, and feed them to her. Still hypnotized by her unmatched beauty, the hunter agreed, and got to preparing the princess's meal. After he was done cutting, he fed her, and after he fed her, a miracle happened. The princess, belly full of bear heart, leaped ten feet into the air, landed, and then jumped twenty, giggling with glee as she did it. When she landed the second time, right in front of the dumbfounded hunter, her arms had grown back, and her torn clothes were replaced by a flowing white gown. The beautiful princess, put back together by the healing magic of sweet vengeance, would marry the brave hunter, and make love to him every remaining night of his life. The hunter was more than fine with this.

VII.

"Yes. I remember the story." I told Lucius.

"Good." Said Lucius. "My beloved Plautilla is the princess. The bully Marcus Gallus is the black bear. I am the hunter. And you, my brother, shall be my arrow and my knife."

VIII.

I was at the baths the day Marcus Gallus chased Plautilla Fulvius and the other girls around the pools, and I was there the week before when he did the same, and the week before, and the week before. Marcus was a molester of some regularity. He was one of your faster growing creatures, my Lord. The boy was two hundred pounds of meat in a six foot sac by age fourteen, and pity be to any of the other children who bloomed slower and later than the hulk. I was, as you know, one of these pathetic autumn lilies, and so as much a target of his attacks as the girls were.

I must confess something. What else is new, huh my Lord? My latest confession is that unlike the gooseneck, whose murder I was mostly indifferent to, the killing of Marcus Gallus was something I relished. In fact, I had imagined killing the mean hearted idiot many times before I actually did so, in those dank sewers beneath the baths. I now regret killing him, but I can't help that my feelings about the boy remain. I did not like this Marcus Gallus. Once, not long before he was dead, he humiliated me in a way that became central to my motivation when agreeing to cut out his heart.

The walk from the palace to the Trajan baths was a lengthy one. We would depart with myself, Lucius, Geta, and a cadre of praetorian guards and as we walked down the main thoroughfare we would be joined by the other children of the court, and their own tutors, and maids.

The only part of the bath days I enjoyed was the very beginning of our walks through the city. It was just me, Lucius, and Geta. Geta would become lost in his endless questioning of the praetorians, who he admired so much. What was battle like? How many Germans had they killed? Things like that. The soldiers were always pigs in shit for Geta Severus, even then. Lucius and I were thus left to entertain each other with conversation, and we never failed at this. What did you read last night? Which philosopher is a fool, which is a hero? Things like that. As enthralled as we both would become in these conversations, they would abruptly halt when our group was joined by Plautilla Fulvius. Lucius would see Plautilla waiting with her maids outside the front gate of her father's home, and he would leave my side and run to her. It didn't matter if I was in the middle of a sentence, he would see her, and he would run, and she would smile. I would spend the remainder of the walk with Felix and Faustus, the simpleton twins, trying to ignore their mad jabber, while discreetly watching Lucius from behind. He would spend the rest of the walk flirting with Plautilla and her little friends in his distinct style, teasing their intellects while complimenting their looks.

"As thoughtless and as lovely as the peacock," Lucius would say, "and equally delicious to eat." The lesser royal girls would swoon, but Plautilla, who was the true focus of his flirtation, would only smile. A polite little smile. A toothless smile, that came from her head, not her heart. It always reassured me, oh my Lord. Lucius may have wanted her, but she did not want him, and as much as their father's may have willed it, a happy marriage they would never share.

Lucius's own pleasure on these walks would be broken when we were joined by the bully Marcus Gallus, who lived closest to the Oppian hill, and was always last to join. He was never pleased to be doing so, but he was never pleased to be doing anything. Marcus was in a perpetual bad mood, and every living being was to blame, down to the street pigeons. I believe Marcus's favorite part of these strolls through town were the many pigeons available for catching and tormenting. He would leap at packs of them, grabbing the slowest with his bare hands, and then he'd break its chubby little wings, and tare them off, laughing as he did it. He would then often throw the corpse, now no more than a sponge of blood and feathers, at Lucius and his girls, or me and my fools, and follow it up with a barrage of insults. He would wonder out loud, "How quickly could I pop off *your* puny wings?".

(I never cared for pigeons, oh my Lord. Or birds, for that matter. They always seemed to be the most unlike humans of all your animal creatures. But still, and though I am the last to judge a torturer, these birds did not deserve the agony they were sent to death with.)

We would arrive at the baths, a bloated entourage of squawking chicks who would grow to rule the Roman roost. Oh, the looks we would get, my Lord. So detested was our noisy rabble of children, that entire families would depart the baths en masse when we arrived. "Here come those entitled little brats to ruin our only day of peace in the long week of work".

And how right they were, dear god. We would move directly to the front of the line, clogging the already crowded apodyterium. At the gymnasia, us princes would challenge the plebs to foot races, or wrestling matches, and when they didn't let us win, we would accuse them of cheating and beat them mercilessly, our guards keeping their plebeian comrades at a distance. It was never a fair fight. In the frigidarium, the princesses would order the pleb women to disrobe and march before them naked. The rich girls would judge and rank the poor women's bodies, and cackle at the fat or disproportionate ones. We were very obviously not welcome, yet I don't think any child in our group was aware of it besides me. Too wanted and loved in their own homes were these children that they failed to see the contempt the outside world held for them

Our first stop at the baths, after changing out of our tunics and sandals, were the latrines. There, sitting inches from one another, the children of the Roman Imperial Court would have themselves a collective shit. I don't understand it, my Lord. I will never understand it. The shamelessness of it. The crude exposure of human baseness. I could never afford it. In all the years, and all the trips to the public latrines, my body never once allowed itself to defecate in front of the eyes its fellows. This is not a popular disposition in Rome, oh my Lord, as you well know. Surely you, who witnesses all men shit, whether in a latrine by the dozens or in a darkened wood all alone, has no preference between public and private defecation. But for me, the distinction has always been a valued one.

We would sit there. A square room, wrapped in wooden toilet benches, the rushing sound of water from the sewer below mixing with the sounds of benighted gases escaping the bodies of the princes and princesses above. We would chatter and gossip as if we were at dinner, or a sporting event. As the children finished their business they would excuse themselves and move on to the next room, to be cleaned, and then massaged with mud and oil by the bath slaves. Lucius was always first to leave the latrine. Fast and efficient, I even envied Lucius his bowel movements. The girls would follow, and then the other boys and I. I was embarrassed at my inability to perform in a crowd, so I would remain bare assed on the seat for the length of time expected of a boy my age before pretending to finish and move on. This meant that I would have to hold whatever I wanted to let go of for the rest of the trip. Most times, oh my Lord, I would relieve myself in the morning, before our journey, but on the days when this wasn't possible, I would spend hours feeling sick to my stomach until we returned to the palace, and some privacy.

If you created an antipodal to my toilet behavior, you called him Marcus Gallus. Marcus reveled in his public shits. Nowhere did I see him joyous but for in the latrine. He was an orchestra of atrocious sounds. He would fart and laugh and spit. He would stretch and crack his back and wrists and legs and feet. And would he stink? Oh, dear god in heaven, he would stink. Marcus Gallus was always the last to leave the latrine. Even the guards would eventually leave him alone to his stinking, the odor growing so great that they feared it as something evil that wanted to enter and possess their souls by way of their nostrils. Marcus would be long finished, oh my Lord, but he would still sit there for at least an hour longer than the rest of us, proudly wallowing in his own stench.

When he was finally finished, Marcus would rejoin us in the garden exedras where we received lectures from visiting intellectuals. Usually things our parents wanted us to hear and believe. Lots of old bearded men droning on about the power of the many gods, and the dangers of you, the only master, the one god. Marcus would shove in between two already seated students, his stench sending them to find new seats, and make a show of how boring he found the proceedings. He'd yawn loud enough for us all to hear him.

No one laughed at Marcus's playing. No one but Plautilla. I saw her, many times in fact, laughing at the brute's antics. When he made farting sounds with his mouth, Plautilla alone would titter. This no doubt added to my brother's frustrations. How could she laugh at the same monster who would later make her scream so?

The day Marcus Gallus attempted to help get me over my fear of shitting in front of everyone, we were being lectured by Erasmus Grigio on the roundness of the sun. Its symmetry made it perfect, and therefore like one of the gods. The moon, only being symmetrical one night a month, was godlike, but less so than the sun. The human face was, like mankind, grasping for heavenly perfection, but falling short. A face aspires to be symmetrical, but never is exactly. Some of our faces are ugly, an eye drooping towards the chin, the other reaching for the forehead. A rosy left cheek, and a right one scarred or birth marked. Yet the beauty that some of us possessed was reaching towards perfection. The more attractive you were the more evolved you must be spiritually. It was novel talk, but total nonsense. Marcus, having the least symmetrical face among us, belched loudly in protest. No one laughed, but I noticed that Plautilla shifted in her seat, biting her bottom lip, which for her age was already rather plump and lovely. Lucius shivered with anger. The wise Erasmus Grigio didn't hear a thing. Like most philosophers still loyal to the old gods, he was near totally deaf.

Seated beside me during this particular lecture was the son of the Emperor's top quaestor, Terentius Varro. When Marcus belched I turned to the child Varro, for no other reason than he was sitting next to me, and thoughtlessly whispered, "This Marcus Gallus make me want to vomit."

Young Varro looked at me with a face of shocked amusement, as if I had cursed god himself, and he just could not believe my nerve. I thought since no one laughed at his joking, Marcus had no supporters. I was wrong. Whether it was out of fear, or stupidity, the Varro boy was a crony of the bully Marcus. Before I could ask why he was so shocked at my seemingly obvious commentary, he was on his feet and shuffling to an empty seat halfway down the exedra, and then when Grigio turned his back fully, to an empty one at the end of it, right beside Marcus Gallus. Varro, a disgusting grin across his face, leaned over to his friend and whispered in his ear, all the while pointing a finger at me. Marcus, smiling at first, turned gloomy as he heard of my insult. His gaze found mine, which must have looked as guilty as could be, starring back at him with worry as I was. Varro leaned back satisfied. Marcus Gallus, furious eyes fixed on me, raised his left palm, and punched it with his right fist. A warning.

I did not know the child Varro well, I don't even remember his first name, but oh my Lord, how I felt betrayed by him that day in the garden. He had taken such pleasure in bringing trouble into my life. My life, that was already so full of pain and trouble, and had so much more coming without his help. I met him years later during a vacation at Antioch, when I had some political power. Grinning, he introduced himself to me as my dear old friend, Varro. I had him arrested and his family deported to North Africa.

After the lecture we moved to the pools. I had to use the toilet, so I did not go for a swim. I didn't even sit on the side and stick my feet in, which I would normally do. I just paced, occasionally rubbing my nauseas belly, and watched Lucius in the pool, splashing and roughhousing with Plautilla and the other girls. Their enjoyment of each other made me sicker. It was bad. I was going to have to return to the latrines, and hope that they would be empty. I turned to do just that and was met with a punch to the gut that knocked the wind from my lungs, the sight from my eyes, and the shit from my bowels.

I heard the girls nearby, they screamed. I must have released a thunderclap of gas, that got their attention. The black spots faded from my vision, and I regained my sight. I took a deep breath. I was on the marble floor, covered in my own shit. I felt relieved to be rid of it, but beyond disturbed to be covered in it. Above me was Marcus Gallus, hands on his hips, trying to maintain his body from exploding with laughter. His ever-present gut was in a seizure, and I thought it might burst and make me an even worse mess. The girl's screams were dimming as they fled from the room and my smells. Lucius fled. I watched him as he hopped out of the pool and ran off behind them. He did not turn. All I saw was his back.

Marcus regained my attention by slapping me across the face with an open palm. He yelled down at me, "I'd rather be a strong idiot, than a weak bastard who shits himself after one punch." He had a point, oh my Lord. He continued, "Weaklings like you make me sick. You make me want to vomit! Actually..."

Marcus got down on the ground and straddled me, not seeming to care that he was getting my shit on his knees. He pinned my arms to the side of my body with his thighs, and then stuck his fat finger into his fat mouth, down his fat throat. I struggled and squirmed beneath his weight, but it was no use. He choked, and then burped, and then vomited all over my face. The royal boys who had remained to watch the show, and who hadn't laughed at Marcus all day, decided that this spectacle was worth a chuckle or a thousand. Their laughter boomed across the pools, and the guards joined them, and so did the plebeians. Even the slaves got a kick out of it. At least, dear god, I was able to bring everyone some happiness.

Marcus was laughing harder than all of them, and he toppled over onto his side, freeing me. I leaped to my feet. I could taste his vomit in my mouth, I could feel his stomach acids burning in my eyeballs, I smelt him deep in my sinuses. I ran for the pool and dived in, avoiding kicks and shoves from the princes who were jovially trying to add to this humiliation. Later they would be able to say, "it was the funniest thing I've seen all year, and I was a part of it. I kicked that little bastard as he ran off in tears."

All around me in the pool, a hazy cloud of excrement.

I left the pools, soaking wet, and ran for the latrines.

(Why, Lord? Why tempt me so to hate my fellow man? How could I not desire vengeance for this outrage? How could I not desire the heart of my enemy taken out of his chest, and placed in a box beneath my bed?)

IX.

The latrine was empty. I had the whole room to myself, and I was free to weep, which I was doing. I was also free to make other sounds, and I made them too. It must have been a pathetic sight. I hope you were busy, my Lord. I hope you missed this part. It wasn't missed by everyone, though, that's for sure. As I sat there I began to hear a distinct sound of suppressed laughter. The gargled snicker of someone trying not to make a sound. It seemed to be coming from below me.

Was it the devil? I tilted my butt up off the wooden seat, and peeked down into the darkness beneath me. Nothing. I sniffled and farted, an extra squeaky one, like a mouse. The gargled snicker burst into laughter, and there was no doubt now that someone was underneath the toilet. I jumped from the seat and landed across the room. The laughter coming from down the toilet turned raucous. It was crazed, but not demonic sounding. I recognized it. I slowly returned to the toilet seat. I peered down into the hole.

A ray of light from the latrine windows shined down into the toilet and revealed a face. It was Felix, one of the twin sons of the Emperor's tax collector. He was standing in water up to his knees. I couldn't see what surrounded him down there, my view of the sewer being limited to the spotlight of the toilet seat.

Felix had a warm smile on his face. He waved at me. Dumbfounded, I waved back.

Felix called up to me, "You make funny noises."

"Happy to amuse." I said. "Is that you, Felix?"

"You could bet on it, my friend!"

"What are you doing in the toilet?"

"Me and my brother Faustus come down here all the time. It's our special place. We found the Greek god, Anteros."

"You found Anteros?" I asked. "In the toilet?"

"We did! Want to come see him?"

"How do you get down there?"

"You jump. It's fun. It's all splashy fun down here!" He jumped up and down, splashing the water around him with his feet.

"How, Felix? How did you fit?"

The hole in the toilet seat was ample, but not ample enough for a person. Maybe a newborn could fit, the less than righteous mothers of Rome knew this well, but a toddler was already too big, and there was no way I was getting down there.

"Pick up the seat, there's plenty of room. You could bet on it."

I lifted the piece of wood that served as a seat. It came off very easily, it rested on two thin beams that ran across the length of the bench, and held up all of the other toilet seats as well. Below the narrow seat was a wide stone tunnel. After that it was a drop of another six or seven feet into the sewer, where Felix waited.

What the hell, I thought. I was already covered in shit. I also wanted to see this Anteros. Felix may have been stupid, but, as you made him dear god, he was no liar. Whatever he had down there, he genuinely believed it to be Anteros, and this made me curious. I climbed up onto the toilet bench, lowered one leg into the hole, and then the other. I lowered my waist in, and pressed my back against one side of the tunnel, my feet against the other. I slithered down the filthy pipe. The smell got worse and worse as I got lower and lower. I started breathing through my mouth, and I could taste the rankness.

"Now jump!" Yelled Felix.

I stuffed my nose and mouth into the top of my tunic, and jumped. I landed on my feet but slipped on the greasy limestone floor, falling on my back with a splash. I was pleased to find that though the smell was no better down here, the water was fairly clean. It was part of a system of the sewer that was constantly flowing, and so stayed relatively fresh. Felix probably laughed at me. I was laughed at so much at that point, that I stopped noticing it.

I stood up, rubbing my bruised back, and had a look around. It was dark, but for the rays of light shining through the toilet holes. I was stunned, dear god, at the size of the place. What great work you do through man. It was an arched corridor of stone that went on for what looked like miles in either direction. I had no idea it would be that huge, and I would soon learn that it was even bigger.

Felix pointed at the entrance to another corridor that parted off from the one we were in. The flickering light of a fire made shadows dance on its exposed wall.

"Faustus has our torch. He's around the corner, praying to Anteros for a true love to appear."

"Well," I said, pinching my nose tightly shut, "let's join him, shall we?"

Felix led the way down the other corridor which opened up into a subterranean coliseum. Pipes were coming out of every wall. Tubes shot up out of the ground, and down from the ceiling, spewing water every which way, rushing in here, rushing out there. In the center of it all was a landing of limestone. Kneeled in prayer at the center of this elevated clearing, a glowing oil lamp beside him, was Felix's twin brother, Faustus.

What a striking touch of idiocy you gave the world in this retarded gemination, oh my Lord. The brothers resembled one another in every way. Big and round, covered in curly black hair that was unruly in all the same places. Their backs, their forearms, their knees, and the tops of their feet. Wide, kind faces, always with curious smiles. Unlike some twins I've known, who resembled one another less and less the more familiar you became with their distinct personalities, Felix and Faustus remained indistinguishable to me for the entirety of the nearly fifteen years I knew them. They were constantly playing tricks on their parents and house maids. Though never in a cruel way, as they were incapable of it, dear god. The deception was always for a laugh, and was soon revealed. Felix would leave his mother's side with a fresh head of cut hair, only to return moments later in the same tunic, but the hair regrown. When they got older they would sometimes trade and share girlfriends without the women knowing, and I suppose this is something they will have to answer for come judgment. But I pray, merciful Lord, that you not hold Felix and Faustus responsible for their involvement in the murder of Marcus Gallus. Though the muscle may swing the axe, it is not to be blamed for the falling trees.

"Hello, Faustus." I said. He turned over his shoulder towards me and Felix, and I saw what his face looked like while in prayer. His brow was furrowed; his eyes were focused as they slowly opened to see me. He seemed for a moment like a normal boy, perhaps even one that was wise beyond his years. Then he recognized me, something sparked brightly in his dimly lit brain, and it so excited him that he began laughing like a dumb hyena. The illusion was broken.

"What are you doing down here?" Faustus laughed louder, and his brother joined him, and soon they were insane with giggling. This happened often when spending time with the twins. Some minor surprise would tickle them and you would have no other option but to wait for the fit of laughter to pass. I waited. It passed.

"What's so funny?" Asked Felix. Faustus shrugged that he had forgotten or never knew.

"Anteros. Where's this Anteros of yours?" I asked, getting us back on topic.

"Ah!" Said Faustus. "Behold!" And he raised both of his arms towards a large, open drain pipe that was emptying water about ten feet over our heads. The pipe was coming from the street above, and it had a series of steel bars across its opening to stop debris from falling into the flowing water below. And there, floating in thin air before the drain pipe, its glorious feathered wings outstretched, was the god Anteros.

I saw their Anteros for the corpse that it actually was almost immediately, dear Lord, but I must say it was convincing. His legs were dangling down through the bars, giving him the effect of hovering. His arms poked through the bars, and the sewage passing by made them bob up and down, like he was giving out benedictions to worshipers below. The dead man stuck in the drain had long, wet hair that covered his face, and made him look as though he were deep in a mystical trance. The oddest bit though, were his wings. He had a long line of thick white feathers growing out of his back and all down his arms. This took a few moments of strained viewing on my part to decipher. The solution was, of course, that he had been shot full of arrows before being dumped. You were there when he was killed, so you would know for sure, oh loyal audience of all, but by design they looked to me like military arrows. This man must have been a prisoner who was executed by the state. He was likely considered a particularly nasty rebel, to be given a sewer drain as a final resting place. Someone was making an example of this man. I wonder now, dear god, knowing what I do of the state, was this executed man perhaps a champion of yours? Some martyred saint, who was tied to a tree, used as target practice, and left to bleed and die in the sewers?

It was easy to understand how Felix and Faustus, with their infantile perceptions, would see the poor dangling wretch as a blessed flying Anteros. It was like when a child would see a lurking demon against his moonlit bedroom wall, only to learn in the morning that it was the shadow of a pile of clothes. In this sense, Felix and Faustus saw nothing but shadows, never benefiting from morning light. I told them years later that Anteros was more than likely a discarded body of a condemned criminal, and still I would find them telling stories of it as if it had been real. I would remind them that it was a corpse, and they would frown and say "Oh, yes, I forgot it was a corpse." Then after a brief moment, "but what a miracle our Anteros was, was it not?"

I envy their forgetfulness, dear Lord, as I envy the twins many things. Simplicity being prime among them. Once, when we were nineteen or so, I watched Felix chase a firefly around a wine pub for near on an hour. He was catching it and freeing it and catching it again, chuckling and drooling, and the whole while teasing the bug, "Gonna get ya. Gonna get ya. Got ya!" He grabbed at the bug a little hard and he smashed it against a clay bar top near where I was getting drunk. Felix lifted his hand off the squashed firefly, its guts glowing a bright green that was slowly dimming. Felix looked long and hard at what he had done.

I tried to comfort him, "No use getting upset, kind Felix. It's only a bug."

"Innocent." Muttered Felix. "Innocent, innocent, innocent." And then he began to cry a loud and whining cry, like a newborn. His brother, who was chasing a mouse out front, heard the crying and came in to see what was wrong. Felix couldn't speak, he just buried his sobbing face in his brother's chest.

"He killed a bug he was playing with." I told Faustus, and pointed at the mess of insect smeared on the bar. Faustus began to weep himself. The crying twins cradled one another and shivered out of the Popina, onto the street, and headed home to grieve.

I went down into the sewer many times in the following weeks and months, sometimes with the twins, sometimes on my own. I would wait until everyone was busy with socializing by the pools, and I would slip past the actively inattentive guards, wait for the latrines to be empty, and climb down the toilet. I was getting to know them well, dear Lord, and with the maps I had procured, I was navigating the tunnels of the Cloaca Maxima as if they were the very streets and alleyways of Rome. At first I would bring with me a piece of linen soaked in lavender and rose oil, to hold over my mouth and nose, but it never did any good, and you would get used to the stench surprisingly fast if you pushed it from your mind.

The central thrust of the plan was obvious from the start of my thinking. I would wait for Marcus Gallus and I to be left alone in the latrines, and I would pull him down into the sewer where he would disappear forever. The logistics of accomplishing this were more difficult. There were several concerns. First and foremost, I was not strong enough to overpower Marcus on my own. Second, say I were to get Marcus through the toilet and into the sewer below, I couldn't remove his heart then and there. I imagined the process would take some time, which it would in fact, and I would need privacy. Someone coming in to do a cursory check of the toilets, might peek down and find me at my work. After being tossed, Marcus would need to be caught, and spirited away to another part of the Cloaca where we could be alone. Ultimately, I needed accomplices, and they needed to be discreet. And who else among us could go as ignored as I could? The only possible choices were Felix and Faustus. Though, I didn't know how I would convince them to assist me in such violence, until the day I discovered the pipe that housed their beloved Anteros.

(Does my planning of evil deeds make them more so, dear god? Does my manipulation of the twins make me more diabolical? More condemned? Surely, motivation and forethought must be taken into your considerations of damnability. All men are tempted by sin, but you must view with triple scorn the ones who spend their idle thoughts not just on sinning, but on how to accomplish sin through deliberate action. Do you have more disgust for the man who in a rage of lust rapes his neighbor's wife, or the man who spends months following her in her daily activities so he can learn her routine, and rape her at a preferable opportunity?

What of murder? What of that squished firefly? Do you hold the murder of that bug in equal disdain as the assassination of a Caesar?)

I discovered Anteros first by his reek. During my exploring of the Cloaca, I came upon a tunnel I had not yet noticed. As I shined my lantern on it and walked to it, I was smacked in the face with the unmistakable stink of rotting human flesh. I entered the tunnel. I could hear the sound of vendors on the street outside the baths, above. A steady river of scummy street water rushed by my feet. In the floor beneath me was a large open drain that collected the water to move elsewhere, and this was most definitely the source of the smell. I peered down and saw the lodged Anteros, and below him, the subterranean coliseum where Felix and Faustus would pray.

Of all the manipulating of dumb people I've been guilty of over the years, I think this first one was my boldest and most despicable. I waited for Felix and Faustus to become lost in prayer, and then I excused myself to do some more exploring, which was usually how things went. I hurried back to the tunnel I had recently found, and I shimmied myself down the drain pipe till I was as close behind the god-corpse as I could stand to be without having to vomit. I cleared my throat and then, god forgive me, pretended to speak as a voice of heaven:

"Dearest Felix! Noble Faustus! Hear the voice of Anteros, for I have come with instructions from the gods!"

I heard first the twins gasp for air, then they began to laugh. Soon they were in hysterics. I knew what to do, I waited for it to pass. When it did they conferred among themselves.

"What happened?" "Someone spoke." "Was it you or I?" "No, it was some third voice." "But we are alone, we two." "Did Anteros speak?" "It couldn't be. Are we worthy?"

"YES!" I shouted. The twins gasped again, and become lost in laughter once more. I wasn't waiting this time. "SILENCE!" I boomed. "Hear me well, foolish Felix, and foolish Faustus! The gods have instructions for you!"

The god-corpse told them a demon was trapped in the heart of Marcus Gallus, and needed to be removed for the sake of Rome. Only the god-corpse knew how to perform this operation. All they needed to do was wait with Marcus Gallus while he was on the toilet, and when they were alone with him, grab him and toss him down below. Anteros would be waiting to whisk him away to have the demon removed. The god-corpse told them to do it on the very next trip to the baths, and no later, or the gods would be angry. The god-corpse told them to mention this crusade to no one, or the gods would be angry. The twins solemnly agreed.

Later, when I rejoined them, I could see the weight the divine mission was on the shoulders of the twins. They were quiet, and reserved, and didn't mention a word of what they had been told, or what they were expected to do. I was relieved that they were so tight lipped, but I was worried, dear Lord, that perhaps they hadn't understood the message, or would forget it when our next trip to the baths came around. But these were faithful twins, and they believed the god-corpse to be the emissary of the gods themselves, and better the twins should die than fall short of accomplishing the will of their winged ambassador. Come heaven or hell, Marcus was going down the crapper, and I would be waiting there to catch him.

X.

On our morning walk to the Trajan baths, I carried over my shoulder a small leather rucksack. No one noticed it but Lucius, who knew what tools were in it, and knew why I had them. Knowing he would finally be rid of his most scorned enemy brought a rare giddiness to my half-brother's face. I was so pleased to have made Lucius pleased. I felt like the hunter in the story of the forest bear. I felt dutiful. I felt proud, oh Lord. I felt righteous. Needless to say, I renounce these feelings, and beg forgiveness, blah blah blah.

In the sack was a butcher's knife I stole from Calpurnia the cook, a small wedge of strong wood, a hand-saw and a heavy mallet Lucius borrowed from the palace carpenter, a length of sturdy rope, and a polished silver amphora that Lucius stole for me to put the heart in after I cut it out. The shiny amphora was an object owned by my step mother Julia Domna, and so in my young mind it had possible supernatural powers. Could she watch me through it? Could the amphora keep track of my actions only to report back to its mistress when I gave up possession of it? The amphora was a lovely globe shape, that screwed opened at its middle, revealing a mirrored receptacle. Lucius thought it would look beautiful holding a bloody heart. I thought of how much I wanted to return it to Lucius, full with one. And I thought, dear Lord, of how bitter jealousy awaited me when he would then give the heart away to another, his fair Plautilla.

I discreetly fell behind the guards and the children of the court, and then ran an alternative route, so I could make the trip to the baths in half the time it would take them. I cut the line, not because I was the son of the Emperor, but because I was invisible. I was small, I was alone, and I was cloaked by my sense of purpose. Anyone who saw me on my way through the baths that day would have noted me momentarily as a boy who was exactly where he needed to be, doing exactly what he needed to be doing, and they would think on me no more.

I arrived at the latrine, it was empty but for two noblemen who were debating the future of grain prices in between farts. I sat on a toilet across from them, and began making moaning noises, clutching at my stomach. "Get ready! I've eaten nothing but figs for days! This is gonna be a bad one!". The noblemen collected themselves, and took their conversation elsewhere. I leapt into action. I slung my rucksack of tools over my shoulder, pulled the wooden toilet seat off the drain, and slipped down it, replacing the seat behind me. I had made that entrance countless times by that point, and so was adept at doing it quickly and quietly.

Once in the sewer, I waited. In the shadows, hiding from the light of day. Underground. Did you see me down there, Lord? It was very dark, and my mission too dangerous for a lantern. Did you see my face as I waited for my prey? Did you see that I was smiling? Were you there beside me? It was so dark; I wouldn't have seen you if you were standing an inch before my nose. If Lucifer was down there with me, would I have smelt him over the shit? Would I have heard his hissing over the rushing water?

And then I heard the children. I heard Lucius teasing the girls as they lifted their dresses and picked their favorite spots around the latrine. I heard Marcus Gallus fling his huge body down on his usual spot, and go right into a chorus of abominable noises. I swear, dear god, that useless heft had the trumpets of hell up his ass. I heard Felix and Faustus. They were giggling and whispering. I couldn't hear about what, and so I didn't know whether to take it as a good or bad omen. Did they laugh in mad excitement over their coming divine task? Had they given me up to Marcus's father? Did they laugh at the foolish bastard down the toilet who was moments away from being arrested?

What could I do? I waited. I listened. I smiled in the shadows. I was thrilled, dear Lord. I only got happier as time went on, the sounds I heard were fitting in with the plan. Lucius finished and left as usual, the girls followed him out, and then the boys. As the boys left, and the of chatter coming from the latrine was dying down, two sounds remained; the tooting of Marcus Gallus, and the laughter of Felix and Faustus. Then came the sound of the guards, growing more and more disgusted with Marcus, and letting him know it. "When we leave you alone to your stink, do you grab a handful and eat? What else could produce such a heinous odor? You've been eating shit, haven't you big fellow?" And Marcus would answer them with the loudest breaking of wind he could arrange, and the guards all ran off, their boots and swords clinking and clanging.

Now the only sounds were of the black bear bully, and my lucky bow and arrow twins.

Marcus yelled at them, "What are you two dumb fucks still doing here? Ain't you gonna run off like the others? Fuck off to spy on the brothels, or wherever the fuck you two idiots fuck off to do when you disappear for hours."

"We go see Anteros." Said Felix. Or was it Faustus? I must say, dear Lord, their voices are as identical as their faces.

"Anteros? That your pet name for some whore dumb enough to sit on your two idiot dicks?"

"No. Anteros, the Greeks old god for returned love. The good kind of love. Would you like to see it?" Asked either Felix or Faustus.

"I fucking well would not, you fucking lunatics."

"Too bad." And this the twins said together in perfect unison, "Anteros would like to see you, Marcus Gallus."

Felix and Faustus stood. Light came down into the sewer through their now open toilet holes. Marcus did not stand at first, but did as soon as I heard the twins clamp their hands on his flesh.

"Get your fucking hands the fuck off of me, you fucking idiots!"

(Dear god, I may be recalling Marcus's words wrong. I don't remember exactly how he put all of his panicked insults directed at the twins, but I think you get the idea. They were grabbing him, he didn't like it, and he was letting them know it with the vulgarities you'd expect from someone of such low character.)

Soon Marcus's screams were muffled and then they were barely audible. When I saw Felix later his hand was covered in bite marks, and I imagine he shoved his fist into Marcus's mouth to keep him quiet. Can one admire this type of dedication, dear Lord, despite what cause it may have been in the name of? Must we always see the big picture, or can actions be judged independent of context?

41

The seat over where Marcus had been sitting suddenly flew off, and the bully came careening down the toilet, head first. My hook was bitten, and here now flopped my catch aboard my boat. Oh, forgiving father, how relieved I was to see him hit his head on the limestone floor of the sewer. I was delighted to hear a devastating crack. I didn't know if it was his skull, or his neck, but I knew he wouldn't be standing up anytime soon. He was knocked out cold, laying in the shallow stream of sewage flowing over him. I grabbed him by his armpits, and dragged him into the shadows.

I took a last peek up through the toilet. Felix and Faustus gazed down into the darkness in silence. Did they expect to see a blaze of holy light? Some sign that they had done good? Receiving none, they broke their gaze and replaced the wooden seat. I could hear their sandals as they softly walked out of the latrines, their purpose served.

My eyes had adjusted to the darkness, and I could see my catch rather clearly. Marcus Gallus's eyes were closed; his chest was still and breathless. His spine looked to be bent unnaturally foreword, so that his chin was pressed against his chest and he seemed without a neck. I put a finger on his throat and found no pulse, I put my hand on his chest and found no thump. The bear was dead, I thought, and without so much as a final growl. He didn't even know it was me who killed him, dear Lord. I felt ripped off. I got passed this quickly by remembering I was not on a mission of vengeance for myself, but one of duty and loyalty undertaken for my brother and future Emperor. I swelled with pride as I took the length of rope out of my rucksack, and tied the dead wrists of Marcus Gallus. I gathered the remainder of rope left after a few good knots, swung that over my shoulder, and got to dragging the broken necked beast.

I needed dryness and a fair amount of light in order to operate properly. The closest place I could think of was the clearing in front of the corpse-god, but I was afraid that Felix and Faustus might grow desperate for some acknowledgment of their job well done, and come upon me up to my elbows in Marcus's chest cavity. The closest place other than that was at a drain let-off at the foot of a muddy hill behind the baths. This would mean bringing Marcus out of the sewer and into broad daylight, but the mud hill was quiet, and I had never once seen a living soul back there. As long as Marcus wasn't making noise, I knew it would be safe to bring him there to remove his heart and dismember his body.

XI.

I laid Marcus Gallus on his back against the incline of the muddy hill, and squatted beside him with my rucksack of tools. In the bright mid-day sun, I investigated his neck more closely. I put a hand on either side of his head and lifted his chin. His neck slipped like wet string, and fell as frightfully far back as it had just been leaned forward.

I opened the rucksack, I took out my tools, and laid them out on a patch of cracked, dried mud. My hammer, my wedge of wood, my saw, my knife, and the amphora of Julia Domna.

I had read Hippocrates, and some work by the great physician Soranus, but not much, and not closely. And I had watched my father butcher several deer on a hunt, but never did so with my own hands. I was an amateur student of anatomy, dear Lord, to say the least. Like soldiers conscripted in a time of emergency, I was going to learn battle by becoming drenched in it. And drenched I would be, for you filled our bodies with much blood, oh engineer of man, and cutting one to pieces will leave you dripping wet.

I took Calpurnia's knife and cut Marcus's tunic from its collar to its waist. His breasts flopped to his sides like an old woman's. His stomach was swollen like a barrel. I could hear his breakfast digesting, dear god, and I checked his pulse once more, and once more was convinced he was dead. Someone needed to tell his stomach. I held the knife tightly and with both hands on its handle, pressed the sharp tip against the fragile enclave where the throat ended, and breast bone began. I pushed, and in went the knife, like it was slicing pudding. There was no blood yet. I cut down an inch and reached the bone, which the knife would not cut. I slide the blade on top of the bone, and cut a straight line down the center of Marcus's chest, severing the skin and flesh. Now things got bloody. I stuck my fingertips into the wound I just made, and pulled the two sides apart from each other, filleting the meat as I went, opening Marcus's tits into two dangling flaps. My hands were slippery with blood. I wiped them on my tunic, and went for the saw. I lined the teeth up to the center of the breast bone, and began to cut. This was awkward work, and hard to get a good angle, but I kept at it diligently and eventually got a clean line sawed down through the center of the breast bone. I knew that I wouldn't be able to wiggle my fingers in between bone as easily as flesh, and that's why I brought the wooden wedge. I put the tip of the wedge, which was sanded very thin by the palace's expert carpenter, into the crevasse I sawed into the bone. The wedge fit so snugly that it stood straight up on its own when I let go of it to get the mallet. I held the wedge securely with one hand, and gave it three good whacks. One on the top, one to the right, and one to the left. With each whack of the mallet I heard the sound of bones shattering as the bully's ribs broke. The gap between bone was plenty wide now, and I pulled each side apart with my hands, snapping any halfway broken ribs all the way through.

Do you shudder at these details, oh sympathetic master? I regret them as much as you do. They are chilling and awful, and yet I must tell them. I can no longer store these details in the library of my mind, and this confession will hopefully serve in purging the archives. Anyway, I'm almost done, so I might as well finish it. Besides, there's one final, important, detail that was particularly stirring to me, and I must share it. It gave me my first real taste of what I and Lucius would come to call admiratio-atrociatas. Shock-horror. Lucius would eventually pursue shock-horror as a religion, as a truth. And I would eventually run from it as the nightmarish monster it is. Marcus Gallus ended his life in the acquaintanceship of it.

I used the knife once more to cut through the muscle and sinew that sat under the breast bone. I pulled squishy handfuls of gore out of his chest, and then there it was, the swollen veiny heart. With its valves and pipes flowing this way and that, the heart made me immediately think of the Cloaca Maxima. I picked up the knife, lowered it against the largest valve of the heart, pressed the blade against it, and then, to my utter dismay and alarm, I saw and heard this dead heart jump and thump like it was a thunderous drum. I leapt away from the body, dropping the knife in the mud.

Lucius would come up with exact definitions for what specific types of cruelty accounted for a true event of shock-horror, but the loose rule was the closer you could bring a man to a painful death, with him still remaining conscious, the closer you got to achieving genuine admiratio-atrociatas.

I looked at the corpse, and took in a vision of shock-horror that I would not see matched for almost a decade. Marcus was alive, dear god. His string neck was tilted up again. His chin was on the top of what used to be his chest. His eyes were wide open, and he was surveying his body's new architecture. His heart thumped again, squirting blood out of its exposed arteries, and onto his face. Marcus's eyebrows raised in dreamy surprise at this, then he turned his obviously unbroken neck in my direction, and looked right at me. I couldn't make a sound, I couldn't move. With his eyes, Marcus asked the questions all men ask while in the midst of shock-horror: am I awake? Is this real?

Marcus took one last look at the gapping mine that was his chest, then laid his head back, and closed his eyes. His heart thumped once more, and then never again.

I cut out the heart, placed it in the silver amphora, then dismembered the body at the joints, and dispersed the pieces in discreet drain pipes throughout the sewers. I stomped on the head until it was unrecognizable and left it at the bottom of a pool of sewage, god forgive my everlasting soul.

XII.

That evening, back at the palace, in the safety of his bed chamber, I presented Lucius with the filled amphora. He dismissed the slaves that were arranging his many pillows for the night. When we were alone, we sat together on his bed, and had a look at the heart. Lucius was delighted, and he laughed with great satisfaction.

"It feels just wonderful, dear brother," said Lucius, "to be able to order a man's heart taken from him and delivered upon silver."

"It feels wonderful to be of service, Caesar." I said. I had never spoken to Lucius in that way, dear Lord, and I liked how it felt to be deferential to him. I looked forward to speaking that way to him more often.

"I'm not Caesar, yet. And if Geta has his way, I never will be." Lucius closed the heart inside the amphora and set it aside. "You've done a fine job. I won't forget it, and neither will the Emperor. I'll see that he's informed of your success."

"Thank you. Well, good night then." I had the keen ability of sensing when Lucius wanted to be left alone, and I always obliged him. This skill was among the reasons I remained his friend for so many years, when most every other man who called Lucius friend found themselves murdered by him.

I got out of his bed, and began to leave, but Lucius called to me by my name. I liked the way my name sounded when he said it. I turned to him, "yes?"

"I should like to give the heart to Plautilla next week at the baths. I fear the flesh will stink by then." He held out the amphora to me. "Put it on the roof of your annex to dry out in the sun. Cover it in wire from the gardener to protect it from birds."

"Yes," I said taking the amphora, "your majesty."

He grinned. I left him alone, and went about setting the heart to dry.

XIII.

The following week I watched Lucius present Plautilla with the silver amphora holding the dried-out heart of Marcus Gallus. I was far from them, across the pools, and couldn't hear a word they shared, but I could see their faces quite clearly. Lucius, at first proud and cocky. Plautilla, at first curious and amused. She saw the pretty amphora and was delighted, and then he opened it, and her face decidedly changed its expression. She was disgusted, and then rather mortified. Overtaken is the word for it, oh maker of words. Plautilla was overtaken with grief. She let out a mournful wail, and this I did hear. She buried her crying face in her hands, and fell to her knees before Lucius, who stood there looking terribly foolish, holding the heart out in front of him. He quickly closed it up inside the amphora, as the other girls of the royal court ran to the aid of their sister. Lucius, embarrassed and enraged, stormed away and left the room. I wanted to follow him, but I knew better.

That night, on the walk back to the palace, Lucius gave the amphora to me.

"You worked so hard for it, you keep it." He said. His eyes were red and puffy, he had been crying.

"What went wrong?" I asked. "Did she find the heart repellent? We dried it well, and covered it with lavender."

"It was not the heart itself that she objected to," explained Lucius, "but its removal. And more specifically that it was removed from the heinous Marcus Gallus, who my betrothed Plautilla Fulvius is apparently in love with, and has been for many years."

I was surprised at first, but when I thought of it afterwards, dear god, I remembered how Plautilla had often been the only one to laugh at the brute's joking. In fact, when I remembered Marcus chasing Plautilla around the pools of the Trajan baths, I now saw not a girl in fear for her life, but one in the ecstatic throes of youthful romance. Marcus was a big, fat, smelly, animal, and Plautilla was simply a girl who loved big, fat, smelly, animals. She would grow into a woman of much the same tastes, and no matter how beastly Lucius may have proved to be on the inside, he was housed in a body that was smooth and gentle, and she would never love him like she loved her slobbering forest bear, Marcus.

I took the amphora from Lucius with honor, and I kept it wrapped in a red silk robe at the bottom of the wooden chest at the foot of my bed.

XIV.

Julia Domna never once came to visit me in my loft, oh my Lord, so you could imagine how unnerved I was to find her sitting on my bed, waiting for me, one afternoon when I returned from a Greek lesson.

My wooden chest was wide open, and the red silk robe was strewn across the floor. The silver amphora sat on the bed. Julia Domna sat beside it, her back to me, looking out the window at the late afternoon sky.

Without turning, she knew that I was there. She spoke, my flesh crawled. "Murdering bastard, stay far from my children, will you?" She spoke as if she was inviting me to a garden picnic. She was wearing a sleeveless blue gown stitched with gold thread. She looked slender but powerful, and womanly in all the right places. Her gowns were famously tight and complimentary to her slim figure.

Julia turned her head over her glowing bare shoulder, and met me with her beautiful almond, brown eyes. They were ten times too big for her head, maybe a hundred times. She could see everything, anything. She looked at you and saw your true nature. She saw your shortcomings as if they were carved into your forehead. There was nothing you could hide from her. Julia Domna sniffed the air and smelt your soul. She smiled at me with a piercing mock warmth, and softly patted the bed beside her and the amphora, beckoning me to come sit.

I crept over to her, each step a mile. There was every reason to believe that she would cut my head off. She had done it to my mother. She had wanted to do it to me for so many years, and now, by my conspiring with her son to kill a child of the royal court, she had the perfect excuse. I sat beside her on the bed, her gaze remained on the sky outside my open window.

"Such a lovely view you have. How generous of my husband to allow you this lovely view. How have you liked it, hmm? Having a view?" Julia Domna tilted her head to me, but kept her eyes on the sky.

I spoke up through my fear, "At night, it's especially lovely, mistress. The stars are especially-"

"I don't mean this view in particular, child. I mean any view. I mean, how do you enjoy the privilege of having eyeballs? Hmm? Has that been nice for you?"

"I don't understand, mistress." I understood just fine, true master.

She continued, "I mean to ask, how would you like it if I took those little eyeballs from you? I could pluck them out, have them tossed with salt and olive oil? Have myself a little snack of your eyeballs, would you like that, little bastard?"

"I-"

"Don't answer, fool." Julia Domna picked up the amphora, and held it in her lap. She opened it and briefly studied the shriveled, putrid heart. She scoffed, closed it again. "All this mess because my husband is a frivolous spender." She stood up, and put the amphora under her arm. "Gaius Gallus has become mad with worry over his missing son Marcus. Plautilla Fulvius told her father that he was killed by my son Lucius, who had some sort of rivalry with the boy. Plautilla and her father are good loyal Romans, they'll be discreet. But still, if this horrible thing did happen, let all traces of it be swept away. To this end I confronted my son Lucius, and he informed me that all parts had been discarded, but for the heart, and that the heart had traded hands, and was now in the possession of his accomplice, the vile bastard who houses himself in my own home."

Julia Domna stuck a long finger in my face. I thought she might poke an eye out after all. Instead she scolded me, "Stay away from Lucius. You're only alive because my husband prefers it, but he will not always be around to protect you. Even kings die, my little bastard." She lowered her finger like she was sheathing a dagger. "For now, I may not be allowed to kill you, but I can make you wish I were."

Three elite guards entered the room on cue. They were guards who had shown a real knack for hating me in the past. One was the earless blue eyed soldier. He was smiling, and holding a short horse whip. God, you saw him, he was practically beaming sunshine in his joyful vengeance. I jumped up off the bed, and ran for the window. Before I could leap out onto the roof, the earless soldier grabbed me by my waist and pulled me back into the room. They tied me to the bed on my stomach, tore off my tunic, and with Julia keeping count, whipped me ten times across the back, until the flesh was split and oozing blood. I screamed and cried, but honestly, dear god, I was relieved. I was being punished severely because I wasn't going to be killed. I would keep my miserable life, and I was shielded from the pain of the whip by my gratitude. After crack number ten, I was untied, and the guards left me and my step-mother alone once more. I curled into a ball, holding my knees, whimpering and trembling, trying to keep my shredded back from touching anything but the cool air coming through the window.

On her way out, Julia Domna kneeled over me, put a hand on my cheek, and with a motherly tenderness said, "You have the face of your father. What a handsome man you'll grow to be."

CHAPTER FOUR

I.

I must sleep a while. Not that a lamb needs rest on the eve before its slaughtering, but I would like to finish this confession with as clear a mind as I started it with. I fear I've not paced myself in my storytelling, and have grown prematurely exhausted.

The day has been long. I spent it with Wojslaw, a monk from eastern Pannonia, and I'm proud to say, dear god, my friend. He asked for my help planting seeds for Jove's flower on the grounds around the monastery. Wojslaw is the wisest and kindest individual I have ever known, and he has helped me to understand you better, my complicated maker. He is a moral man, and a devotee of the one true god, and if you let him start telling you about it, good luck getting him to ever shut up. Such a lover of religious talk for its own sake, during a six month long vow of silence, imposed on him by the elders of his sect, Wojslaw crept from the monastery and into town once a week for ecclesiastical debates with the prostitutes and wine merchants. He'd talk about god with a horse if he thought it understood him, or at least seemed open to conversion. Wojslaw had a long-suffering nobleman for a father, who was from a ruined family that lost its wealth but maintained its education, which debtors are unable to repossess. To ease his mind at the end of a stressful day he would have his son Wojslaw talk to him while he drifted off to sleep. Wojslaw always had monologues prepared on this or that spiritual topic to deliver to his drowsy father, and it was a part of their nightly routine for the entirety of his childhood. "It's been a rough day today, my son. Calm your father's busy mind with the words of another's." And Wojslaw would orate, and as the years passed, he became more than good at turning feeling into thought, and thought into speech.

(Did you give this boy to this father in order to train him in the art of talking, oh divine exponent of our righteous character? It would seem too orchestrated a combination to be accidental, that such a deep knowledge of god fills the chest of a man who is doubly blessed with the words to share it with his brethren.)

No man or woman who ever talks with Wojslaw goes unaffected. He talks of a god of mercy and of pain with an enthusiasm that emanates from serious study and contemplation. He is a man who thinks long and slow and then speaks incredibly fast, for he may die before he can tell you all that he has discovered within the depths of his mind and soul. He is a pleasure to listen to, as you must often do yourself, oh proud creator. Many tell my friend, Wojslaw, that he speaks with the voice of god. He blushes with modesty, and reminds them of his stammer, which is, as you well know my Lord, incessant and beyond his control. A burst of audible air from his gullet appears between his every thought, as if for dramatic punctuation.

"What a silly god- TUH- to give his evangelist- TUH- a broken voice- TUH."

Wojslaw jokes, but we know about your affinity for all things incongruous, dear god.

Once he discovered there was a new tongueless stranger at the monastery, Wojslaw and I became fast friends. I was another sleepy daddy, who would hang on his sons every word without any of his own in return. This image must seem rather funny to you, dear god, for as you know, Wojslaw is over thirty years my senior.

The sun set as we finished planting our trees, and we ate bread and drank wine on the western hill, your pink sky for scenery. Wojslaw talked with wit of you and your ways, and I listened. When we returned to the monastery there was news that old friends of mine were in the village, and they carried with them strong wood, sharp nails, and nagging grudges. They were asking for the bastard son of the Emperor Septimius Severus. My death lay in wait.

I must sleep a little while. Don't worry, dear god, the infection on the stump of my tongue makes it hard for me to sleep more than an hour at a time. The pain overwhelms my dreams and wherever they have taken me, I am suddenly gripped by the sensation of losing the tongue for the first time, and am roused awake. I may find myself in a dream of a hunt in cool weather. I close in on the great deer. I draw my bow, the prized antlers in my sights, I fire. Just before the arrow reaches the animal's skull, a horrible pain seizes me and my mouth is suddenly flooded with blood. I wake up to find that a blister has burst and puss is oozing down my throat, or worse, the wound has reopened. Sometimes I'll wake Wojslaw, and without any protest he'll take me into his chambers. We sit together on his bed. He talks. I listen, holding a bundle of cloth stuffed in my mouth, waiting for the bleeding, or my pulse, to stop. Despite the countless linens I've stained dark red, my heart remains defiantly thumping.

Wojslaw is the first of my fellow men that I feel I can honestly call a friend, and I thank you for him, dear god. Before I met him I had only ever pretended at friendship. I had masqueraded as a friend to others, and they returned that which they received, a mock warmth that never rose above shallow coquetting. The closest I ever came to friends were the young men that Lucius and I spent our adolescence with on the streets of Rome, past sunset, drunk on visionary elixirs. Among them were the dimwitted twin sons of the Emperor's tax collector. Out of stupidity, or perhaps depravity, the twins were always up for a night on the town with the soon to be Emperor and I. They were always good for laughs, could drink like empty barrels, and were worth four men when it came to a throw down with a rival. They fought hard and dirty, just like me. Felix and Faustus would have called me friend, but I doubt that with their feebleness they could be trusted to apply the term aptly, oh Lord. I certainly did nothing to deserve their friendship, leading them again and again into murder and mayhem for the sake of my own hidden benefits. When we were children I saw the twins as useful globs of malleable clay, and as they grew I saw them as much the same, albeit larger globs.

Though I loved Lucius, he was never my friend, and I never his. My bastardhood made me a solitary prisoner in the imperial palace, and Lucius took advantage of my helplessness, no more than that. It's true, he confided in me, trusted me with his most private secrets, and most valued political strategies. He kept nothing from me. Yet despite our apparent intimacy, Lucius chose me as his right hand not out of friendship. There was no special quality Lucius saw in me, nothing he admired or respected. I was around, and I was trustworthy in so far as I was utterly harmless, that was it. What could I ever do with the information he shared with me? The only influence I had in the world was due to my connection to him. When Lucius confided in me, it was like confiding with an external region of his own mind. When he confessed to me, it was as if he was whispering into a hole he dug in the ground. Who could I tell, besides you, oh Lord? Who would listen?

For my part, I was even less a friend to Lucius than he was to me. In my single-minded obsession with him, I turned Lucius into more of a statue than a human being. Something to worship, not make friends with. This gave him yet another advantage over me, for one is never prepared for a statue to grow, age, and change. Lucius was always surprising me, though I think I can fairly say I surprised him last. And it's the final surprise that counts, am I right, dear god? What proof against a genuine friendship is there better than the surprise of a dagger in the back?

Nonetheless, if you were to ask me when I was nineteen or so, I would have told you that Lucius was my best friend in the world, even though I knew well he wouldn't say the same about me. That bothered me then, and it bothers me tonight. If you were to ask Lucius who his best friend was in those formative years, he would have answered without hesitation, "The pink-wolf, of course. Dexius Gladius Januarius."

Yes, my Lord, the great soldier Dexius, who famously wore his legionary helmet and armor wherever he went, even during peace time. He was called the pink-wolf for the way he faded the red of his uniform with lemon juice to appear as pink as a carnation. His scarf, tunic, and cape, all as pink as the Spring gown of some pampered Empress. Dexius grew his black hair long, and curled it into thick locks, which he would tie with pink ribbons. His helmet was bronze and silver, but atop its crest was an arched plume of horse hair dyed a vibrant pink. His legs were plucked of every hair, his skin was tanned dark brown, hiding the scars that covered most of his body. His shoulder plates and chest armor were polished with oils, and sparkled in the moon's glow. Before a night out, Dexius would pale his face with white ash, and then rouge his cheeks with the dregs of red wine, like a whore would before an appointment. He wore silk wristlets, and pink anklets over his caligae. He wore a rose behind his left ear. From a distance, say across a crowded party, he looked like a dandy mockery of a soldier. Likely some lavender bloke, wearing a uniform, but calling it an outfit, a costume. Good Romans, drunk and angry and looking for fun, might see the pink-wolf in his splendor, and think they've found themselves an easy target. They cross the party, screaming insults at the soldier in pink. Calling him a disgrace to the uniform. Calling him a disgrace to the legions. Calling him a disgrace to manhood. A good beating ought to teach this fairy how to dress, they think. But as they get closer to Dexius, the good Romans realize it's they who are about to learn a lesson in appearance. For the pink-wolf is pink in color only, and his fangs are as sharp as his gray brother's. Sharper.

Beneath all the pink and the polished armor is a body of stone muscle, hardened by disciplined training, and nearly a decade of battle under the harshest conditions imaginable. Dexius fought in the mud of Germany. He fought in the ice of Briton. He fought in the swamps of Gaul. He fought under the sweltering sun of Africa. Fighting is who he is. It's what he does. But when Dexius Januarius finds himself in a civilized place like Rome, he finds a proper fight elusive. He walks the streets, looking for another pair of fists to play with, and learns that his size deters civilized men. Trouble exists in cities, just like it does in the wild, just like it does on the battlefield, it's just a little more hidden, just a little more comfortable in the shadows. No one in Rome wants to fight a man of such obvious strength and ferocity, so Dexius decided to stop looking for trouble and start tempting it out of hiding. Trouble comes looking for a pink piglet to gobble up, but instead meets a wolf in a pork jacket, grinning and ready for a tussle. Lucius and Dexius had much in common. Together they invited trouble to do its worst and then sliced it to pieces with their swords. They enjoyed the same things, and each admired the others abilities at ruthless violence. I was afraid of Dexius, and jealous of his fearlessness.

All devils must be given their due though, dear god, and this pink devil threw one hell of a punch. It was quite a majestic thing to see in action. I've even seen the pink-wolf kill men with nothing more than a swift fist to the head. Once, a soldier on leave in the city insulted us with his loud, drunken singing. We dragged him to the thoroughfare, Lucius and I held his arms, and pulled his head back by its hair, so his chin poked straight out. Dexius punched this rowdy soldier in the cheek and cracked his jaw clean off his skull. He was left with a dangling flesh-sack of bone fragments where the bottom of his face used to be. He shook a little in the dirt, spitting up teeth and blood, but then all at once got stiff as a log and died. Felix and Faustus were watching and they applauded. Lucius and I couldn't stop laughing. Good times.

I must sleep, yes. My thoughts are wandering away from me and I must sleep for just a little while. I've arrived at the part of my prayer that will deal with my adolescence. Mine and my brother's. We caused such havoc in those days. We were young, and handsome, and rich, and powerful, and had not a care in the world, and oh dear god, did we raise hell. My late teens and early twenties flash by in my memory as a picture show of ripe breasts bulging through torn tunics, and peach asses presenting themselves from upturned togas. Fine clothes, fast horses, and sharp swords covered in hot blood. Playing, and fucking, and laughing, and killing! What fun!

Forgive me, oh my Lord. I am tired. I lose myself in reminiscence.

Sleep. Yes. For a little while, god. I must sleep.

II.

Here is me. That is, the bastard. And here is my brother. That is, Lucius, now twenty one years old, now married, now known as Augustus. Not to me, though. Always Lucius to me.

And here are our disciples, that are the twins Felix and Faustus, those foolish giants; and the pink-wolf, that is Dexius Januarius, the comely warrior.

And we're all dressed in legionnaires uniforms. Armor and helmet and all, though none have served in battle but Dexius. Also, none wear a pink plume but he.

And we're sitting in the den of the witch of potions, and the sun is setting, and we're making up our minds what to do with the evening. The witch of potions serves us dreams in mugs to sharpen our wills and ready our bodies for another evening of shock-horror on the streets of Rome.

Tonight we're drinking the witch's most special mead. That is, the one I've just swallowed, and which tastes of stale grass and copper. She has been brewing it for a decade, so she says, and it's finally ready to pour down the throats of future kings.

"Drink. Drink, and gaze upon the world which lays atop the world." Says the witch of potions, refilling our mugs with her frothy mead. "Drink." And we do.

And now comes a quiet time in the den, as we sit and wait for the mead to begin its trance.

And here is the witch of potions, busying herself over a new concoction. She mixes this tonic with that elixir, she crushes dried mushrooms of blue and violet into fine powders. And as my mates are staring at the walls, and smiling at nothing, and twitching with the coming on of visions, I see the witch. And here is the witch's face, and here are her long ears, and her sluggish nose. And I wonder how anyone could possibly be this old? Her skin and muscle are slack, and free from the bone. I could reach over, tug on the end of her dangling chin, and pull her wrinkled visage right off that skull of hers. She wouldn't even notice. She'd even be relieved, like throwing off a cloak made heavy by the rain.

And here is me, and here is my own face, and my own skin. I touch it and am relieved by its stiffness. Its smoothness. Lovers I've had, after touching every part of me in a frenzy, have told me how lucky I was to have such smooth skin. I didn't feel it till now, here in this den, touching my young face while gazing at the witch's oldness. What luck to be young.

The witch of potions looks up from her busyness and meets my gaze with her hollow black eyes. She parts her wire lips, licks them with a dry tongue and asks me, "Does my mead yet find you, young prince? Have you met it in your stomach? Has it exploded bolts of lightning in your chest, and mind, and fingertips?"

I close my eyes to better feel the effects of the mead, and find the witch her answer: My stomach churns noisily, summer rain clouds brew thunder in my gut. My chest is a fever of commotion. My pulse has quickened to a thousand beats a second. I can no longer hear a separating of thumps, just one constantly resounding vibration. My mind's eye is a colorful swirling madness, a greasy pond of white reflected moonlight turned green and orange in the rippling water. My fingertips dance against each other, sparking like flint as they strike. I could torch the entire Teutoburg forest with a snap.

I open my eyes to answer the witch, but before I can speak, here is the word of Lucius, "Yes." He tells the witch and twists a smile. "The mead is well met, indeed."

Felix and Faustus hoot with laughter and agreement. "Well met! Well met, indeed it is!"

The pink-wolf, solemn, hulking, arms folded, but pleased by the mead into nodding agreement.

Lucius finds my eyes with his own. He speaks, "And you, my brother? Do you feel it?"

Lightening and lightening and lightening, and I say to him, "Oh, yes. I feel it."

...

And here's me on the street. And there is that moon, and there is the glowing face of my brother, Lucius. And we're walking, and stumbling, and leaning on one another so not to fall. Felix and Faustus are laughing at the stars. The pink-wolf marches with a lost grimace across his painted face, amused to distraction by the click of his boots on the stone walk beneath.

Suddenly the wolf halts his walking, and plants his paws, and sniffs the air. Lucius stops beside him. We all stop.

"What do you smell?"

And now the wolf is moving again, and we're following him down a side alleyway, off the street, between closed shops. And the wolf follows his nose, and we follow the wolf.

And now we see what the wolf smells. An old, piss soaked, drunkard, roasting three pigeons on a spit over a small fire he's made. The wolf smacks his jowls.

The old drunkard thinks he's alone, but we are slowly coming upon him from the shadows. He lives in this alleyway. It is his home for the night, and my friends and I thrill at our unseen trespass. The old drunkard is resting on a patch of dirt he's piled for his bed. A neat stack of pigeon feathers, which the drunkard has removed from his dinner, sits beside him for company. He drinks wine from a stone flask, and belches. To no one, the old drunkard speaks:

"The world grows, so it does. The cities grow. This city swells with noise, and with numbers. We are too many. We are too, too many. And all of these new heads, thinking and thinking, and still not an original idea in fifty years. War with the Germans. Rape the Babylonians. Endless slaughter upon the Jews. Build a bath, raise a temple, pass a decree of nothing. The world grows, but doesn't change, and this old man would die of shock if he heard an original thought."

We reach the edge of the shadows, and Lucius stops short of visibility, and we all stop behind him.

The drunkard rotates his pigeon dinner, their skin crackles, and the air fills with the smell of cooking fat. He reaches to the stack of gray feathers, and selects the longest one. He sticks the feather in his matted hair. The mead starts playing tricks on me, turning the old drunkard's dirt heap into a royal throne, his feather a crown.

Lucius closes the cheek guards of his helmet over his face, covering all but his eyes. We listen from the darkness as the old drunkard yammers on to the street cats:

"Where have all the kings gone? The men to lead me? The men I would follow? In my life I've heeded no call other than that of the wind, and the whims of my heart, but I don't wish it were that way. Where is the master whose path I would willingly ware? Send me back in time, oh powerful Saturn, so that I may be servant to a worthy keeper. So that I may belong to a Julian, or a Claudian, or an Antonine. Where in the modern world are the Octavians who turn Augustuns by action, not by name change? Where is good Nerva, good Trajan, good Hadrian, good Marcus? Where have they run off to, with their honor, and restraint, and wisdom? Good Romans ask, who are these new animals who live in your palaces, and claim your titles? Who are these strange beasts, who don your purple robes, and call themselves royalty? Where have all the kings gone?"

"To death." Answered Lucius from the shadows, startling the drunkard to alertness. "Shall we send you to meet them?" And Lucius steps forward into the light of the pigeon fire, and we follow.

And we're circled around the drunkard and his camp site, Lucius standing before him. The drunkard tries to stand, but Lucius puts a boot on his shoulder and forces him back down onto his butt.

"What, what, and what of it? What is this? What does five soldiers want with one old man?" The drunkard spits with every word.

"It's your words that siren us to you, old man. Your seditious ramblings about the Emperor. Also, your dinner, which caught the senses of my comrade in arms." Lucius nods at Dexius, giving him approval to finally descend upon the scrumptious looking pigeons. He takes the spit off the fire, and begins pulling chunks of greasy meat off the breast of each bird, tossing them to Felix and Faustus.

I am not hungry. The mead has caused a flutter of nausea in my stomach, and a confusion in my thinking. As the cooked bird turns to mush in the chomping fangs of my friends, I mistake it for the flesh of the old drunkard.

The drunkard protests this devouring. "Rob a man the fullness in his belly? Rob a man of his right to speak freely to the night? You make my point through your daring, soldier! Who leads you? Who is your master? A thief. A thief who marches his soldiers into Rome to take it for himself. To make himself king by force of an army. The servants of thieves are nothing more than that."

Lucius delivers rebuttal. "And what of your beloved Gaius Julius? Did he not breach the Rubicon, so that other men of similar worth may breach it again and again?"

"What has been broken once, can not be broken again. Take Rome from the sea. Break her with a navy, that would be a bit of originality, at least. Compare the thug on the Palatine hill to our father? Our Caesar? Ridiculous!" Now the drunkard is studying the pink-wolf, who tosses aside a wing bone, and licks his fingers. "Now, you've finished. Those cooking pigeons were all I had in the world, and you've taken them. Now go on! Leave an old man to his drink."

Lucius ignores this plea, and returns to the debate at hand. "And the Augustus that you love so dearly? What was his legacy for Rome? The sadistic recluse, Tiberius? The mad Caligula, and the fiddler Nero? Should not an Emperor be judged by the progeny he leaves us?"

"And what will our judgments be then of the Severen clan? Hmm? A king that leaves us a bastard, a queer, and a murderous punk!"

Nausea aside, insults aside, this bastard feels a rush of happiness to be included.

Lucius opens his cheek guards, revealing a face every Roman knows. They have seen it pressed onto their coins, and raised before their temples. The son of the Emperor. The murderous punk prince of Rome. The drunkard's tired eyes double with recognition.

"Sir," says Lucius, drawing his gladius from its sheath, "you injure me."

Lucius thrusts his sword into the top of the old drunkards stomach, so that just the point pierces his flesh. The drunkard, overtaken by the instinct to stop this invasion into his body, grabs the blade with both hands, and tries to pull it out and away. Lucius pushes ever so gently forward on the handle of his sword, and the smooth steel buries itself deeper into the bulbous belly of the old man, slicing his fingers and palms as it makes its descent. Blood is splashing. The old man is groaning, and gritting his teeth. He squeezes his fists around the base of the sword and tugs as hard as he can, to no avail. His right thumb is severed, pops off, flies through the air, lands in the fire. Slain right through by the gladius, the old drunkard is now pinned to his dirt throne.

"Say hello to King Romulus for me." Lucius smiles and lets go of his planted sword.

Losing his breath, the old drunkard whispers to his grinning murderer, "You've killed me. The peaceful abyss waits. Yet, what horrible vision sees me to the end? The arrogant smile of Tarquin, the last of the old Roman kings. May you and yours suffer the same as that old tyrant."

Lucius does not cease his smiling. He steps away from the skewered old man, and his followers step towards. We stomp the old drunkard with our boots until he is dead, while Lucius hunkers down and picks through the bones of the roasted pigeon for a snack. When it is finished, Lucius retrieves his sword from the dead man's gut, and the feather from his ear, to put behind his own.

...

A starlight orgy is being held at the colosseum tonight. The skin and flesh of Rome's most beautiful elite will be there, so we're making haste through the forum.

My vision is cleared askew by the witch's mead. We pass temples and basilicas. We pass the Curia Julia, the seat of government. I know their symbols, I know their history, but tonight they are nothing more than stacked brick and stone. Tonight, the forum, and the senate, are miniature sets for some childish puppet show. And tonight, I wonder for the first time, when have they ever been anything but?

Tavertine arcades give way to the open air of the Flavian amphitheater. Waiting by the entrance are servants looking to take our clothes, and our armor, and our weapons. We breeze by with our swords, and our chest plates, and our helmets, and do we turn heads? The most lustful women of the party discard half sucked cocks to greet the fascinating new arrivals. Five uniformed legionaries, the pinkish Dexius heralding like an imperial banner that the son of the emperor has arrived with his notorious coterie.

African musicians beating drums, a writhing wildlife of dancing nakedness moves to the beat. Torches burning, buckets of wine are being passed and shared. Carpets laid on the arena floor. Young Roman professionals fuck comfortably over the sand where gladiators kill each other. Tits and apricots and dicks and plums and holes and olives and holes of a different sort.

And now our happy band splits so that we may each do our own worst. I see Felix take a blonde girl, I see Faustus take a brunette girl. I see them switch and switch back, and pair anew with a red headed girl each. I see Dexius find a boy, and then another boy, and then another. A taste he acquired in a military tent, encamped under desperate circumstances, bonding with those men who would risk their lives beside him. The finest boys are happy to bend over for a chance with the legendary pink-wolf, and they line up by the dozens. Dexius will have each and every one of them, buggering with his fingers the ones he cant reach with his cock.

My tastes are far more conservative. I seek and find the highest possible combination of beauty and inebriation, never sacrificing a deficit in one, for a surplus in the other. The equilibrium between willingness and potential enjoyment is paramount. The mead has transformed my strategy of action into quantifiable mathematics. Enjoyment is a dialectical equation. Happiness is a ratio.

And here she is. And here is her fine peach ass, but her flat chest. Also, here is her giggling friend. And here are her massive tits, but her stone wall of an ass. And I say to myself, "added together, these will do nicely."

There is no privacy, but I lead my two girls to the edge of the orgy. I recline on dusty pillows by a bowl of grapes, pop a few in my mouth. Sweet and juicy. Is it the witches potion or are these the most delicious grapes I've ever tasted in my life?

"You, with the small tits, suck on your big breasted girlfriend's nipples." And this one eagerly obliges my order, and the other one is moaning and gritting her teeth.

My vision drifts, and scans the party goers, sucking and fucking. And here is a playful screaming. And here is a nude, smiling beauty, emerging from the crowd. She looks like Lucius's childhood love and current wife, Plautilla. But rounder in the hips. Much rounder at the hips. She runs, and laughs, and is chased by a snickering Lucius, mad and horny from pursuit. He is close behind his pray, he reaches out and pinches her lily white ass, leaving a red mark. "Ouch!" Screams the Plautilla look alike, running back into the forest of debauch. Lucius, face dripping with lust, disappears after her.

I'm hard. I return my gaze to my girls. I join them. We three get close, we three are kissing. I bend the big assed one over at her waist. I pull aside my armor, and my tunic, and take out my cock. I fuck her standing, pushing her face forward into her friend's cleavage.

And here again comes round-hipped-Plautilla, running naked across my field of vision. No more laughter now. Whimpering now, and tears. Along with her pinched ass, she has acquired bruised thighs, bloody knees, and a black eye. Out of the crowd behind her comes Lucius. He grabs faux-Plautilla by her shoulder, she scrambles to get away, he grabs her by her hair, she spins around to face him, and he punches her in the nose. He shoves her to the dirt. He kicks her in her filthy, swollen ass. She stirs to her feet, and fleas in a panic, back into the crowd that has now turned deaf to her cries for help. Lucius happily pursues her out of my sight.

I cum. I pull out. I wipe myself on her lower back, and walk away without a look or word of thanks.

Tucking my cock back behind my tunic, and under my armor, I walk to a bar on the sidelines of the action, for a drink. After a while gone on wine, I'm joined by my brother.

Lucius is sweating and panting. He takes my wine and chugs it for refreshment, and I notice the blood covering his hands, and the bits of flesh between his knuckles. Has he killed the girl he was chasing? I can no longer hear her cries.

"Enjoying yourself, brother?" He asks.

"How could I not be?" I answer.

"Does the mead still sway you?"

"Like the tall trees in a storm, oh my brother."

"Good. Let us test its proclaimed paralysis of fear. I grow bored with beating old drunkards and women. Let us find a proper enemy to draw blood from." Lucius turns away from me. "What swine is worthy of our fists and boots and blades?"

As Lucius surveys the coliseum and its revelers, I am surveying his face in profile. Why is that nose so familiar? Why do your eyes seem more my own than the ones I find in a mirror? When you breath in, my lungs fill with air. Where you step, I must follow behind. Was I you in a past life? Will you be me in the next?

"Let's... kill... him!" Lucius has made his pick and is pointing. I follow his finger across the party to its target.

And here is Titus Millius, the corrupt quaestor turned gang lord. And here is his entourage of hired goons, yanked from his personal army, made up of retired praetorians and high priced foreign mercenaries. Five of them are here tonight, getting their fair share of sexual distraction, but keeping at least one eye each on their master and protectorate.

Despite their exposed cocks, the guards wear steal shoulders and chests to put our own armor to shame. They carry daggers roped to their waists, and spears lay nearby, within close reach. One black goon looks to be a sagittarii, with his bow over his shoulder, and his quiver beneath the swinging tits of the girl he's banging.

The goons are dispersed, but still form a perimeter around their patron, Titus Millius, who is currently holding down a shrieking pregnant girl that he's raping. Did Millius bring the pregnant girl from home, or more likely, was she provided by whoever is hosting the party? Special requests must be met for special benefactors. The pregnant girl looks to be from the far east, but it's hard to tell for sure because her face is so contorted by suffering.

A memory seizes me of a public display from the past, with Titus Millius loading a goon who had betrayed him into a sac along with three feral dogs. He had the barking, screaming sac thrown into the sewers. His reputation for brutal shows of extreme violence rivals even that of the emperor's eldest son. And so they must fight.

"Good." I say finally. "Perfect."

My brother pats me on the shoulder, an obedient friend is a noble friend.

And here we go, and here we come, confidently strolling towards battle. And here is Titus Millius with his brutalized far-eastern. And here are his goons with their growing suspicions and tightening grips. And here we come, the royal inheritor of Rome, and his bastard lieutenant.

Lucius draws his sword mid stride, and so I draw mine. I ask him, "shall we give fair warning?"

"To those you'd like to lay or kill, whom wouldn't like to fuck or die, give only surprise." And here is Lucius's wild glorious smile, and here is his heart pounding in my own chest.

We're upon Millius. He's got the pregnant girl like she were a dog. She's all but given up, wrapping her arms around her belly and taking the worst of it like she were already dead. She hopes he'll just finish, but I know the spirit of a monster like Titus Millius, and bet that if she'd like to end him faster, she'd do better to show a struggle. Shall we be this young mother's heroes this evening? No. I think we are too late for that.

Millius sees us. He does not cease his thrusting. "Ah! Do I see the elder Augustus come this way?!" He sounds friendly enough. "And do I see his bastard?" That was less friendly. "And do I see their swords?" Less friendly still, but it's too late. Lucius raises his sword.

"Your vision is strong for an old man, Titus Millius. How are your reflexes?" Lucius swings his sword down at Millius, who apparently has fine reflexes for a man his age, let alone one with his cock stuck in a girl, for he raises his own sword immediately. Lucius and Millius cling and clang over the sweaty back of the still penetrated pregnant girl. I join in with my own sword, and Millius is able to fend us both off. It is quite a thing I see before me. A hairy chested man of forty, up to his waist in unwieldy pussy, all the while holding his own in a double sword fight with men half his age. Is Millius quick as cupid, or has the mead slowed our attack to a crawl? Millius's hired goons have seen our offensive, and they are grabbing their daggers, and they are grabbing their spears, and they are leaving behind disappointed lovers, and they are advancing on us. We will need reinforcements.

"Felix! Faustus! Come!" I scream to the crowd between slashes of my gladius.

Millius makes a grand sweep at us with his blade, and then does a flip backwards, finally dismounting from the pregnant girl. She falls forward on her stomach, and grabs at her womb seeming to be struck with pain. Her maternal water seeps out of her womanhood. "Oh no." She whispers, and I hear her. I want to lift her and carry her to safety, but I will not. I feel nauseas with want to help her, but I will not help her. Instead I turn to the approaching goons who would like to kill me.

And I scream again. "Here! Felix and Faustus! Here!" And still no response. Where are those two retards? Crawled up some cavern of a slut's ass where the sound of man will not travel?

Lucius chases the bare assed Millius into the orgy. I suppose I'll stay here with his five bodyguards and give my life for my brother.

The first goon is upon me, and he must be drunk or an amateur, because I get my blade right in his gut, and he drops his spear. I slay him right through and he looks at me with utter disappointment and reproach. He goes for his dagger and cuts my forearm trying to bring it up to cut my throat, which he bumbles, hitting nothing but my cheek guard. I head butt him to his nose, and pull my sword out of him with a shake and a turn, making sure the wound will never heal. Not bad, I think. Even if they kill me now, at least I'll have gotten one of them.

And here are three more goons coming at me from all directions. And here's the mead returning with new powers. And here's me with eyes on the back of my head. I hold south, and then attack north at the exact right seconds. And here is the detailed retelling of how the battle went, and here is me reading it before it ever began. This goon swings at my west, and I block it with my forearm steal, swing my sword, cut off this goons arm at its elbow. That goon swings at my east, and I return my bloody gladius to defend it, cutting an elegant slit across his throat, bringing a spray of hot salty blood to cover my face, before he gargles off to suffocate and die. I must look terrifying. Face covered in blood, my enemies piling up around me. The orgy guests are certainly taking notice. The smart ones run to get their clothes and go home before things get worse, which they always do. I grin wide so that my white teeth will contrast my red drenched face. The world is certainly taking notice of me. I must look terrifying.

And what is this? A heat at my lower side. Is this an itch? No, it has quickly progressed past the annoyance of an itch. Am I on fire? I'd better have a look. I turn slowly over my shoulder, and what is this? Goon number three has got his spear between my armor and has stabbed me. There it is, right above my hip. I've been stabbed. And he's still got his hands on the spear, and that can't be good. He would like to lean on it and put it through me. Finish me. Why hasn't he? Why is he motionless? Has the mead now reversed its effect? Has time sped up for me so that others now seem to move as slow as a tortoise? If so I am thankful. I make an abrupt turn of my body, yanking the spear out of the goons hands. I pull its metal out of my hip, and toss it aside, too pained to hold it. I drop my sword and clutch at my bleeding side.

Time returns to a normal count, and goon number three is upon me anew. I try for Felix and Faustus. This time I whistle, loud and high, and then the goon is right on top of me with his dagger.

I am grappling both of my hands around the wrists of the goon as he plunges his dagger towards my chest.

I wonder how Lucius is doing in his fight?

...

Here is me. That is Lucius. And here is my enemy, that is Titus Millius. And we are blazing a trail of horror through the orgy with our swords. Cling, clang, cling, clang, and sparks fly, and women scream as we interrupt their lovemaking.

Millius is my match as a swordsman, and equals me at finding joy in cruelty. We cross swords while passing a fat pig of a whore, and I pause to cut off her tits, just to see how she would look without them. Not pretty. We cross swords while passing a proud stallion with a hard on, and Millius pauses to cut off his cock, just to see how his expression would change. It melted right off his face. We trade friendly winks, and go on trying to kill each other.

Though, I don't think the party organizers like our blood sport as much as we do. I can see their agents assembling on the coliseum floor with their long spatha blades.

Fuck, Millius is a hell of a swordsman. Far better than I expected. If I get killed tonight, dad's gonna be pissed.

I could use a hand. I wonder where the pink-wolf is?

...

Here is me. That is Dexius Januarius. That is, the pink-wolf, if you like. And here is a fine lad to lay with. And here are his silky brown locks, and here are my callused raw fingers running through 'em. All the lads I met at this party have been fair, but none finished me the way this one did. This one here, with the curly brown hair, mud brown eyes, and tiny scar across his nose. I could kiss that scar all night.

But, wait. What the fuck is this shit that comes to disrupt my peace? Who starts a sword fight at an orgy? Damn, and damn, and damn. No time for love, old warrior, old Dexius. Duty calls you. Your master has started battle with a gangster, and he has gained the attention of the staff.

The emperor won't like this. I'll have to cause a bit of mayhem, a bit of a rumpus to distract those who would kill my Augustus.

I say to my boy, "Looks like I must get back to ugly battle, dear and beautiful one."

"Why go alone? Here is a young man who would give his life for you, and here around us are dozens more of the same wild breed. And did we not bring daggers of our own?"

And my boy with the scar on his nose wraps my rock heart with a softness like a warm water, and I kiss him with my grievous face, and he accepts me despite it. He shows me his dagger, and I tell him, "go on, make some chaos with the other wild-boys in the name of the pink-wolf."

And while I go to defend Lucius, my brown eyed boy is telling his friends the plan. Soon the orgy is overrun with naked wild-boys, stabbing a leg here, a thigh there. Slicing open a neck here, a wrist there, and dashing off before they can be caught. They run and laugh, and the naked orgy goers are bleeding and panicking. The place is erupting in shrieks of pain and confusion. Everyone is running for the exits. Torches are kicked over, and oil lamps are exploding flames. Rich, naked Romans are running and screaming for their lives. Tits and dicks flopping soft with fear. Blood, and fire, and chaos.

And to top it all off, you're in love! Oh, Dexius, what a night you're having! Ain't living a grand adventure?

Here's me, the pink-wolf, and here is my sword. The party guards know me as a friend of Lucius, and know me as trouble, so here they come to cut me down and put an end to this disaster. The key to killing 'em is not speed, or skill, but belief. Belief in Dexius Januarius. Who are these twats to think they deserve battle with the likes of me? As I tare through 'em, I pull 'em close and kiss their cheeks. I stab 'em in their guts, and slap their bottoms, and giggle girly like, sending 'em to the after world humiliated. I cut this ones noggin clean off him and then I fan myself with a demure left hand, his headlessness offending my lavender sensibilities. That'll give 'em a start. And when they come in for more combat, I grab 'em, I hug their faces against my bosom, I kick their legs limp beneath 'em, and I hold 'em tight. We spin, we swing, we dip, we twirl, and damn if we ain't dancing.

And now I'm upon Titus Millius, who has gotten the better of my master, Lucius. He is over him with his spatha. Lucius has lost his own gladius, and his helmet has been tossed. Millius is about to make the killing blow to my prince's throat. Lucius doesn't look all that upset about it. More curious, than upset. Eager to discover the mysteries of death, is he? They will have to wait. I put my sword deep into Millius's back, pull it out, and stick it right back in again. One more time for good measure, out and in and out again. Hell, that felt good, two more times. And one more, for luck. And another. That should do it. The spirit of Titus Millius tumbles out of its lost cause of a body.

I give a hand down to Lucius and help him up to his feet.

"Terrible timing, Dexius, my friend." Says Lucius to me. "I was just getting to the good part."

"Where are the others?" I ask him.

"My brother is still locked in battle. Gone missing are the twins."

...

Here is me. That is Felix, brother of Faustus. And oh, how my brother would love this honey melon I'm eating. I have found a quiet place, below the amphitheater, where the gladiators dress before battle. I have hidden myself away with a big, ripe, honey melon. And now I'm eating it. And its juice is cold, and nice.

This girl was nice to me tonight. And that other girl was pretty. I wonder, will I ever marry a pretty girl who will be nice to me forever? I hope father will be able to arrange that. I do hope so. I would like to sleep beside a pretty girl. That would be nice. That would be nice.

This honey melon is nice. How big of a bite can I manage? Yes, that's a very big bite, indeed! I wonder how big a bite Faustus could bite? No bigger than my big bite, I'd wager. Shall I return to the orgy and see if he'd like to share-

No! That was the whole point of finding this quiet, dark place. There was me. Felix, good and shagged, and now hungry, and watching that nice table of pretty fruit. But they were slicing, and sharing, and everyone with their tiny little slices, polite little nibbles. No, not for me, that would not be enough. For me, a whole melon. For me and Faustus, we would have needed two melons. Or more. And our friends? Would they want melons? Big and strong Dexius, the pink-wolf, how much honey melon could that man eat? A lot. Three melons? And to feed Lucius? How many honey melons does the son of an emperor demand? Many. Many melons. More than this one melon, that I hold here, and which I have bashed open and eaten. And I lick the juice from my fingers, and wish I had stolen myself two melons.

Two melons. Like mother. Like the nice, pretty girls at the party. Melons, ha! Melons! Ha!

Where am I? Have I been laughing? Here's me. That is Felix... in my father's cellar? No, not there. Beneath the baths? No. Beneath, yes, but beneath what?

And as I try to remember, I am wondering where my brother is? And as I am wondering, I am given sudden visions of the sewer god of love and I am seeing his lovely winged feathers.

And where am I? And why is Faustus not with me?

And how many melons for the bastard?

...

Here is me. That is, the bastard. Again, and still. Still the same bastard. Still with a goon's dagger to my heart.

I wrestle with the goon trying to kill me. His strength is great, and great, and greater, and suddenly gone. His dagger falls into my hands, and is mine. The goon has lost interest in it. He now just wants to lay on top of me without moving, like a premature ejaculator. I look over his satiated mass to see my dumb friend, the lucky twin, Felix. Or is it Faustus? Whoever it is, they have stuck their sword through the heart of the third goon, and spared me the piercing of my own. I push the goon corpse off of me, and stand up.

The coliseum has turned aghast, people are brawling to get over one another, and out into the streets. Wild young men are running about naked, cutting guests indiscriminately, and being chased to no avail by the security cadre. And I sense the pink-wolf is somehow responsible.

I turn to my savior. "Felix?" I ask.

"What about him?" Answers the twin. It's Faustus. Faustus saved my life.

And here is a sound that comes before a recognition. Thwack. Loud and crisp. Thwack, just the sound, and then I see the arrow materialize in his back. An arrow has planted itself in the sturdy, armored, back of Faustus. Thwack, thwack, thwack. Three more arrows breach his armor across his shoulder blades, just like the wings of his beloved sewer pipe Arteros.

"What about my brother?" Asks Faustus. He falls to his knees, blood sprays from his nose as he exhales. "Something has happened to me." Faustus falls onto his face. I duck down beside him for cover. "Yes." He whispers to me on the ground, "something has definitely gone wrong with me." Faustus closes his eyes. Faustus dies.

I look up to where the arrows came from. It's that black sagittarii. I should have killed him first. He is reaching into his quiver for another arrow. One for me. I grab my sword and get on my feet. I run right at him and release a war cry that rises atop the screams of the amphitheater. The sagittarii loads his arrow, aims, and pulls back on his bow just as I reach him. He releases. The arrow finds a home in my armpit, and my blade finds a home in his skull. He sucks in a few breaths of air he'll never put to use, and keels over dead.

I pick up his bow, break it over my knee, release another war cry. I am invincible. I grab the arrow lodged in my armpit, and yank it loose from the muscle it's torn and hooked itself into. I launch the arrow into the night sky, it flies over the clouds, and hits a goose, which comes cawing down to earth. I examine my wounded armpit. A piece of bloody flesh dangles, I flick it. My shoulder bone makes a grinding sound when I rotate it. It appears that I am injured, but the mead has somehow eased me of all pain, and I feel nothing. I am invincible.

Faustus wasn't so blessed. I return to my fallen friend. And here comes Lucius, and Dexius. And I'm glad they are alive. Lucius pokes at the dead twin with his boot. "He dead?" He asks.

"He's dead." I answer.

Lucius surveys the continuing pandemonium around us. "Well, let's get out of here before the imperial guard shows up. My father would be terribly embarrassed to know we caused this."

"We need to tell Felix of what has happened." I say.

"There is a mysterious bond between twins. Perhaps he's already aware. He should be brought to his people for proper burial." Dexius is kneeling to lift Faustus. He does so with ease, tossing him over his shoulder.

My stomach churns. I am nauseas. I do not feel invincible anymore. I feel as though I could drop dead at any second. I feel as though I have died already, everybody knows it, and I'm late on the joke. Here's me, in hell.

"You know a way out. Don't you, brother?" Lucius is speaking to me.

"What?"

"So we won't have to pass through the bustling crowds? We can make an exit through the sewers, yes?"

"Yes." I answer. "Through the sewers. But, what about Felix? He's probably looking for his brother."

"So? We did whistle for him, didn't we? What good is a dog who doesn't come when called?" Lucius talks, and I am getting sick. I would like to vomit.

Lucius goes on talking, "Felix will look for his brother, and when he cannot find him, he will return home. And there at the gates of his family's villa he will find his brother waiting. Come, let us make haste so that we can deposit our friend's corpse, and be on with our evening. There is a whore of some renown and much beauty that lives on the other side of the Alban hills, in Lanuvio. I'd like to pay her a visit. The night is still young, yes?"

"Yes." I answer. "Still young." And now I am vomiting. Lucius and the pink-wolf are laughing at me. The vomit comes in leagues, and when it is over, I feel much better.

Here's me, guiding my brother Lucius through the rear arcades of the coliseum, and to the sewers below, and to our escape from this madness. And Dexius follows close behind, with the dead Faustus flung over his shoulders. We leave a show that would have satisfied any paying audience.

And as we depart the orgy turned killing field, I spot that far eastern pregnant girl, who Titus Millius had been raping when we came to murder him. She has found a quiet place in the shadows. She is humming a lullaby to the cooing newborn baby boy wrapped in her arms. I wish we had taken Millius's head to give him as a birthday present.

...

We spot three fine brown horses tied to a post outside the amphitheater. Lucius wants to steal them and go see a special whore who has caught his interests. Dexius says there's a boy with brown hair and a scar on the bridge of his nose who he would rather spend his evening with. To please Lucius, he offers to first bring the corpse of our friend Faustus to his parents, so we can be on our way, unburdened. It's at least an hours journey to Lanuvio, even with the horses.

I can tell he is disappointed that Dexius will be parting our company, but Lucius agrees, "Fine. That will give us enough time to visit the military hospital at the foot of the Alban hills." Lucius turns to me like a consolation prize, "We'll raid the medical tents and herbal supply. Refresh ourselves for the trip." I brew a smile from my still uneven stomach.

And now the pink-wolf is mounting his horse, and departing with dead Faustus strewn across his lap. His body bounces violently as they ride off into the night. Faustus seems to smile coyly at me, like a child play acting that he is a tree. He is remaining as still as possible, but I can tell he chokes back laughter. I expect Faustus to open his eyes, and wink at me. Does he realize this play is real? Does the poor fool yet know that he's actually died?

And here's we. That is, me and my brother. And we're riding our steeds down avenues and alleyways, that turn into suburban villas, and finally country farmland.

We make a stop at the imperial military hospital, and Lucius uses his influence to gain access to the apothecary. We fill our loculi with oils, and powders, and herbs, and tonics. We take a swig of this, and a snort of that. This one tastes of spoiled oranges, that one of sulfur. We pack the poppies given to the wounded, so we will be down for the epic night of sleep that will conclude our escapades. For now, we use what soldiers do before battle, so we will be up for the exceptional prostitute Lucius has spotted, and who we're traveling so far to visit. As we shop Lucius is whispering to me about the legends of her beauty.

"She is of dreams. You will see her, and remember her and not know from where. I tell you, brother, you have met her as a goddess, naked and in your dreams. Her innocence is of a virgin. We will lay firstly hands on her, and mystify at how such an untouched thing can be for sale."

The euphoria of the witches mead has worn to a rumble of the stomach, and an aching of the skull, and these newer medicines are a welcome stimulation of my spirit.

And we're riding again, and the hospital is behind us. We pass marshes, and swamps, and lakes. And we're kicking our horses. Faster and faster. Their hooves cracking the lime cement of the Appian road.

And here we come upon a fence, and Lucius slows his horse and I slow mine. And we stop, and dismount, and tie them to the fence. From here we walk. Beyond the fence is a little artichoke farm. And beyond the fields of artichokes, are rows of coriander and mustard seed. And beyond these crops is a small stone farmhouse, a steady plume of gray smoke drifts out of its western wall. Is this house on fire? No. As we get closer, I see it is the smoke of a controlled fire, drifting out of a heated wall, and a small hypocaust. The wall is built with local stone, probably gathered by the brothel keepers themselves, certainly not a professional mason.

"Here we are." Lucius points at the farmhouse we're approaching. Aside from the cobbled together heated wall, it's no more than a common, plebeian, homestead. The fields of crops were plentiful, and the house looks sturdy enough, but this is the land of a poor, working family.

"Unlike any brothel I've ever seen." I say to Lucius.

"Wait until you see the whore."

We continue to walk. We walk past the buckets of harvested artichoke heads. We walk past the carpentry shed, and the chicken pen. We walk past the sleeping mule. If this is a brothel, they sure are doing a good job of making themselves look like a farm.

And the medicines are working. They come on strong now. My heart is faster than the horses that drove us out here. I no longer feel tired, but this drag is worse. I can't feel anything. My arms and legs step and glide without any tension or weight. These are not my arms. These are not my hands.

The outside world is changing, too. The sheds, the pens, all turn to squares and rectangles, I need to remind myself they are real things with purpose. The artichokes are wax husks of crowned circles. The mule is a complicated mess ovals and infinitely repeating triangles. Those are not artichokes. That is not a mule. Some bad artist has placed me in a painted replica of the world. Everything is covered with a dreadful vale of forgery. These are not my hands. That is not my brother. This is not a brothel. Where has he taken me?

We're at the door. In the glow of the threshold lantern I can see that Lucius is smiling lustfully. Same face from the orgy when he was chasing Flauxtilla.

Lucius is knock, knock, knocking on the door. Very friendly, like a neighbor's come to borrow some eggs for a pie. Though, what neighbors would come this far, this late? There's no other farm for miles in any direction. But this is a brothel, so they expect callers at all hours, I suppose.

A voice comes from within. A man. An older man. "Yes? Who's there?"

"Military, sir." Lucius says, and winks at me. What is he up to? "Better open up and have a chat. Imperial business." And he knocks twice more, instructively this time.

"What sort of Imperial business? What's this about?" Says the man behind the door. Is he the door man? Is it a secret whorehouse? Underground? Not paying their taxes to the palace?

"We shouldn't have worn our outfits." I say.

"They're uniforms." Says Lucius. He pounds on the door. "I'm serious now. My man and I are legionnaires, sent by the Emperor himself. Now you open up, or I'll kick this door in!" And he pounds, and pounds.

The man inside laughs. "You'll have to, cause I ain't opening shit. It's the middle of the night. We're all asleep. Fuck off till the morning, would ya?"

"Are we not here during their operating hours?" I ask and Lucius ignores me. He looks angrily determined. I can tell his heart is going as fast as mine. He sees that door and it looks like a piece of papyrus. Why not kick through it? So, he takes a step back, raises his right boot, and kicks, kicks, kicks. Dust explodes off the bottom off his caligae into the air, but the door stays put.

"Fuck off!" Says the man inside.

I want to go home. "Let's go home." I say.

"No. Tonight I promised my brother the finest whore he's ever had, and tonight he shall have her."

Lucius steps back from the threshold. I follow him as he begins to circle the farm house. It's nothing more than one big box. There are sky windows on the roof, but it's a chilly night, and they are closed, and probably locked.

"There must be some way in." Says Lucius, single mindedly scanning for a weakness in the structure.

I feel no judgment. Right and wrong are numb, but still exist for me as logical ideas. This is wrong. Right? Factually. This is not a brothel, and this is wrong. Despite my indifference, I'll try once more to end it. "Stop. Lucius. Let's leave. This isn't the way it should be."

Lucius turns to me, annoyed and dismissive of his yapping bastard. "It'll be however I please."

Silence. And Lucius looks away from me before I look away from him. And he is checking the remainder of the homestead. He see's something that removes the resentment on his face.

"There." Says Lucius. "Good. Perfect. I couldn't have planned it better myself." He's pointing at the heated wall, and the oven beneath it. "The hypocaust. That's how we'll get in. You love crawling through dark places, don't you brother? Crawl through the oven, and bash through the inner wall of their very living room." Lucius seems positively giddy at the idea. "Oh! It will give them such a fright! And when they're distracted by shock, you simply unlatch the door and let me in."

I look at the hypocaust. Its fire glows in the night like it's made for me. It is a siren to my very nature. Crawl through here and save the kingdom for your brother. Yet, what kingdom? What brother? These are old feelings. I am empty now. Shall I kill my brother here and walk back to our horses? Ride to Bari, stowaway on a boat to Athens. Start a new life with the nobodies?

"This is not a brothel. Is it?" I ask.

"My father is the emperor of Rome..." says Lucius, "... the world is my brothel."

I am turning from my brother to the heated wall. I am walking over to the mouth of the oven. I kneel down beside it, carefully gage its hotness with the back of my hand. Hot. I crouch down further, and peak deeper into the arched, brick, oven. There is a row of burning, dry logs, and then a small tunnel of smoke that brings the fires heat up into the channels hidden in the wall.

I am taking off my armor. I am taking off my caligae. I'll carry my sword with me, but toss the belt and sheath. I look at my tunic. With its frayed ends, it would likely catch fire. I am taking off my tunic. I am naked but for my subligar.

I look at Lucius. He seems pressed for time, tapping his foot and biting his fingernails, while he watches me undress. "Save your flesh for the whore." He says to me.

"I don't want to catch fire." I say.

"Get on with it. I'll meet you at the front door."

"Take my clothes." I say.

"Oh, alright, fine." And Lucius gathers my tunic and armor, and leaves me to my task.

I kneel down, look into the pit of fire. I use my sword to move the flaming logs over to either side a bit, careful not to adjust the fire too much so those inside remain unsuspicious. There is a thin tunnel through the burning. I lay flat on my stomach and, sword first, crawl into the oven.

Heat, and heat, and heat, and I'm covered in sweat before my abdomen has even entered. The steal of my sword blackens with soot before me. Sharp biting at my elbows, gnawing at my arms. Knives stuck in, and twisted. Burning, and burning, and burning.

I'm in the oven up to my ankles now. My body remains nestled between the two roaring fires, but my head has passed through to the slim passageway inside the hollow of the heated wall. I turn on to my back. My shoulders are cooking. My thighs are cooking. The pain reaches an intolerable burning, and then, what is this? A cascading

65

numbness. The drugs. The lovely, lovely drugs. I grin at my indifference to the flames. I wiggle my legs, pulling my toes into the oven, teasing the fire with them, like testing a pool before a swim. I feel no heat, I do not wince. Fire? What fire? Soldiers do not burn.

I lay my sword down by my head. I push myself forward, squeezing up against the false inner wall, and yanking the rest of my body through the oven and into the smoke filled hollow. I stand up, a wall at the back of my head, a wall at the fore of it, and the whole space clouded with hot, thick, smoke. I fill my lungs with the stuff, a good deep chest full, and pleasurably exhale it back where it came from. I feel no tightness, I do not cough. Smoke? What smoke? Soldiers do not choke.

Now, it's simply the matter of bursting through the wall and opening the front door for Lucius. It had better not be stone or worse, metal. Soldier's are strong, but can they shatter steal? I push on the wall with both hands. Bricks, but ceramic bricks from the feel of it. Smooth, and thin, and likely hollow so the heat will get into the house. A wise construction, shame to break it to pieces. I press my back firmly against the wall behind me, and then one foot at a time, I'm climbing the ceramic wall, crouching my body, and becoming suspended and stuck between the two. I can already feel the ceramic wall buckling beneath the soles of my bare feet. It is creaking and whining ever so quietly, and then without warning comes the first crack, like a bolt of lightening. My feet push forward, increasing the pressure. Another crack, and another, and another, and the ceramic shatters. The wall comes crashing in on the farm house, and I am riding on it's wave of debris and smoke.

I tumble forward and clumsily get on my feet. The military herbs have made it easy for me to recover my senses and assess the room I've landed in. And here is the bear rug, and the dinner table, and the eaten pot of stew. And here are the family beds, and the wash basins, and the store closet. And here is the family. A father, at the dinner table. A daughter with him. The father is bald, short, wide shouldered, burly. His face is covered in scars. His bald head is covered in scars. His right arm is gone at the biceps. His stump dangles from his tunic. With his left arm he is reaching for a wood axe on the table. He is slow and surprised, I am double quick and in charge. I even take a moment to eye his daughter. She is as beautiful as a goddess from some dream, and I immediately know she is the one Lucius is here for. She is young, perhaps sixteen. She looks like Plautilla did at that age. But she is not the youngest in the house. Who is this just beside me? Who is this young boy on the floor, among the mess of ceramic? There is a son, and he is ten perhaps.

The father with one arm is coming at me with his wood axe. What shall I do? I bend, and in one sweep I pick up my sword, and the fallen little boy. I raise them up against one another, specifically the tip of my blade against his tiny neck. Yes, that will do. The father with one arm is ceasing his advance.

"Drop it." I say. The father considers. I poke the blade into the boy's neck. He whimpers, and bleeds a drop, and his father drops the axe.

"Thank you." I say, not really sure what else to say. I drag the little boy by the scruff of his neck, my blade still at his throat, across the homestead. I walk past the beautiful daughter. She is crying. Already? Does she sense the villain who waits at her family's front door?

"Wipe away those tears, dear. Don't give 'em the satisfaction." Says the father. "Don't give 'em a single tear." The daughter follows his command, and wipes them.

I walk slowly past the father, fevered rage fills his head with blood, turning every bald inch of it crimson. As I pass him, I kick his axe across the floor and far out of his reach. He is surely a veteran. And missing arm or no, I don't want to test his battle experience.

I am at the door. The little boy is an obedient prisoner. He watches his father, never breaking their gaze, and silently drifts where I will him. Keeping the sword on the boy, I unlatch the door, and open it.

"Hello." Says Lucius as he enters. He already has his sword drawn. He takes in the homestead. He sees the bear rug, the eaten pot of stew, the dinner table, the veteran's daughter. He smiles shyly, and nods at her, like you would your childhood crush. He asks, "How are your evenings?" No one answers him.

Lucius turns to me, sees my hostage. He puts his own sword against the boys neck, and hands me my tunic and armor. I lower my weapon, and get dressed while Lucius speaks with his captive audience. "A pleasure to meet you, sir. I see your deformity. Pardon my rudeness in asking, did you serve?"

"Aye." The one armed father is answering slowly, carefully, but his breathing is that of a marathon runner. "Fought for my country. Served good and honorable, and gave an arm for it."

"Yes, very good." Says Lucius as I'm putting my chest plate on. Lucius keeps his sword on the little boy who watches his father, and continues his pleasantries. "And how does a veteran come to do such work, may I ask?"

"The land is a gift from the emperor. All soldiers who fight to a certain ability, at a certain age the government gives them a spot of land to farm and-"

"No, sir." Lucius interrupts. "I mean, how does a veteran come to be a pimp?"

"Excuse me?" Asks the one armed father. I am finished dressing. Lucius looks at me and motions at the boy. I put my sword to his throat, and Lucius lowers his.

"Don't be deceptive, sir. You are a pimp of some renown, are you not?" Lucius walks over to the father. "Yes, I've heard of you. I have been told stories about the simple beauties of your women. Yes, I've heard of your brothel, good citizen. And I have come to sample of your whores." I now notice that at Lucius's side he has a coiled length of rope. The same type we used to tie the horses.

The veteran looks at the Lucius like he's mad, but speaks to him like a rational old friend. "Listen, my comrade, you men are soldiers, and I am a soldier. We are brothers. Whatever you may have ingested, and whatever it has done to your way of thinking, it is wrong, and you must see that. All will be forgiven, if you release my boy, and leave our home. Now. Soldier to soldier, I don't want any more trouble in my life than I've already had. Just leave. If you want the advice of a seasoned soldier, that's it. If you don't want to find any trouble, my advice is that you leave now."

Lucius steps even closer to the father, he looks over his shoulder at his daughter, then back at the man. He says, "And what advice have you got for the man who seeks trouble?"

Before the veteran can answer, Lucius delicately takes his hand to hold. The veteran pulls his hand away, shoves Lucius back from him, winds up for a punch with his one arm. Lucius steps back fearfully, and yelps, "Cut the boy!"

I grab the boy's hair and put the blade across his neck like I'm going to slice it open. The veteran stops his punch, his fist hangs mid air.

Lucius turns to me and says, "How about we cut off his little arm? Hmm? The right one, just like poppa? Like father like son?"

67

I grab the boy's arm, raise it, and hold the blade under his armpit. The veteran lowers his fist. Lucius steps towards him, reaches for his hand and takes it. "Come. This way."

"It's alright, my children. Remember your mother, and be strong." Says the father. The daughter begins to cry again, "Father," she says "do not let them have us."

"Worry not my daughter. Dry your tears, and make no more, and they shall never have a part of you."

The farmer's daughter wipes the tears from her face.

Lucius walks the veteran by the hand to a wooden chair sitting beside the bear rug. "Sit." Says Lucius. And the father sits. Lucius takes the coil of rope and uncoils it. The father sees that Lucius would like to tie him up, and jumps out of the chair. He makes a dash across the room, headed right for the axe. And he'll get it too. Lucius is close behind him, but he's going to make it. He'll grab that axe, crack it into my brother's skull, and this will all come to an end.

Unless I stick my foot out, at the exact right second, and trip him. Shall I trip the veteran trying to save his family, and rob him of his last chance at survival? I'd like to let him pass me by, I'd like to let him get to his axe, I'd like to keep my foot right where it is, and do nothing. But this has all happened already, and the choice has already been made. I stick my foot out and in the way of the one armed veteran. His right ankle hits my boot, and then his left, and there he goes tumbling forward, face first.

The veteran hits the tile floor, breaks his nose, and knocks himself into a daze. Lucius scoops him up. He doesn't put up a fight. Lucius drags him across the room and sits him in a chair just beside the bear rug. Lucius does a fine job of tying the veteran, and his one arm, to the chair. He ties his legs to the legs of the chair. He ties his waist and chest to the back of the chair. Once he is happy that the veteran is secured, he puts a boot on the side of the chair, and kicks it over.

The veteran father cries out as his head whacks against the hard floor. His son yells, "Poppa!", And I grab him tighter. He begins to weep. The daughter makes a move towards helping her father, but Lucius picks up and swings his sword at her. She stops at the end of it. He grabs her by her nightgown, and pulls her to the bear rug, he throws her down upon it. She does nothing more than sigh as her butt hits the ground.

Lucius reaches down to her and grabs a bit of her nightgown, pulls it, and cuts it with his blade. He tares the remainder of it, and strips the young girl of her clothes. I see the facts of her body. She is young and beautiful. But I feel nothing. She is a collection of circles. Some rounder than other girls her age, but what is roundness? What is size? What are proportions? Here is a naked animal, and here is my brother, the butcher.

The daughter covers her nudity, but not frantically. She is slow and methodical, and almost ignorant of her attacker. She is unoffended, as if a curiously strong breeze has blown her clothes off.

"Don't cover up such beauty. I came for the goods, did I not?" And Lucius grabs the girl's wrists and yanks them away from covering her shame. She accepts this new offense with equal disinterest, lowering her arms to her sides, as if sun bathing, alone on a private beach. She arches her back with grace, and shakes her long hair loose from her shoulders. Lucius is suddenly furious. He smacks the beautiful girl across her face. She looks away from him. She rallies her strength, and tries as hard as she can, but as the redness in the shape of a hand appears across her cheek, so too do tears appear in her eyes.

Lucius smiles. "There's what I'm looking for." And he leaps on top of her, touching and kissing every part of her. And she is letting him. She sometimes shifts her weight this way or that, beneath his ravishing, as if he were an annoying fly landing on her. Lucius looks up from his kissing to her distant face. Sensing his gaze, the girl yawns, bored. Lucius punches her in her liver. She squeals, and begins to weep. Lucius, satisfied and excited, goes back to his kissing.

I am still holding the boy. He is crying. He has wet his tunic with piss. I have got the boys piss all over my boots. He is staring at his father, waiting for him to wake up. His little body quakes. His chest is sending shock waves through his limbs, and I can feel their pulsating.

Lucius is inside the farmer's daughter now. Girls who lose their virginity to men they love, in the grip of devotion and romance, still quiver with pain when the moment of penetration occurs. This farmer's daughter, on the bear rug with my brother, makes not a sound. Cries not a tear.

The one armed veteran father wakes up.

"Oh, she's wonderful! She's just as I dreamed!" Moans Lucius in a fit of frantic ecstasy. He see's the father has woken. "Oh, good, maybe now she'll cry a bit more. Go on, beautiful, cry."

The father is dizzy and half asleep. He tugs on his ropes, there is no hope. The father sees his weeping son, and joins him. He watches his daughter as her soul is butchered. He grits his teeth and moans in agony. He screams, and shakes in a wild fit, doing nothing more than rotating his chair on the floor.

Though her father and her brother seem to have no problem with it, the girl refuses to cry, and it's making Lucius angrier and angrier.

"Cry, damn you! Do I not invade you?! Does it not hurt?!" Lucius grabs the aloof girl by the back of her hair, still not a peep. He pulls her up onto her feet, and over to the dinner table. "Cry!" He smacks her across her face, and she spins around and splays out on the table, spilling the left over pot of stew. Potatoes, bits of beef, a pool of brown gravy, and now the daughter's pretty face. As Lucius rapes her from behind, he is banging her head into the stew covered wood table. Still, she does not cry, or put up a fight.

"Cry! Damn you! Cry, or I'll kill the lot of you!" Lucius is demanding, and the girl is not obliging. She has gone as limp as a rag in the wind.

The veteran is weeping and screaming, "Cry, my dear! Cry for the monster! Cry!"

But the girl is not listening, and Lucius is losing his patience. "Cry!" Bang! He thrusts her forehead into the table. Blood is mixing with the stew. "I terrify you! I am a wolf who comes to devour you in the night! Cry!" But she won't. Bang! "Cry!" Bang! "Cry!" Bang! "Cry!"

And the father screams out, "Cry, my daughter! Cry!" But she still does not cry.

Lucius holds the girls face down into the blood and gravy and appears to cum, mumbling, "cry out, cry out."

In my mind I hear my own voice repeat him. Cry out. Cry out. I release the little boy. His legs turn to jelly beneath him, and he crumbles to the floor, splashing into his puddle of piss. I step away from him. Cry out, I repeat to myself. Cry out.

69

Lucius steps away from the girl, and the dinner table. She falls to the ground. Lucius kicks her. She does not move.

"Claudia?" Says the one armed father to his daughter. "Claudia, speak to me girl, are you alright?"

Claudia is dead.

"Oops." Says Lucius. He looks at me. He smiles, and says again, "Oopsie-doo." And he laughs, and walks over to me, and pats me on the shoulder. "Sorry about that, my brother. You haven't had your turn yet. No worry though, clear the mess away, and I'm sure she'll still be warm."

The father's weeping changes, it becomes mournful and defeated, like a dying old dog crawled under the veranda to die.

"Will you have a go?" Lucius asks me.

"No." I say. "Let's get back to the city."

"Suit yourself." Says Lucius, and now he is setting his eyes on the shocked, motionless little boy.

"Hello there." Says Lucius. "Shame for you to see your father this way. Blubbering like a woman, and defeated. Still, I'm sure he looms large in your psyche, as mine does in my own. We are both sons of warriors, you and I. And as a son of a warrior, I know what it's like to always try to be just like your father, and to always fall short. Your father is a great soldier, who has given parts of himself to the glory of battle. What have you ever given, boy?"

The little boy says nothing.

"Today, one son to another, I am going to help you on your way out of the shadow cast by your father." Lucius smiles at the boy, and the boy does not react. He has gone to the same cold void that the medicine has sent me. The boy is simply not here. He sees Lucius talking to him, but comprehends not a word.

Lucius looks at the crying father, who does comprehend. The veteran of wars, cut down in his living room, comprehends well. "Please. Mercy." Begs the veteran. Lucius grins, grips his sword, and grabs the little boys arm by its trembling hand.

"Like father, like son, hmm?"

Lucius raises his sword and brings it down on the upper arm of the little boy, hacking it halfway through the bone. The boy explodes with an alarm of screaming from the bottom of his soul. The father screams along. Lucius yanks the blade out of the arm, raises it, and lowers it again, this time severing it. The homestead is saturated with blood, and hair raising screams. Lucius tosses the little arm next to the squirming, screeching boy.

Lucius stretches, cracking his back, arms and knuckles. He turns to me, and over the shrieking, says, "Shall we hit the road?"

"Yes." I say. And as we leave behind the dead daughter, the armless son, and the bound father, my soul aches to cry out, but does not. Instead, in a whisper, it is convincing itself that it does not exist.

…

On the journey home I am quiet. We drive the horses so fast that they are all but broken by the time we reach Aurilean's wall. We slice their throats, and Lucius curses and spits at them while they whinny and die.

On our walk, Lucius is worried that I'm quiet because I'm angry at him. "Don't be sore because you didn't have a turn with the girl." He says. "I got a little carried away, but that's no reason to be bitter."

I tell him that I'm just tired, and having a bad reaction to all the potions and herbs. He says he understands, but still wants to make it up to me. He buys me a room for the night at a proper brothel, with a proper whore. He buys himself one too, and says good night for the evening.

"I'll see you in the morning sun, oh my brother." Says Lucius.

"Yes." I say. "See you." And my whore takes me by the hand and walks me to her quarters.

My whore is dark skinned, and her clothes are covered in a fine layer of desert sand that shakes loose as she removes them. She holds me to her naked breasts and tells me everything will be alright. I suckle at her tits and what is at first milk now turns to a grainy mud.

I lift myself to kiss her. Our lips touch. Our tongues meet. I push mine into her mouth. She caresses it with her own. Then she bites down, clamping her fangs into the meat of my tongue. She tares my tongue right out of my mouth, chews it, and swallows it. I fall back, away from her. Away, and away, and away. And my mouth is filling with blood. And my mouth is filling with blood. I choke, and I cough, and I bleed. And dear god, will I die, or will I wake? Will I die, or will I wake?

III.

I wake.

Yes. I am awake.

It was a dream. I do not bleed. My tongue is severed, but not newly so. I am here, in the monastery, in my room, in my bed, oh dear god.

I have dreamed. Did you watch, oh my Lord? Did you see me and my brother? Did you meet the pink-wolf, and did you see our friend Faustus die, and did you see the misery we brought to that country homestead? Must I confess the night again, now that I have relived it?

In truth, it was not of just one night that I dreamed. The den of the witch of potions, the alleyway of the old drunkard, the coliseum orgy, and the artichoke farm. I did not visit these places on the same night. My sleeping mind put these scenes together, dear god, for this is how I remember them. Though I spent the bulk of five years this way, I recall them as one long, single night of horror.

How long have I slept? It can't have been more than an hour. The moon is still at the top of my window, and has not passed over head. The night is still young, and so too is my prayer, dear god.

71

My sleep has left me thirsty and hungry. Let me go to the kitchen for some wine and bread.

CHAPTER FIVE.

I.

Is she not among the dearer of your dearest creatures, oh god? Did you hear how she spoke to me? With such warmth and compassion. Did you witness the caring in that old nun's brown eyes, every time she laid them upon me? Were you there with us, just now, in the monastery kitchen? I went for my mid-night bread, and wine, and found Sister Lousada, shaken from her own troubled dreams. She greeted me with a smile, and we sat, and she told me of her visions, and asked me about mine. Though I could not tell her with words, she felt my suffering, and hugged me, and kissed my cheek. Did you send kind Sister Lousada a nightmare simultaneous to my own, so she would be awake to comfort me at this late hour?

(Or is the hour early? Is it yet morning where you are? At what hour do you usually wake, oh my Lord? Up and at them with the sunrise, I'd imagine. But which sunrise? The one in Rome? The one in Athens? Or Lubdugnum? Or Antioch? What time are you usually in your bed by? Have you a bed? A blanket of dappled night sky? Do you even require rest? Do you sleep at all? If so, do you have dreams, oh slumbering keeper? Are we the ghosts who haunt them?)

Sister Lousada was born a Jew in western Hispania. Her family having fled there from Judea after the Roman siege of Jerusalem, and the first destruction of their sacred temple. Her family stayed true to its old world faith for over a century, until Lousada met and fell in love with a dark skinned Mauri, and the two eloped south. Finding no comfort from either of their former communities, the young couple rejected religion altogether, and raised their children, three sons, without god, in the city of Gades.

When an outbreak of variola fell upon them, Lousada played devoted nurse to her husband as he died, and then to each of her three children, as one by one, they too succumbed to the vile sickness, and died. Never growing ill herself, Lousada sat constantly bedside, rubbing tonics on their coughing chests, collecting and removing the jugs of diarrhea and vomit, and anointing the puss filled blisters that rose and burst all over their little bodies. When they died, she herself buried them, first washing and wrapping them in accordance with her families traditions, which she had so long ignored, but never forgotten. After her third son died and was in the ground, she left Gades for the country.

Lousada got a job as a bar maid in a small village, and began practicing her old faith once more, carrying out the ceremonies and rituals that fulfilled her ancestors, but which now seemed empty to her. Her family was robbed from her, and in these meaningless tasks she found no relief or condolence.

As you know well, dear god, for it was you who sent him, one night the monk Wojslaw wandered into the public house that Lousada was working and wallowing in.

Good Brother Wojslaw saw the suffering in the eyes of this quickly aging bar maid. He engaged her, he sought her out for friendly conversation when he passed through town, and he tipped her generously after each meeting, even though everyone could tell he was a poor man. One evening Lousada confessed to Wojslaw her loss of faith, and how the agonized deaths of her family had led her to hate god and his ways. She accused you of putting us here to suffer and die, never knowing the depth of the pain you are asking us to endure. She has a point, oh Lord, and Wojslaw nodded that he understood just where she was coming from, but told her that there was a new development in the character of god.

And then the monk told, and the woman heard for the first time, the story of your son, the man-christ, Jesus of Nazareth.

Lousada went that very evening with Wojslaw to the monastery. She has lived here all twenty two years since, giving her broken life over to you, oh great redeemer. To you, and to your son.

When we come to you, oh true god, must we come broken? Can a man or a woman rightly come to god whole and intact? Even your son, your very spirit made flesh, was barred from heaven until sufficiently broken. The son of god, his soul and his body torn to shreds, begs his father for help and is met with silence and torture. Your own son! I ask you, dear god, what chance do the rest of us have who aren't even blood relations?

Perhaps you're like most Jewish dads, always expecting just too much from your son, holding him to the highest of standards, every accomplishment just short of total success. Still, humble as man may be, do we not function similarly to your sanctified progeny? We suffer, we pray for mercy, and receiving none, we break. It is in this breaking that your nature is revealed, oh loneliest sufferer of all.

I feel a terrible sadness over take me, oh god. A deep pity for my fellow man, and for my creator, and for his son, and for my wretched self. How crippled I am in my thinking that the honey flavored happiness absorbed from my visit with Sister Lousada, has become fermented in me to a bitter punch of misery. She was woken by dreams of her dying sons, crying to her, but still she grinned. Still she cared to comfort me. She filled herself not with the latter days of illness, but the earlier ones of birth, and celebration. The words of Lousada repeat in my mind, dear Lord:

"I lost the crop of my family, but not the love harvested from it. My husband saw in the eyes of his wife, even as he lay dying, devotion and love. My three sons knew, as they slipped out of my arms and into god's, that they had a mother who loved them. I was that mother. Me. They were my sons, and he was my husband, and I was their mother, and I was his wife. For this I will praise god until I am dead. And if there is no heaven, and all is here and now and for a short while, still I am content. For I have given love, and I have received it. God made a Sephardi girl, and he made for her a black husband, and he made for them three sons. And upon this family he heaped great love, and great death, and I ask you, did he not bless his own son with the very same? Shall we not rejoice in his will?"

(Rejoice? I don't know, dear Lord, I don't know. Is your will in league with plague and disease? Shall we rejoice at the arrival of your holy agent, pestilence?)

Despite my doubt, I smiled in agreement. Lousada smiled back, sighed, and poured herself one last glass of wine to take with her to her chambers. She put a soft wrinkled hand over my own, and squeezed. She said good night. I pray you give her peace and sweet dreams, dear god.

II.

My visit with the nun Lousada has turned my thoughts to women. My mother. My step-mother. The women I've had, the women I've wanted. The ones I've killed for, and the ones I've killed. Their hair, their mouths, their breasts, their hips and legs and feet. The feet of the women I have lusted over fill my mind like a sandal merchant. Every toe, every arch, every ankle. I think, dear god, of the feet I have kissed, and of the ones I have driven nails through.

Using the sensation of memory, oh master of illusion, you return my missing tongue to my mouth, and I can taste again. I can feel my tongue plunging into their pretty mouths, running down their soft cheeks, and necks and nipples.

I can feel, oh my Lord, the tongue that tasted her blood, and so had to be removed. Her blood. Her blood that was innocent and chaste, that I expected to be similar to sweet berry preserves, but that nonetheless tasted of the same salt and metal which flavors even the most evil of men's blood.

Her. She. The girl whose name I dare not remember. The christian girl.

If only my mother had kept me, turned away from her love of Septimius Severus, and fled with her son east, away from the murderess, Julia Domna. If only I had been born in the desert, with the people of the sand. My people. If only I grew up beside the christian girl, in that tiny village of tents and mud huts, baked in your most orange sun, oh Lord. Instead I was raised against my nature, in a city of slick marble, beneath the hateful gaze of a treacherous step-mother.

My distrust and outright fear of the empress who the world called my mother, raised in me a primal lament over the existence of women in general. I longed still to please, and posses them though. My step-mother first among them. If I could win the love of the lioness who hated me most, I could win any of the pack's affections. Every happy advance I made was an attempt to conquer and control a country whose locals despised and rebelled against my occupation. And when they welcomed me as a hero, I would become bored and make a quiet but rapid withdrawal. Those women who plotted against me, and undermined my command at every turn, these were enemies worth crusading against. And I would do so using whichever sword was better suited. The one sheathed at my side, or between my legs.

It makes me laugh aloud to think of my previous self, and how much he seems a stranger to me now, oh Lord. Warring against and conquering women and making his way in the world, like the ambitious prince he fancied himself. These days I couldn't woo a fig off a branch.

I had futilely hoped that as my will to take girls to bed in reality disappeared, I would also experience a diminishment in my urge to do so in fantasy. Quite the opposite. I often wake with a desperate want for the loveliest women of my past. I tell you, Lord, some have grown old and no longer resemble the image of youth and beauty I retain in thought. Some are women I have murdered. Many are dead and in the ground, the vivacious bodies I conjure are in actuality gray skeletons wrapped in decaying garments. I push these memories away, and replace them with a nameless, faceless, body. The tits of a statue, the ass of a foreigner, and I finish myself off as quickly as possible. I do this not for the pleasure of the thing, oh Lord, but to be rid of the desire. Am I to carry these frustrating wants with me through the waking day? Allow this morbidity to be ever present? No. When the long gone beauty of these women returns to me, control is needed, and so too is my hand.

I've lost the vine of what I'm trying to get across. Why am I telling god about my jerking off habits? What purpose could that possibly serve? More structure is needed in this prayer. This is not some fickle far eastern meditation, free to roam and wander as my subconscious sees fit. I am trying to communicate something to you, oh Lord. This is not a formless mingling of spirits, it is one intelligent being speaking to another, albeit an infinitely higher one.

This prayer was supposed to be meant as an apology. Too often tonight tonight I have tried to express my character to you, as if it will compensate for my sins, instead of simply confessing and flatly apologizing for them. I've tried to show you how I see this world you've made, and what I think works about it, and what I think I'd throw overboard were the ship mine to command. Such utter arrogance. I feel a rising shame, oh my Lord. Who am I to tell the creator of the universe anything but, "thank you so much for my arms and legs", or "I'm sorry I fucked up so badly"?

You did not come here tonight for jokes and fairy tales. You came here tonight for a confession, and you shall have one. If you are still listening at all, dear Lord, it is to decipher whether my change of heart is genuine, or vanity. Have I truly recognized my crimes as such? The only way I know to prove my commitment to repentance, oh loftiest of jurists, is to continue to detail my strayed path, and become witness to my own prosecution. From here on until morning, I will try to put things as plainly as possible. An accounting of the wrong I've done, without all of my desperate flourishes.

III.

In the new spirit of things, I'd like to now review the year Lucius spent in Briton with Geta and our Father, and away from me. It was the year I crucified my first Rabbi, slept with my step-mother, and assassinated my father's best friend, Gaius Fulvius, with a spear up his ass. I should say, oh god, that I took pleasure in none of it. Well, mostly none of it. Some of it was alright. At the time, some of it was alright.

I'm already fucking up. This prayer is shit.

Sorry. I should curse less, as well. Brother Wojslaw would laugh himself into a fit if he could hear how I speak to his one true god, and Sister Lousada would likely weep. I beg patience, Lord. After all, this is my first time speaking to you directly. We are, at the end of the day, unacquainted. I have always been shy and awkward around new friends, and here is no difference. Blame my stumbling on an eagerness to be honest. Please, I beg patience, Lord.

IV.

The three great sins of my lonely year in Rome without Lucius, are not unrelated, and indeed there is much connective tissue between them. I was twenty one, and was busily employed by my father's cousin, the second most powerful man in the empire, Gaius Fulvius. When my father recruited me for the position, he referred to it as an agent of military intelligence. Gaius was more direct with me. He told me on our first meeting that I would be an assassin. I said yes without hesitation.

I had impressed my father, and Gaius, when I murdered the goose-necked boy in front of them. Lucius had informed them of my success in using the sewers beneath the baths to kill the bully

Marcus Gallus, and they would not see such talent go to waste. I was put to work killing merchants, killing priests, killing Senators. Anyone who spoke out against, or was a stone in the sandal of, Emperor Septimius Severus. Most of the jobs required no special skill, just an opportune moment on a dark, empty street, or behind a basilica. Sometimes I'd kill them right out in public, my face uncovered, in broad daylight. I'd cut down some headstrong politician as he walked unguarded to worship at some temple, and stroll off through the forum, covered in his blood, no one daring to stop me. Occasionally men were too important, or too beloved by the citizenry to be outright murdered. In these scenarios I was particularly prized by Gaius, who would send me to the sewers beneath these wealthy men's homes, to drag them down their toilets, never to be seen again.

Fulvius and I worked together closely, and I respected Gaius as a man of decisive action, and loyalty. He never seemed to me to want anything more than to be number two, and serve his Emperor, his best friend since boyhood. Gaius and I were natural friends for one other reason, we were both bitterly hated by Julia Domna.

My step-mother was constantly warning the Emperor against the deceitful snake, Gaius Fulvius, who smiled to his face, but scowled in the shadows. She spoke poison of the man from before he was even appointed Prefect, to well after his death, remaining enemy to his very name and legacy. She said she saw Gaius as a threat to her husband's autonomy. She often compared Gaius to the legendary Sejanus who made such a puppet of perverted old Tiberius. When an emperor becomes too reliant on a strongman in Rome to keep his political house in order, he is at this man's total mercy. This Fulvius was much too powerful, commanded much too much respect from the military, and could be nothing but a threat to her family's dynastical control of the empire.

I know I promised, dear Lord, that I would cease with all my editorializing, but I must pause to call horse shit. I always felt the true motivation for Julia Domna's hatred of Gaius Fulvius was simple, petty, personal rivalry. It wasn't out of matronly protection of her husband's power base, but out of competition. She saw herself as second in command. More than that, she saw herself as first in command behind a puppet throne. Gaius Fulvius was trying to weasel his hand up the puppet that she had slaved so hard, and for so long, to lay her claw inside of. She would kill and risk death to keep hold, and hell to the man who tried to loosen her grip.

It was the hatred that these two pillars of influence had for one another that lead me to do such horrible things in that year of loneliness and sin.

V.

There was a dinner party held one evening at the palace, and it was here that the whole affair began.

I was standing with Gaius Fulvius at a side bar, meant for drink refilling on the way to and from the privy. Our conversation was privileged, so we felt this appropriate. The main hall, where the banquet was getting underway, was far too crowded with the dropping eaves of the royal court. They were enjoying appetizers of cow udders stuffed with salted sea urchin, and jellyfish eggs in honey and oil. I'd lick my lips if I had a tongue, oh my Lord.

"The bitch hates me for the sport of it." Gaius said to me, and I knew who he was speaking of. "And I am powerless. Would that I met this queen on the battlefield. A yapping bitch dog in some sacked village. There, bent over my knee or my sword, she'd learn finally her place."

Gaius Fulvius and Julia Domna's political rivalry had to play itself out in the shadows. The Emperor Septimius Severus wanted no sight of it. It tormented him that his best friend in the world and most trusted lieutenant, and his beloved queen and love of his life, could hate each other with such irreconcilable vigor. Neither Gaius nor Julia could go to their Emperor and simply ask for the other's head, as they had grown so accustomed to doing. Restricted from direct violence, the rivals settled their disputes through politics. They opposed one another in every way possible. Bureaucratic appointments, budgetary allocations, and mostly rhetorical issues. Gaius would be heard talking of his appreciation for Egyptian architecture, and women, and immediately he would be attacked by orators in the queen's pocket, as being in collusion with outsiders. When Gaius found himself on one side of an issue, he could always trust to see Julia opposite him.

"This Rabbi, now. When has she ever had any love for the Jews? Suddenly she protects this seditious one, simply because I'm the one who ordered him deported? How many Rabbis are deported from Rome back to their desert huts, every year? Never a word from her. But I send one Jew packing, and I've got this bitch hounding me at every turn."

"She's relentless." I was listening, but I was also watching the entrance to the hall. Lucius was nowhere to be seen. He left alone the night before, and hadn't been back to the palace all day. Plautilla, his wife, was at the party, flirting with some fat slob praetorian, feeding him dates and laughing at his bad jokes. Geta was there, chatting it up with some retired military men, doing of a bit of flirting himself. It had been made clear to everyone invited that both sons were expected at this dinner. I was preoccupied with worry that Lucius had decided to play rebel, and gone out for a night on the town without me.

"Something will have to be done." Said Gaius.

"About what, sir?" I asked dumbly.

"Are you even listening to me? This Rabbi. He is dangerous. He grows a following of devotees in Rome. I'd not like to make a martyr of him, and double his power. And so expulsion is our best option. Our only option. Still, your step-mother defies me. She takes this Rabbi into her council, assigns him her own litigators, pays the court fees, and bribes quaestors. They've got an appeal before the Senate! A Jew before the Senate! Mockery! Jest!" Gaius chugged his wine. I laid a supportive hand on his shoulder.

"You'll find a solution, as you always do, sir." I filled his goblet from a jug on the bar, spilling some. I was distracted by the guests, now arriving in greater numbers. Still no sign of Lucius.

Under any normal circumstances, with any normal rival, Gaius would send me to solve the problem with a sharpened dagger, but here that was obviously no solution. Best friend or no, Septimius would find it impossible to forgive any man of killing his wife.

For her part, Julia Domna could probably get away with killing Gaius, if she had only been able to pull it off. A husband who is truly devoted to his wife, like Septimius was to his, could find a path to forgiving her most anything. After all, she was the mother of his children, not Gaius Fulvius. But, as was the nature of her brand of influence peddling, Julia Domna could not simply order someone killed. She had no army of her own. She had some loyal bodyguards, but they were without any real experience at coordinated violence. If she wanted to be rid of someone without the help of her husband, she would need to first find some benefactor she could sway or blackmail into assisting her. Once she had a middleman on board with her scheme, they would make the appropriate connections with the gangsters, who would contract the assassins, who would do the actual killing. This was a slow, and untrustworthy process, and when the target was someone as well connected and informed as Gaius Fulvius, it was destined for failure. In lieu of murder, Julia Domna would have to latch on to causes that would bring irritation, humiliation, and defeat to Gaius Fulvius. Even if that meant clinging to the knotted fringes of some Jew.

Gaius drank what was left of his wine in one big gulp, and then smiled. "Speak of the vile cunt and she shall appear." Gaius raised his empty glass to the banquet.

The double doors at the back of the hall opened wide and Julia Domna entered, flanked by a dozen of the prettiest little flower girls dressed in white, four lute players strumming romantically, and a well timed release of cooing doves.

The party broke into applause at the queen's arrival. Gaius went to take a shit.

VI.

The evening progressed, and so did the dinner. I can smell the ostrich boiled with onions and raisins, oh Lord. There was still no sign of Lucius. I couldn't eat.

I was as noticed as the furniture at these types of events, so I spent most of the evening watching. I watched the other guests fawn and revel over one another, chatting and gossiping, and stuffing their stupid faces full of meat, and nuts, and Gaulish wine. I watched my father, who lay beside my step-mother. She played her part well, keeping up with the conversation around her, while maintaining a cool air of distance. Her husband said not a word, and seemed more distant than the moon. Septimius didn't seem interested in playing any part tonight, besides that of a bored toddler. He was drinking, yawing, burping, and scratching his ass with the same hand he was using to eat his curd cheese with, something everyone in the room seemed to notice, but for the emperor. I watched the queen lean over to her king several times, and with an unshakable smile (unshakable because it was painted on, oh my Lord) she would whisper an inquiry, "Sleepy, my love?" Which was met with ever louder snarls and growls, and then more chugging of wine. The emperor was in a bad mood, and seemed eager to do nothing but plunge himself deeper down into it.

"No one to talk to? Aye, big brother?" I turned, and Geta was laying beside me, filling the empty spot that had been set for Lucius. He was smiling his famous smile, and picking a grape skin from his big white teeth with a splinter of wood. Geta and I shared similarities of appearance that Lucius and I did not. Lofty foreheads, square jaws, and flat noses. The older we got the more we resembled our father, and therefore each other. Geta was, of course, younger and more handsome, and so a constant reminder that I wasn't even in possession of the best possible version of my own face.

Geta saw that I hadn't touched my food, and began to pick at my leftovers with his splinter of wood. "Sin to waste good food. Nervous stomach? Worried about the absent chickling, like a good mother hen?" Geta popped a bite of parrot sausage into his mouth and chewed and laughed. He wasn't being mean, or a bully, he was just being the boy that he was and would be until his death. He was kindly playful in his rudeness.

(I always liked my brother Geta, dear Lord. Truly. And whatever complicity I may have had in the events leading to his eventual murder, I never ceased in that liking.)

"You wouldn't happen to have a clue, would you? About where he's been all these hours? I'll let you have the rest of my dinner." I slide my plate closer to Geta.

"Well..." He considered the plate carefully. "Very well." He ate every last bite of food on the plate, chewed it thoroughly and swallowed it down with a big gulp of my wine. Then he said, "I haven't the foggiest." We both laughed.

Geta patted me on the back and said, "Cheer up and be merry, brother. I know how fond you are of dramatics. And watching our father as closely as you have been, I'm sure you're well aware that he's a kettle near boil."

We looked over at Septimius. He now seemed to be muttering to himself, angrily. Julia Domna lay a comforting hand on his shoulder, and he swatted it away like a pesky fly. She recovered her dismissed hand as gracefully as anyone could, but we all saw it, and it no doubt stung the queen's ego. Too bad Gaius was still in the privy, he'd have killed to have seen it. I can't count the hours I've wasted waiting on that man to get off the toilet. You blessed Gaius Fulvius with one of the most brilliant political minds of the epoch, oh god, but cursed him with the guts of a pebble eating mule.

"Isn't that novel, brother?" Asked Geta, amused at himself. "About a kettle on the boil? The water is hot, and hotter, and hotter still, and suddenly it's boiling. Who decided when the water should begin its rolling? And that it should do so under extreme heat, whether here in Rome or there in Egypt, or wherever you like? I find that fascinating."

Our odd way of thinking, Geta's and mine, was another shared quality. Though always a soldier, and never a scholar, I found Geta's interests of thought to be quite deep, and spoke of a curious, if untrained, mind.

(By the way, Lord, what of the water boiling? Does it work as I'd imagine? Somehow linked to the water's own sense of pain? Like putting flames to the feet of a man? Bring the torch close, and he squirms. Bring the torch closer and he wails. Bring the torch right against his feet and hold it there, and then the man, like the water, shall in his own way boil.)

"And what will the decisive event in the boiling over of this very evening turn out to be, aye?" Asked Geta speculatively.

The answer came in the form of clanging sword fight that burst through the rear double doors.

Dexius Januarius, the pink-wolf, crashed into the banquet hall, rippling back muscles first. He was immediately recognizable by the sheer size of him, set aside his flashy pink plume. He was in the middle of a sword fight, and didn't look like he was going to pause it in order to say hello to all of us. The pink-wolf moved quickly backwards into the room, his opponent pursuing him, kicking over bowls of fruit, jugs of wine, and screaming princesses.

The opponent was an athletic young man who I didn't recognize at the time, oh Lord, but turned out to be Pompeius Musclosus, the legendary chariot racer. He could handle a sword as well as he did a horse whip, and was giving Dexius a worthy challenge, matching him in speed and focus. So focused on one another, that they didn't flinch at protests when they stepped up onto the very banquet dinner table, taking their fight to higher ground. The queen's maids and slaves swarmed around the dueling warriors, slapping their ankles and throwing cups of water at them. "Cease! Cease!" They did not cease, oh Lord.

The queen didn't show any signs of distress, but kneeled up, and stood, and took a conservative step away from the table, and the princesses of the court followed her. The king looked positively awakened, delighted at the sudden war game playing out before him. He was laughing, and pounding his fist on the table, cheering them on. "'At a boy! Kill 'em! Kill 'em!" Geta and the other princes of the court followed him, clapping their hands, and shouting hooray. The Praetorian guards, seeing the king's approval, held tight and let the squabble go on uninterrupted.

Another three new guests joined us in the banquet hall. Lucius, drunk and stumbling, with a bare breasted bar-wench under each arm, giggling and acting as crutches to their tipsy master. One wench was holding a small stone flask. The other wench had recently been with child, and was still producing milk, which dripped down her tits. My brother was alternating his suckle from bottle to nipple. They were blurting out drunken cheers of their own to their champion, the pink-wolf.

Jealousy struck me like a bucket of cold water to the face. If not my brother's favorite, who was I? I felt as those damned to purgatory must, oh Lord. I was dead, but not yet gone. To be excluded from Lucius, was to be excluded from living, without the relief of death. Even now, years later, I wonder obsessively, dear Lord. What marvelous adventures did Lucius and the pink-wolf get up to without little old me that night? I imagine them working beside one another to construct a tower of blocks to the treetops, and then one to the clouds, and finally the moon, where they would share a drink and a toast to their great friendship. Did Lucius purposely not invite me? Was he punishing me for something, oh god? Testing my loyalty, like you tested Job? Hoping I would remain devoted despite my pain? Or had he simply not thought of me at all? Had he forgotten me? That would be much worse.

Lucius's entrance disturbed my father as much as it disturbed me. At the sight of his oldest son and his two wenches, the emperor lost all his vigor for the swordplay. His smile dissolved, and his fists loosened.

"Enough! Enough! Enough! I've had enough!" The emperor's voice bellowed through the great hall. The place went dead quiet. Children and toddlers who had thus been unagitated through the entire fight, now began to squeal and cry out for their mothers, who attended to them quickly, shushing them, and dragging them out of the hall.

The fighters, sweating and panting, and halfway to killing each other with the very next blow, immediately lowered their swords, and turned sharply, like the good soldiers they both were. Their chests heaved as they gasped for breath, but they stood up straight and at attention.

The emperor spoke again, quieter this time, but no less commanding, "Has the world gone mad and forgotten who is king?"

The queen laughed and whispered to her maids, who giggled along with her.

The emperor noticed this, but brushed it off. He took a big step up onto the dinner table along with the pink-wolf and his charioteer opponent. "What is the meaning of this, good Dexius Januarius?"

Before the pink-wolf could answer, Lucius spoke up for him.

"It was meant as a gift. From me to you, my father."

The emperor stepped past the warriors, and hopped down off the other side of the dinner table. "Ah, yes. Of course, I saw you come in with these two whores, and I thought this mischief was somehow your doing." The emperor walked over to his son, and the now trembling bar wenches, who tried to cover their heaving shame behind folded arms.

"I know how much you love war, my dear father. I simply wished to bring you some entertainment." The two wenches scurried off the way they came in.

The emperor was now standing directly before his son. Septimius was shorter than Lucius, but so to is a lion shorter than a giraffe. "You seemed to be enjoying the mischief until I showed my face. Does my involvement displease you in someway so as to sour your enjoyment?"

"I tell you son, that it does. It displeases me greatly."

A shudder passed through the entire hall. The very air we breathed, dear lord, thickened with the drama of this very public display. I caught the eye of Geta from across the hall. He was standing with some chuckling soldiers, he was smiling, he winked at me.

"It displeases me to have a son, unexperienced so totally as he is in the ways of war, sending another man to fight in his name." The emperor pointed an accusatory finger up at the pink-wolf.

"Is that not the job of a Caesar, father? To send men to fight for his various causes?"

Septimius Severus slapped his son Lucius across his smug face. Now there was more than a shift in the air of the room. A collective, audible, gasp rose from the crowd, followed by resumed silence.

Julia Domna revealed herself briefly, but only to those who watched her as closely as I did. You couldn't even say that she moved, dear Lord. You couldn't call it more than an intention of movement. Her son was slapped, and though her body may not have moved, her soul practically launched itself across the room to his rescue. Of course, Julia Domna was never one to be swayed by the whims of her soul, and so she stayed put. But it was there, oh Lord, the mother in her flinched and blinked in a flutter.

The drunk father let his drunk son have it, "How dare you tell me about the job of a Caesar! You, who has never been in battle. I, my son, have fought in many battles, side by side with real men, who fight and kill real warriors. Not pimps and gangsters, and poor defenseless women and girls. I've fought on a battlefield, my little boy. Not in the streets of a city my father was supreme master over."

Lucius took the berating with a lowered head, his eyes on the tiled floor. That did him no help.

"Look me in the eyes, you cunny jellyfish, you!" Yelled the emperor.

Lucius looked up with eyes wet with tears. That was the last straw for the emperor. "Oh, hell! No! No! No! No son of mine!" And then he called to the pink-wolf, "legionnaire!"

The pink-wolf turned and hopped down from the dinner table. "Yes, sir?"

"Give my son your blade."

"Yes, sir."

And the pink-wolf gave a confused Lucius his gladius, and then took a step back and out of this situation.

"Get your little ass up on that dinner table, and fight for your goddamn supper, would you?" The emperor pointed at the charioteer, still standing on the table, still holding his sword, still waiting to finish a fight.

The queen had enough, and showed her protest the only way she could. She cleared her throat in the most unnatural of ways, it sounded like a rooster crowing. "Come, come, ladies. The men have succumb to their more barbarous of natures, and it's time for us to take our leave. It's a matter of dignity, you see." She bowed at her cynically grinning husband, who waved a gracious hand in her direction. "Good evening, Caesar." Julia whipped herself around, and marched out of the hall, followed by a lovely army of princesses. On her way out, Julia Domna passed Gaius Fulvius, who was returning from the privy. "Leaving so early, my lady?" He asked. She did not answer.

The men were now alone in the hall with their savageries. Lucius was well trained and not unexperienced with a sword, and the charioteer was tired from his row with the pink-wolf. On the other hand, Lucius was piss drunk, and this charioteer was one of the most winning competitors to come around in a generation. There was a fairly good chance that Lucius would be killed here. I was nervous.

Lucius, understandably, was nervous. He took a look at his father, wagered that he would kill him if he didn't fight anyway, and climbed up onto the dinner table with the pink-wolf's gladius in hand. The pink-wolf found himself a jug of wine, a plate of rare oxen thigh, and laid down in a corner at the back of the hall, facing away from the action.

The fight began, the worn swords clanging anew.

(Do I bore you once more, patient listener? I bore myself with all the clinging and clanging of swords. How many swords can cling and clang in my mind in the exact same way?)

To put briefly what you yourself can remember, oh Lord, Lucius was winning the fight at first, then luck turned the way of the charioteer, and he had my brother down, and near death.

The final blow of a sword fight tends to make neither a cling, nor a clang, and usually no more than a mellow sort of squish. This fight had no squish, dear Lord, as you well know. This sword fight ended with a heavy thwack. The emperor, seeing that his oldest son's life was about to be taken at his own dinner table, shook himself sober from his drunken rage, took a sword from one of his praetorian guardsman, climbed up onto the table, and with one powerful swing, cut the charioteers head clean off his shoulders.

Blood covered the table, the food, and mostly Lucius, who crawled out from under the fallen charioteers decapitated body.

I looked for the pink-wolf, and he was gone, oh Lord. Nowhere to be seen. In the spot where he had been laying, now sat his empty plate, jug, and a large puddle of steaming piss.

The room was silent but for Lucius's heavy panting. He got onto his feet. Face dripping with fresh blood, he looked his father in the eye, and then, dear god, he giggled.

So devilish was this giggle. So off putting. So unnerving was it, in its timing, and in its pitch, and in its confidence. So disturbed by it was the emperor, that I believe, dear god, his following declaration was sparked entirely in reaction to the frightful peculiarity of that giggle.

The emperor stepped back from his son, and turned to the crowd. "My countrymen, war is a mess of blood. War is a tangle of intestines. War is clean flesh ripped by filthy metal. War is glorious beyond all other works of man. But war must be seen. It must be ravaged, chewed up, swallowed, vomited and spit out, and then the surviving spittle worshipped as the nectar of the gods. My sons are two Augustan, to be sure. Given to me, and to Rome, by the same gods, no doubt. But given as babes, are they. Babes, unknowing of the ways of war, and so unknowing of the ways of the world." Now he turned back to his son Lucius, and delivered this part to him, "Babes must be taught. War shall be their teacher. War shall be their guide. Here, today, I announce my plans for a new war in Briton."

The crowd around me rushed with chatter. I looked for the face of Gaius Fulvius, and found it, looking as pleasantly surprised as I expected it would. Fulvius had been pushing the emperor to go out on a big, long military campaign. He didn't care where it was, just so long as it happened, and soon. You see, dear god, all of Septimius Severus's military victories had thus far been against rival Roman generals, whom he fought against for the throne. To secure his legacy as a conqueror, the emperor needed to crush a foreign power.

Also, Fulvius saw the emperor's boredom growing, and was eager to have him out cutting heads off, where he was at his happiest and most useful. And if in the process this left Gaius all the more uninhibited to rule over Rome as the dictator he was fashioning himself as, all the better for everyone. Julia Domna was not going to like this news at all.

"At the start of the month we shall begin preparations for an all out assault on the Caledonians. For too long they have been unbending to the will of civilization, and it is time for us to bring to them order, modernity, and unrelenting cruelty." The emperor filled a cup of wine, and raised it. "I shall lead an army north, and with my sons beside me, I shall bring death and destruction to the highlands!"

There was a thunderous hooray from the crowd, and everyone lifted their drinks to toast war. Finally, still dripping with blood, Lucius looked across the hall at me. Our eyes met. He smiled, dear god. I was alive again.

VII.

I did not get to see Lucius off before he left for war, oh Lord, and it saddened me. There was a gigantic precession through the circus maximus, with tremendous pomp and celebration. The city, and Julia Domna, were wishing good luck to their departing princes.

My master, Gaius Fulvius, was present at the festivities, but I'm sure his mind was with me, and my crucial mission of preparing the always more important after-party.

In the month leading to the emperor's departure, his wife pestered him into expediting her favored Rabbi's court proceedings. Fulvius protested, but Septimius saw nothing to fear in a weak, old Jew, who was loyal and indebted to the empress. Septimius signed the proper orders, let his wishes be known to all involved, and the Rabbi was quickly freed from military arrest, and given a full reprieve from accusations of treason, and from threats of deportation. The Rabbi's freedom, and Julia Domna's political victory over Fulvius, was a departing king's gift to his queen. It was, as you know, dear Lord, the final gift he would ever give her.

The old Rabbi returned to his family in the Jewish quarter. Relieved of his legal troubles, he was free to preach in the square, and teach at his community temple. His relief did not last, dear god. For Septimius was gone, Gaius Fulvius was now in charge of Rome, and that murderous Severan bastard was heading over for a visit.

On this mission I had with me several tools, oh Lord. Most useful among them, the surviving half wit, and half gemini, mighty Felix.

In the year since the death of his brother, Felix seemed to double in appetite, and in weight, but also in hours spent at the baths, training and wrestling. He was big before, now he became gigantic. He became doubly strong, doubly fast to fight, and doubly unreasonable in every manner. When his brother was alive, Felix would turn to mindless laughter when he became confused or surprised, now that he was dead, he turned to mindless violence.

There have been many incidents. I'm sure you have watched these scenes with disappointment and pity, oh god. At that dinner party held by Felix's long suffering mother, you saw, oh Lord. They unveiled that new, wall sized, polished silver mirror. Felix arrived, drunk and stupid, and upon seeing his crystal clear reflection arrive beside him, he thought his brother Faustus had returned from the dead. "Praise the sewer god!" Screamed Felix. "Brother! You live!" And before anyone could stop him, he ran, arms outstretched to hug and embrace his brother, who was also running with open arms towards their long overdue reunion. You saw the end of this embarrassing anecdote yourself, oh Lord. You saw that bump form on poor Felix's forehead. You saw his broken wrist, and his renewed grieving. You saw him tare that beautiful mirror down off the wall, and shatter its mean illusions. You saw him beat anyone who tried to lay a calming hand on him. You saw his inconsolably destructive nature. And you saw, and I pray you forgive me for, how I put this nature to work for me time and again.

I had killed so many by then, dear god, that I became a sort of elitist about which tasks of murder I deemed worthy of my skills, and which could be delegated. When I was assigned to kill a target I felt beneath my talents, I would simply tell Felix that new information had surfaced concerning the murder of his brother. I would tell him that the target was somehow complicit in the crime, and it was suspected that the target himself had fired the single, fatal arrow that killed good Faustus. I would give Felix some wine, and send him off into the night, confident that in the morning my target would be dead, his face pulverized by the bare fists of what must have been two men, but was actually just a single giant. This was a reusable technique, as Felix had also become more forgetful than ever, and I could produce an endless number of killers who fired the single, fatal arrow. God, forgive my manipulation of my friend's troubled weaknesses.

Other tools with me that day, oh Lord: five praetorian guards, one tall beam of wood, one short beam of wood, rope, five nails of iron, a hammer, and a shovel. Also, most importantly, a painted sign post that read, "Hands off! Property of the queen!".

I strolled through the empty ghettos of the poorer pleb districts, Felix and my soldiers following behind in two short columns. The dwellers of these filthy neighborhoods were all at the departure celebration. The fires were squelched, the shops were closed, the houses were locked up. Dogs were milling about, stretching, sniffing for scraps of food along their newly inherited streets. We passed the Porta Compana, and the ducts of Asienta, where flowed the foulest water in all of Rome. Its stale, reeking stench, trumpeted our arrival in the Jewish quarter.

The Jewish ghetto was more alive than the rest of the city proper, maybe only a quarter emptied by the days events. The rest, who were uninterested, or offended by imperial pageantry, had stayed behind to go about their days as usual. My red cadre of praetorians and I broke this commonness. The Jews in Rome who paid their taxes and kept their anonymity, were left to their quiet lives, and the sight of soldiers in their neighborhood was a rare, off putting occurrence. We garnered many concerned whispers as we walked up the slim road, towards the synagogue.

We were expecting Julia Domna's guards, and a skirmish, but found no one protecting the front door of the temple, but for a fat old man, dozing off on a patch of grass. His armor and sword lay by his side, fast asleep. He yawned when he saw us, and did not stand. He told us that there were a dozen private bodyguards, himself one of them, who had been assigned to protect the Rabbi and his temple. They were hired by agents of Julia Domna, and paid well, but had disbanded the moment they heard the start of the emperor's departure ceremony. The eldest among them, whom we found napping on the grass, had stayed behind, feeling sleepy, and not up for the long march back to the Circus. "I figured you all wouldn't kill me," said the old guard, "if I turned over the key to this here temple without any fuss." He figured wrong. I took the key from him, drew my sword, and stuck it through his chest. He groaned, and cursed at me. I pulled the sword out, and he turned over onto his side to die. We used the key and let ourselves in.

(Sorry about killing that old, napping fellow, dear god. Quite unnecessary. He probably had grandchildren. Oh well.)

We filled the small foyer of the synagogue, which was really no more than a larger than average pleb house. We pushed through two swinging doors and found the main hall, a living area converted into a temple. There were simple engravings of the Jew's candle holder, and their crossed triangle stars, carved into the stone near the ceiling of the room. At the front of the hall was a small, open, dark wood cabinet. Before this shoddy alter was the Rabbi. I forget his name, oh Lord, for I was never able to properly pronounce it. It was like, Rabbi Elisha Ben, something-or-other-with-a-G.

Rabbi Ben was with two younger Jews. They were handsome and strong looking, surely the pride of their flock, with short black curls and wide jaw lines. They were praying together. Rabbi Ben was reading in a strange language from an unrolled scroll, using a golden wand to follow along with the words on the parchment. I entered with my gang, and the praying ceased.

"Rabbi Elisha Ben G..." I said his name aloud, and butchered its pronunciation as badly as I later would the man it called. Still, the skinny old Rabbi stood, and nodded at me. His young associates gently rolled up the scrolls, and as the Rabbi slowly walked across the room to greet me, they placed it in the empty cabinet of the the dark wood alter, and closed it.

Rabbi Ben was before me. I can still see his benign little smile, oh Lord. I can see his body of skin and bones, his shiny bald head, circled by a crown of gray tufts. He wore a black tunic, and a belt of knotted white string. His students wore the same.

"Are you Rabbi Ben?" I asked again.

"Yes. I am the man you are looking for." The Rabbi spoke to me in Greek, which was a surprise. "I have been expecting you." He continued, "I shall accept arrest without protest." Then, Rabbi Ben put a friendly, weak little hand on my armored shoulder.

I can't say exactly why, oh god, but I filled with a terrible anger. My intentions for this old Rabbi were bad, to put it mildly. Should he not have been gripped by awful terror at my very presence? What nerve this old Jew had. And then, looking again at his benign smile, I decided it wasn't nerve at all, but stupidity. He thought I was here to arrest him again. He had no idea what I had in store. This made me even angrier. I decided it was time to give him a hint of his destiny.

I placed my right hand on the Rabbi's brittle shoulder, returned his benign smile, and began to squeeze. I put my thumb deep into the socket, and twisted, and turned, until I heard a pop of dislocation. The Rabbi's thin line smile melted and then opened wide into a horrible quivering O shape. I wound up my left hand, and punched him hard in his gut. He folded forward over my fist, gasping for air. He clung to me, trying to maintain his balance. I shifted slightly and Rabbi Ben toppled onto the floor, like a bundle of twigs.

The handsome young Jews rushed to help their master, but were grabbed and held. One was held by two praetorians, the other by Felix alone.

Looking down at the shocked Rabbi, I yelled my orders. "Collect this old sack of bones to the street. Go to the dark wood cabinet, remove the scrolls. Tear them to shreds. Piss on them. Cut the throats of these two, so that they should witness the scrolls destruction as they bleed to death." Panic now seized the young Jews, and they put up a desperate fight to get free of their captors, to no avail.

As my men carried out my instructions, I walked away from the screams, and back out into the streets. It was hot in that temple, and my forehead was wet with sweat. I remember feeling quite good to step out into the air, dear god. Forgive me, I must confess, I felt excellent. There was a slight breeze, and my damp brow was cooled. I remember closing my eyes, and stretching my arms out as wide as they could go. A deep breath, full lungs, and the world was mine. In the midst of commanding death, I felt very much alive.

A small crowd of Jews had formed across the street. They were faining disinterest, no one eager to become involved on behalf of the Rabbi or his temple, but they were certainly going to keep an eye on the situation. I smiled at them. I waved a little hello. They snarled, some of them spit. I chuckled. Come on over here and spit, I thought. You don't want to fuck with me when I'm feeling this good, I thought. God forgive my encouragement by their fear.

Felix and the other soldiers rejoined me outside, two of them dragging the bewildered Rabbi Ben between them. Felix, fists dripping with blood, was shaking piss off his dick, and he painted a terrifying picture for the onlookers across the street, who shook in unison. I laughed, and pat him on the back. Felix grinned, grunted like an ape, and tucked himself away.

We walked back up to the Porta Capana, where the road to the Jewish quarter merged with the main thoroughfare. In the next few hours this road would be filled with massive crowds of Romans, returning home after the departure celebration. Here we stopped, dear Lord, and prepared a cross to nail old Rabbi Ben to.

A slender but deep hole was dug into the dirt of the roadside to mount the base of the cross in. The shorter plank of wood was nailed across the top of the longer one, forming a T shape. At the top of the T was nailed the painted sign to tell all who passed that the slaughtered Rabbi had belonged to the queen, and look at what good it had done him. It would send a message to the people of Rome, and to Julia Domna herself, that Gaius Fulvius was their supreme commander.

Things were just about ready. Rabbi Ben stood quietly by, watching the men work, his hands unbound, the idea of running was a joke. He was looking back and forth, from the construction of the crude device that would torture him so, to the crowd of his own people who would watch until he was dead. Without words, dear Lord, using a very dignified, polite kind of gaze instead, the Rabbi was asking his fellow Jews to do something to help him out of this. They responded with their own polite looks, which told him gently, but starkly, that he was on his own.

The Rabbi turned to me. "Sir? May I talk, sir?"

"Talk, Rabbi. This is your party." I spoke with such confident abandon. Forgive me, forgive me, forgive me.

The Rabbi spoke urgently, and was very short of breath, but was making an effort to conceal his distress. He was folding his trembling hands together and hiding them behind his back. At the time, I was disgusted by the old man's failure at masking his fear. Now, so close to my own death, oh god, I honor his nobility in even attempting to hide it.

"Shall I speak in my defense?" Said the Rabbi. "Shall I tell you how I am a harmless old man, caught between two feuding politicians? Shall I tell you that my crimes do not warrant such harsh punishment?"

"No." I said. "That won't do you any good. Gaius Fulvius wants you on a cross, and so on a cross you go."

"I understand." He said. "I really do understand your position. Following orders and all. Perhaps you would be open to the idea of a bribe? Some amount of money in exchange for my life? I could leave on a boat for Judea this very night. Gone forever. How much would my freedom cost in coin?" He talked like he was haggling for a carpet, but the fear was growing in him, and his face turned white, and his eyes became unblinking. The fog of destiny was clearing, and this old Rabbi didn't like what future was being revealed to him.

"To be honest, Rabbi, I am paid extremely well. From the looks of your shoddy temple, I don't think you could afford me." I turned my back on Rabbi Ben. The wooden horse was ready for its rider.

Felix and the highest ranking Praetorian stepped close to the Rabbi, casting a long shadow over the shrinking Jew. He looked up at them like a sick dog. I moved back, and they ushered Rabbi Ben over to the cross, which was laying flat out on the dirt, just in front of the slender hole in the ground.

"Lay down, crossed legs, arms out, palms open." Said the high ranking Praetorian. He had gone through this procedure many times, and spoke with a bored authority. None of us had crucified someone before, and Fulvius sent this experienced man along, an old friend of his, to show us how it was done.

Rabbi Ben was staring down at the cross like it was a cold lake, and he was being goaded into diving in. He looked at the crowd of onlookers, which had grown, and moved closer, but was no nearer to lending the old man any assistance. Rabbi Ben was frozen, but for his involuntary rattling.

"Go on! Lay down!" Yelled Felix.

The Rabbi was a statue for a few more long seconds, and then finally said, "I'm terribly sorry. I don't think I'll be able to." He turned to Felix and the Praetorian with genuine apology in his eyes, which were wet, as he was beginning to cry. "I'm quite nervous, you see, and it's made me rather stiff. I don't think I can do it. Will you help me to lay down? Please?"

The experienced Praetorian took Rabbi Ben by his arm, and was going to help him to begin the process of his own murdering, but Felix was impatient. He pushed between the Praetorian and the Rabbi. "Lay down, we said!" Felix shoved Rabbi Ben with all his might, knocking him onto his ass with a choke of pain. When the Praetorian grabbed Felix by the shoulder, the dumb giant turned and punched him across his chin, knocking him on his ass too. Then he kicked the Rabbi square in his chest, laying him out flat on top of the wood.

The other soldiers and I laughed at the Praetorian who got punched, and I of course did nothing to discipline Felix. The experienced guard thought of punching Felix back, but that wasn't going to end well for him. So, pissed off and insulted by the retard who pushed him, the only one among us with any knowledge of crucifixions, spit, said "Fuck this", and walked off towards the nearby public house to get drunk. I wish he had stayed, dear god. If only one of us had known what we were doing, perhaps the Rabbi's killing would have gone more smoothly. As it was, Felix and the other untrained executioners got to work, nailing the Rabbi to his cross.

There are many crucifixions in my long tale of suffering and murder. Dozens soon to come, and dozens more after that, oh Lord. This early one stands out to me because it was the first I was responsible for, and supervised directly. But also, I dwell on it for the hysterical incompetence of it. What a morbid farce, oh god, for a man to die in such a comically excessive fashion. Did you laugh, my darkly humored master? Admit it. You laughed. It was too terrible to do anything but.

The errors of our inexperience made for Rabbi Ben, what should have been an excruciatingly painful death, an unbelievably excruciatingly painful death. Firstly, the nails were all wrong. Too short, too thin. They were driven through the Rabbi's palms, not his wrists, where they would have had more bone to hold onto. The guard who secured the left palm was squeamish, and didn't hammer deep enough into the wood. Felix secured the right palm, and was too eager, and hammered so hard that the Rabbi's palm was crushed to a pulp, and the nail driven nearly all of the way through, gripping the wood with nothing more than skin. Similar problems lower down. He should have been nailed at his ankles, not the top of his feet. The nails shortness was especially a problem here, as they needed to pass through both feet, and then the wood, a task they failed. Finally, heavy rocks should have been placed in and around the hole at the base of the cross from the get go, to keep it from toppling over at a strong wind. All of these obvious mistakes would have been avoided by someone with some experience, but he left to have a drink, and so things went how they did.

The cross was raised the first time, and the Rabbi did not scream. He did that while the nails were being driven through his flesh. Now that they seemed there to stay, he was defeated, and quiet. Too lost in pain to speak, perhaps, oh god. The pain caused him to forget himself, I think, and his situation. Perhaps he thought he was a boy who had climbed a tree, or a carpenter up his ladder. He gazed down at us dumbly, spit dribbling long and silky from his mouth. His face was empty, like a child, like an orphan. Lazily, the Rabbi looked at his wounded right hand, then his left. He whimpered, and hung his head in a distraught remembrance of who and where he was. This was no tree, this was no ladder.

The Rabbi closed his eyes and appeared to pass out. The Jewish onlookers sighed in relief. Then, his body began to shake. Every part of him was convulsing. He was tugging his limbs reflexively away from their bondage. First to come free was his pulverized right hand, tearing right down the middle web of his fingers. The Rabbi woke up and began to scream, clutching his hand to his chest, shifting his weight awkwardly. Some Jews in the crowd began to scream along with him. The shaking of his legs and feet caused the bottom nail to yank itself out of the wood, releasing his body to fall and then swing rapidly to the left, as that hand was the only part of him still stuck to the cross. He was screaming, and dangling there, bleeding, when the last nail holding him up came loose. Before we could get under him to catch him, the Rabbi fell onto the dirt with a dry thud.

Wailing, and pleading in his native language, the Rabbi was now insane with panic. He was slipping in and out of consciousness as we nailed him to his cross for the second time. Some Jews from the crowd were yelling at us to just cut his throat and be done with it. Put him out of his misery. I could not do this, oh Lord. My mission was not just to kill this man, but to make a message out of him. He needed to go up on that cross under that sign that read, "Hands off! Property of the queen!", And he needed to stay up there long enough for the people of Rome to see him.

The second time he fell, both of his hand nails gave out simultaneously. Much to the shock-horror of those watching, the nail driven through the Rabbi's feet did not give out. So, when Rabbi Ben's arms were released, he fell forward, diving past his waist, tugging his legs out away from the wood, and his ankles. This caused him to crack both of his shin bones in half, and they came piercing through his pale, wrinkled calves. This woke the Rabbi from another daze, and he was alive again, screaming in agony. The crowd screamed with him, many turned to be sick, many fled to scene.

The experienced Praetorian who had left us to our own efforts, stepped out onto the veranda of the pub he was drinking in. He watched our failing over a cup of ale, with a satisfied grin. If he wasn't a close comrade of Fulvius, I would have had him nailed up next. Ass. Sorry, god.

As we nailed the still living Rabbi to his cross for the third time, he protested only with his eyes, the life in which was far away and drifting farther. The only sounds he made were short gasps with each refreshed nail, followed by the continuation of a steady laborious breathing. It was getting very difficult for him to keep his grip on this world.

This time we put the nails in his wrists, and what was left of his ankles, and at first, it seemed like it would work. That was good, because the departure festivities would be ending soon, and we needed to have our message set up, and be on our way. Then, a wind came. Did you send it, Lord, to complete the joke? It wasn't enough that he fell twice. Are things funnier in threes? Whipping through the boulevards, gaining momentum, the wind caught itself in the back of Rabbi Ben, like boat's mainsail, and pushed him out to sea. Or, rather, pushed him face first into the dirt a third time, a heavy beam of wood smashing down behind him.

The experienced Praetorian, over by the pub, started to laugh. It was a wild, whole hearted laughter. He couldn't believe how badly this had turned out. Sure, when he walked off, he had hoped his absence would be felt, but there was no way he would have guessed it could have gone this poorly without him. We crucified that little old man three times in less than fifteen minutes. It truly was funny, and the Praetorian's laughter made me all at once aware of just how funny. God forgive me, I laughed. Felix laughed. The other Praetorian guards laughed. The Jewish onlookers couldn't help themselves, and in a wicked stupor, they laughed along with us. I swear to you, dear god, though he lay face in the mud, covered in blood and his own torn flesh, as near to death as a man can be without ceasing to be, Rabbi Ben laughed too. Then, he shut his eyes for the last time, and died.

Finally, we got some rope, said fuck the nails, tied the dead Rabbi to his cross, and stood him up sturdy with a heavy base of boulders. Message delivered.

VIII.

In the months which followed there was a purge in Rome. Anyone with any power who was not loyal to Gaius Fulvius, fled the city, or were killed. Assassinations and show trials swept the streets clean of dissent. The sun rose daily on the fresh corpses of Senators, killed and left miles away from their homes, near drains and tunnels of the Cloaca. Rumors spread that Gaius Fulvius had conjured some underworld demon, who dwelled in the sewers. Forgive me my smile, oh Lord.

Gaius now had total administrative control of the Italian armies. One of the first things he did was to order every reserve unit stationed in the countryside transferred close to him, inside the city. With these new soldiers he created his own police force and intelligence apparatus, flush with loyal veterans.

Julia Domna had vast reserves of influence to spread around in defense of Fulvius's power grab, but not enough, and not of the brand needed to stop it. The empress would spend weeks scheming with a tax collector a way to covertly siphon her funds not approved by the city's dictator, and Fulvius would spend not a moment to reach for his sword. It was time consuming and exhausting to manipulate and maneuver a bureaucrat, and so quick and easy to just kill them. Fulvius was better equipped to kill his enemies than was Julia Domna, and so he bested her at every turn.

Fulvius used the military to take control of the economy, and used the economy to take control of the culture. He seized private grain supplies, forcing market bosses to side with him in tributary disputes. People who used to pay off the queen for legal favor, were now taking their business to where true power lay, with the king's most trusted Prefect. Seemingly overnight, statues were raised by brown nosing patricians glorifying Gaius Fulvius, and coins were even pressed with his face. Meanwhile, shrines to Julia Domna and the royal family were vandalized and painted over with vulgarities. I myself painted several cartoon cocks in the mouths of my step-mother. Monarchy was losing popularity overnight, and I, dear god, felt liberated.

Julia Domna's world was shrinking. She was isolated to the imperial palace, living a life of continued decadence, no doubt, but essentially a prisoner in her own home. The roads to the palace were under the control of Gaius's police, and the empress was under constant surveillance. Her every move was accounted for and reported to central intelligence daily. Correspondences were intercepted and read, so she was unable to send word of her situation to her husband. Innocent visitors to the queen were arrested, interrogated, and sent on to their mistress, beaten to near death. Girls who stayed loyal to her court were raped. Privateers who were hired to protect the queen were paid double to ransack the palace, kill some servants, and run off with whatever valuables they could grab. Everything was done to rid the earth of Julia Domna, but for that final shuffling loose, news of which would have been impossible to keep from the emperor.

Through his boldness, Gaius Fulvius made it clear to Rome, and to Julia Domna, that he did not see himself as a temporary leader. Once they were discovered, which they inevitably would be, his crimes were not likely to be forgiven by the emperor. Whispers spread that Fulvius had his eyes set on civil war. When the emperor and his sons returned to Rome, would they be granted entry by its new king?

One day, Gaius called me to his offices. "The bitch has laid an egg. I'd have you crack it before it hatches of its own will." He said.

"Bitches have puppies, not eggs, sir." I smiled. Gaius smiled back.

Our friendship was in full bloom. Our shared enemy was on her knees. We had dreamed of this day, and now here we were. Gaius had done more for me than any man had in my life, dear Lord. More than my father, more than my brother. True, Gaius had instigated me into worse sin than I had ever previously been guilty of, but I was probably headed down that road anyway, with or without him. Gaius trusted me with power and responsibility. I was an intimate of his at intelligence analysis meetings, always being asked my opinion on the best method of murder. I often thought in these days of what it would be like if civil war did come, and I was asked to side with Gaius against my father and brothers. Perhaps Gaius would be successful, and when the empire was his, my place in history would be affirmed. Perhaps an empowered Gaius Fulvius would appoint me Prefect. No longer would I be remembered as the shadowy bastard of the Severan clan, but the day lit son of the Fulvian administration. My bastardhood would no longer be a mark of shame, but a triumphant symbol of rising democracy, and falling monarchs. Bastardus Filius Reipublicae.

(Sadly, none of this was to be. The machinations of Julia Domna, which turned out to be matched in ability by none but your own, oh god, would engineer my fantasy towards self-immolation.)

"Be she barking dog or pecking hen, she remains a trifling beast that will not cease in agitating me. A quaestor's journal has been confiscated and a plan has been uncovered. On the first of the month, Julia Domna intends to leave her castle, and brave the streets. She will march from the palace to the Senate, gathering to her side as she goes, the more prominent widows of those we have killed. Wives of Senators, patricians, merchants. Daughters of the court who claim their chastity stolen by my order. At the Senate, with these whining victims howling and balling behind her, she shall decry me as usurper to the throne, and list my crimes for the record. I have nothing to fear from the Senate, but her wild accusations will undoubtedly reach Briton, and without the proper context may threaten my position in Rome. We may have a strong little army in here with us, but the emperor has quite a large one out there with him."

Julia was cunning, and it seemed a cunning plan, to be sure. It made good use of what tools remained available to her. It would be impossible to keep a Senate testimony hidden from the emperor, no matter how far away and preoccupied he was. If she were to speak, it may very well have been catastrophic for Gaius's plans. She had to be stopped. If only we had gone to the end with our boldness and just killed the egg laying bitch. It would have spared me, and my country, great hardship and terror.

Leaving murder aside, we were limited in our choice of responses. Gaius couldn't simply stand in the way of Julia's testimony with parliamentary rules or the like. It would appear petty, and the people would resent him for it. To stand in her way with soldiers would make him appear the mock dictator that he was. The answer was that Gaius would do nothing. I would be the one to act. I jumped at the opportunity.

Gaius and I formulated a simple but adequate plan. On the morning of her testimony, I and a gang of assassins would dress in the clothes of beggars. Donning theater masks, we would ambush Julia Domna and her precession of protesting victims as they walked to the Senate. All would be slaughtered but for the empress. She would be beaten, and robbed. The violence would illustrate to her finally the dangerous precariousness of her position. We would escape to the sewers, our faces unseen. The following hour, Gaius would announce that the gang of criminals who attacked the queen have been arrested, and justice meted out. The queen would be asked to remain in her palace apartments indefinitely. For her own safety, of course. It would then be leaked through bribed officials that Julia had wanted to visit the Senate so she could announce the organization of a charity fund for veteran's wives, which Gaius Fulvius thought was a noble idea, and in her absence would be taking up the cause himself.

"Good." Said Gaius. "Use comedy masks. Don't do her the honor of tragedy." He stood briskly.

The plan was settled, and I was dismissed. As I left his command office, Gaius rushed out himself, through a back entrance, which led to his privy. His intestines were acting foul again, and during our meeting he must have been quietly suffering to hold himself inside himself. His next appointment will have to wait, I thought, Gaius will be on that toilet for an hour. I marked this, oh Lord, in a way I hadn't before. All of the time he spent, squatted in the same place, distracted and immobile, it was a weakness. A weakness that an enemy could make fine use of. And a friend, too, oh god.

IX.

Several years earlier I had moved out of the palace, and was living quite happily, with the pimps, thieves, and other rogues of society, in the Suburra district. I first leased a room on the top floor of a tall insula, and in less than a year saved enough to buy the entire building. I hired a sharp old lena I could trust, and she set up a half barbershop, half hand job joint, in the tabarnae at the ground level. It was a steady income, oh Lord, and it felt good being a landlord. I was happy as master of that apartment building, my tenants revered me as fair and easy spirited. Maybe I should have stayed there, oh god? I could have spent the rest of my days collecting rent, and enjoying the free services of my very own brothel and beauty parlor. Like so many other earthly paradises I have visited in my tiresome life, it was not to be my home, I was only passing through.

There was a great abundance of theaters and actors in the Suburra, and it was from one of them that I borrowed the comedy masks. "You will return them?" Asked the actor, and I answered him with my sword through his chest. I made no effort to hide the corpse, no one begrudges the killing of a professional liar. Forgiveness, god, for depriving Senaca's play of its Hercules at that evening's performance.

Four smiling masks for four stone faced assassins. I did not bring Felix with me. This mission was too important. There was too great a chance that he would become overly excited and remove his mask, or otherwise betray his identity as that giant retard who hangs out with the bastard lap dog of Gaius Fulvius. The men I did choose to accompany me were known loyalists to Fulvius but were instructed in the importance of maintaining their anonymity in this operation. I remember, oh god, how much of a point I had made about the masks to my men before we set out. You heard me, Lord, with my own mask already on, my speech muffled, "This mask is your face today, soldiers. To remove this mask would be to remove your face from your skull. Should you be apprehended, and your mask taken off you, you are expected to claw out your own eyeballs, and tare off your own cheeks, so to become unrecognizable to your captors. Am I understood?"

The stoic soldiers put on their masks of fixed grimaces, and nodded that they understood. Did I understand, oh god? No, I certainly did not. For, after all my worry, and reiteration, it was I who happily removed his mask at the climax of the attack.

We ambushed the peep of chicks as they entered the Via Sacra, where the road was narrow, before it opened up to the temples and government buildings. We surrounded them when the road was at its tightest, and leaped from the shadows and alleyways, our daggers drawn. There was no where to run. It didn't matter, because not a one of them tried. Upon the sight of us, and our weapons, and terrifying comedy masks, the widows did not flea, but rallied and circled themselves around their queen, Julia Domna.

"We shall protect you, empress!" They screamed. "We die for our majesty, Julia Domna!" They shrieked. And then we gave them what they wanted. They died like lambs. Easier. I've seen lambs kick a farmers thumb broken rather than have its throat cut. Not these women. Their husbands had died terribly, in some cases their sons and daughters. They had been raped, and beaten, and all very recently. These were women who had, of late, been crying out for death. Here I came, oh god. The answer to their prayers.

(I had heard many of these widows say outright that they had considered suicide as a way of coping with their varied loses, oh my Lord. Some had been rumored of attempting to do so. One had been found by her servants, wrists cut, but all wrong, and in the way where you survive but with embarrassing scars. A terrible sin, suicide. Straight to hell, if I'm not mistaken? So, taking just a brief pause for logical thinking, let's say these women hadn't been slaughtered that day. Even if Julia Domna's plan had gone off successfully, would they have been any more reconciled to life without their loved ones? If left alive, I'm confident some of those widows would have committed suicide. And then where would they be? Not up in heaven, reunited with their husbands, where they went after I was done killing them. But down in hell, to suffer for all eternity. I must say, that in this one case, perhaps my killing was the lesser of two evils? Does my logic offend you, oh my Lord? Yes, it must, for I am filled with shame at its conclusions. Yet, my mind still arrives at them, without being driven. Is it equipped to be automatic in this way, oh maker of me? Why a brain so easily prepared to connect, through the lovely gift of logic, sin with justification?)

We agreed before hand that the best show was the bloodiest show, and to this end, the widows were all to have their throats cut at their main vessel. When we were done, and the flock of widows deflighted, the street was painted red. Our daggers, our beggar's rags, our grinning masks, all covered in the blood of good patrician women.

The only thing still standing in the street, with a pair of tits, was my step-mother, Julia Domna. She was drenched in the blood of her courtesans. Her hair, which had been done up in a decorative hive for the day's events, had fallen, and become unraveled and soaked. It was slopped over her forehead, and dripping a mixture of blood and dye. Her makeup was half washed away, and she looked like she had been whipped down the center of her face, where a crack of red blood had splashed and left itself. In the shock-horror of it all, she had peed, and her light violet toga became a deep purple around her crotch. She had stepped out of her left sandal, and her foot was bare, and nakedly dipped into a sea of blood rapidly forming on the colonnade. She looked at me. She was not crying, but her eyes were welling with terror. As my masked companions got to work digging through the pockets and purses of the widows, completing the facade of a robbery, I stepped closer to Julia Domna, for a better look at her defeat.

How my heart rejoiced, oh god. How my heart rejoices still at the long desired fantasy of that fleeting instant. I had crushed her. The all powerful she-devil of my childhood. My tormentor. My hater. Here she was, in tatters. Humiliated, with her own piss running down her legs. And there I was, my gloating face hidden behind a mask. It was not right. The true joy of this moment would come in her knowing that it was I, that useless little bastard, who had made such a fool of her. A part of me too strong to overrule decided that I could not miss this opportunity, oh Lord. She must see me, I thought, she must see me. I removed my mask.

My step-mother showed no sign of surprise at the revelation. She remained quietly terrified.

I could imagine the anger on the faces of my still masked companions. "Fucking idiot", I heard them mumble. They wrapped up their collections, and began making their exit, back into the hills.

I was unfinished. I put my bloody dagger to the lily white throat of Julia Domna. Her breath was shallow, but rapid. Her chest was heaving. My eyes grabbed hold of hers, and they entangled. I pressed firmly with my knife and cut her a little, and she bled, and winced in a shock of pain, but did not move. The blood made its way down her neck. I pulled her close to me by her waist. I stuck out my tongue, leaned in close, and licked. I licked the blood from the droplet at the top of her breasts, up the muscles of her throat, to just underneath her chin, and the wound itself, where I laid a gentle kiss.

I stepped back, I was shaking. I wiped the salty blood from my lips, and swallowed what was in my mouth. I had lost myself, oh god. Where had my mind gone? I was possessed. Yes. That was the only way to describe the sensation, oh master of the universe. A terrible demon had taken grip of me, and set my tongue to work, collecting blood to feed its unholy appetites. I did not yet see the serpent, oh my Lord, but I must say that on that day, I sensed his malevolence more strongly than I ever had before. It was not the first time this invisible reptile had made use of my sword, and of my tongue, to quench his lustful thirst for misery. It would not be the last.

I turned and fled behind my companions, feeling relieved that I had accomplished a great work. A masterpiece.

Did you stay behind with my step-mother, oh Lord? What was her affect after I was gone and out of view? Did she laugh, oh god? Did she laugh at my stupidity, and the unfolding of her plan?

X.

I allowed my masked accomplices to keep the booty they plundered from the widows, if they also agreed to keep my secret, that I had removed my mask. Revealing myself to my step-mother undermined the whole point of the mission, and Gaius Fulvius would be less than pleased to hear of it. I was in trouble. Claiming myself as the culprit of this terrible crime, should have led to my death, oh god.

The night after the ambush of the widows, I could not sleep. Julia Domna would certainly announce that it was her wretched step-son who had betrayed her. He had unmasked himself, and there had been witnesses. And was her step-son not the right hand of Gaius Fulvius? And did not the right hand, like a good dog, obey none but its master? And then Gaius would be faced with a choice. Kill the queen bitch, and declare a war he was not yet prepared to win, or cut off his right hand, and disown it. Since the former meant his likely death, I was sure my master would go with the latter. I was not his son. I was not even his brother's son. I was his cousin's bastard, and that night, tossing with worry, I lost all illusions of what bonds tied Gaius and I.

I thought I would be arrested in the morning. I got out of bed and paced the room. I entertained wild ideas. I thought I would ride east, to the deserts of my ancestors, and never return. But I thought I would miss Lucius too much. Perhaps, I could ride west to Briton. I would inform my father that the noble Julia Domna was in trouble, and I had stolen away to deliver warning of the insidious plans of Gaius Fulvius. Perhaps we could ride back to Rome together, with an army, to retake the city, and liberate our beloved mother. Wildest of all, why not kill both Gaius and Julia before morning? What good were either of them to me alive?

When morning arrived, no one came for me. In the afternoon, no one came for me. In the early evening, my old lena brought me up a note that had just arrived from a Praetorian messenger. The note was unsigned, but I knew that it was from Gaius. It read simply, "Good job, my beloved nephew."

I finally got some sleep. It was the sleep of a champion. The sleep of a victor. I had horrified my enemy, and put her in her place. She was so afraid that she had decided to do what was best for her, and just keep her yapping beak shut. I slept through the entire evening, and late into the night. When I awoke, an hour or so after midnight, I was starving. My lena heated the leftovers from that night's supper special, and I ate stewed pork on the curb bench in front of the building. It was a cold night, but the food was warm, and so was my spirit. I had finished eating, and was reclining in my chair, when I saw the palace slave girl walking up the side path.

Was her name Aurial, oh god? Her mother's name was Agatha, that I'm sure of. Agatha was a fixture of my childhood, always just behind my step-mother, head tilted down, eyes on the ground, waiting to be needed. She was a statue, until some piece of clothing on her mistress came out of place, or a door needed to be opened, or a glass of wine refilled, and then Agatha would buzz with efficient movement. Agatha lived for no other reason but to serve Julia Domna, and when she died, her daughter took up the family business. I had moved out of the palace by then, and never got to know the daughter. Was her name Aurial, oh god? You know the girl I mean, of course. The slave girl, the daughter of Agatha, who shared her mother's lack of all characteristics aside from unwavering service to the queen. Was it Aurial? She wore her hair in short, tight curls. Fuck it, you know the girl I mean. I'm just going to call her Aurial, and hope I'm at least close.

Aurial marched right up to me, and wordlessly thrust a folded piece of parchment in my face.

"The fuck is this?" I asked.

"From my lady." She said, and shook the note rudely. I snatched it from her.

"Fine." I said. "Now fuck off."

"No." Said Aurial. "I am to wait. You are to read, and give answer, immediately."

I groaned, faining annoyance, because I was actually quite intrigued, to say the least. I unfolded the note. I read it with growing pleasure. I kept the note for nearly a year after receiving it, and then I burnt it to ash. While I kept it, I considered it as fine a trophy as the silver amphora heart that Lucius had given me so many years before. The words were few, oh my Lord, and I have memorized them:

"My son, I am defeated. My enemies surround me. I must see you. Come to the palace under cover of darkness, so that I may throw myself at your feet, and beg mercy. If you honor your father, you will come see me this very night. Have pity on a lost woman.

Your loving mother, Julia Domna."

I should have known that bitch was up to something, oh god. Part of me did know. The smarter part of me. It spoke first, and said loudly, this is a trap, go see your loving mother at her palace and you won't leave alive. Another part of me was hopeful. It spoke second, and said seductively, you've won, go see your loving mother and claim your long desired prize.

I should have torn the note, given Aurial a swift kick in her slave ass, gone straight away to Gaius Fulvius, and reported the queen's attempted communique. I would have been rewarded for my loyalty, and avoided the catastrophe that awaited me.

As it was, oh Lord, I pocketed the note, pulled on my boots, belted my sword to my waist, and headed for the palace.

XI.

Aurial led the way through the unguarded gates, across the barren courtyard, and down the center hall of the imperial palace, towards the queen's private suite. It was dark, and none of the gas lamps were lit. Had they run out of oil? It was cold, the hypocausts were not burning. The halls were quiet, emptied of servants and slaves. Had they run off, or had they been sent away?

Everything looked smaller. The ceilings seemed lowered. The fresco paintings, which were so life like to me as a youth, were now unconvincing cartoons. The entire palace seemed a fake of itself. Was this the grand castle I had been a child in? Had I new eyes?

(I often wonder, oh Lord, what would Rome look like to my newest set of eyes? Now clearer than ever after years spent away from the city, in deep repentance in the countryside. Were I to gaze upon the great temples of my childhood home once more, how would they appear to me?

Would I see them as standing ruins, lingering in denial of their own long past collapse? Would I even be able to see them at all, oh god?)

We approached the double doors that led to the queen's lair. Aurial reached into her cleavage and removed a small brass key. She unlocked the doors, and moved to open them. Fear washed over me and I put a hand on Aurial's shoulder.

"Stop." I said. "Wait." I unsheathed my sword, and stood back from the doors in a defensive stance. "Go on." I said. "Open them both, and open them wide."

Aurial looked at me with such boredom that I became certain there was no imminent danger. She opened both of the doors wide, and revealed a room so massive, and so dark, that it appeared infinite. At the center of this void was the queen's linen canopied bed, glowing from the flame of a small lamp within.

Seeing the utter emptiness, I lowered my weapon, and my guard. I stepped into the room behind Aurial, who called out to the bed, which reminded me of a campfire in a deep wood, "Oh mistress. Are you awake, my dear mistress?"

The queen's little fingers poked through the linens surrounding the bed, parting them. Her fingers had never seemed so small to me. Then came her unmade face, and her bandaged throat. Her cheeks were pale, her lips were gently pouting, her eyes were big and wet and sweet, and when they saw me they bloomed and wilted, at once. It was my hated step-mother, Julia Domna, and to me she had never appeared so outrageously beautiful. Then she smiled. Like her fingers, like her palace, it was a smile that appeared little to me. But for its littleness, it was also delicate. God forgive me, it was precious.

"Yes." Said Julia, in a voice I had never heard before. "I was asleep for a small while, but I awoke not long ago. Another terrible nightmare." Had my step-mother always sounded so girlish? Had I a new set of ears to go along with my eyes, oh Lord? Was it really her? Had she sent an impostor to assassinate me? If so, she had sent a little girl.

"I have brought the bastard." Said Aurial, pointing at me with a fat thumb over her shoulder.

"Now, now, Aurial, what did we talk about?" Asked the queen.

"Sorry." Said Aurial, reluctantly. "I have brought your son." She sneered at me. I couldn't help but smile.

Julia smiled at me again, and then parted the linens of her bed's canopy even further, revealing the silk toga she wore, which clung to her body like smooth purple skin. Behind her was a plush oasis of lavender blankets and pillows. She put out one of her delicate hands, palm up, and then her fingers danced in a come hither motion.

"Come, my boy." Said Julia, in that same girlish voice. Then she closed the linens and disappeared.

My heart was pounding. I looked at Aurial. She shrugged like the clueless imbecile that she was and is. Sorry, god, I really don't like that slave bitch. She never wanted anything but trouble for me, and for no reason.

As if following previous instructions, Aurial briskly walked out the double doors, closing and locking them behind her. Alone in the darkness, I sheathed my sword, and climbed into the light of my step-mother's bed.

Julia Domna's seduction of me that first night was a slow coiling snake of a thing, oh my Lord. At first, I felt terribly awkward. I had never been so close to her, in such an intimate setting. I don't think I had ever been around her with her sandals off, and now here she was, bare footed and lounging in her night dress. And there I was, sitting with my legs crossed, trying to look at ease, with a heart like a scared mouse. I was afraid, yes, but god forgive me, I was piqued.

She began by charming me with compliments, ever comparing my good looks to my father's. She was shy, but giggly. She talked of how low she felt for the years of strife between us. She had been petty, and allowed her jealousies to cloud her affections for me. "Truly," I remember her saying, "you have been nothing but a good boy, and I have been nothing but a villainess."

At some point she touched my cheek, began to cry, and gently rested her face on my chest. I was frozen. Was this a trick? Was I a fool for letting her get this close to me? Was she seconds away from unleashing her fangs, and going for the vein in my neck? No, she was weeping. I raised my arms and wrapped them around her gossamer shoulders.

"Lay down with me." She whispered. "My sleep has been so troubled lately, without a man beside me."

And so we laid down, my step-mother and I. And soon she was asleep in my arms, or so it seemed by the slow steadiness of her breathing. I couldn't fall asleep at first. I was too excited, too aroused. Forgive me, Lord, I did not want to miss a single toss or turn of her body. I began to act asleep, and in my commitment to the role, I eventually dosed off.

When I woke up, Julia Domna was still asleep, and still in my arms, only now she was completely naked. Her purple evening toga was a ball of discarded fabric at the far end of the bed, like it had been kicked there. With her eyes closed tightly, she writhed into me. I undid my belt, pulled off my tunic, and dropped my loin cloth. I held her naked body against my own, and buried my face in her hair. I pretended to be asleep, and then, once more, I was.

When I woke up next, I was on my back, the empress was straddled atop me, and I was inside her. Still dreamy with the fog of sleep, I was not me, and she was not her. All that existed was the pleasure between us, and the want for its climax. My mind was a billion miles away, and maybe that was part of her plan. Would I have fallen into her trap had the luring not been punctuated by disorienting periods of sleep? Probably so, god, probably so.

Before and after I had my own step-mother, I had many, many women. But my shameful confession is that none ever equaled the erotic tension I experienced in that canopied bed that first evening, or any of the evenings that followed over the next year. And there is the despicable core of this most heinous sin. My enjoyment of it.

I curse my own desires. Damn them to hell. I spit on the floor in outrage at their insistence.

XII.

My state of being during my affair with Julia Domna is humiliating to recall. I spent the first month of it undoing my hard work of years prior. I sold my building of apartments in the city, and used the coin to hire some bodyguards I could trust to protect Julia Domna and the palace. I visited the toilets of minor lieutenants of Gaius Fulvius and disappeared them from the world, easing the grip around the queen's neck, while not raising the suspicions of my previous master. With my masked accomplices, I robbed and murdered couriers of Fulvius, so that the delivery of bribes to Senators and other officials became unreliable. This caused whispers among the ruling class that perhaps Gaius didn't have Rome as tightly under his thumb as he'd have them believe, and some returned their support to Julia Domna.

In my position among the heads of Gaius's intelligence apparatus, I was able to deliver distracting misinformation to allow Julia Domna to restart her operations. She was able to travel freely through the city, making surprise visits to personally collect taxes from delinquent mill bosses. Those who had been disloyal to their queen during her time of weakness were disappeared down their toilets, or crucified in the streets at night.

I spent my days doing a half ass job for my Uncle, and my evenings rebuilding the power base of a woman who was once my worst enemy on the planet, but had become my sole purpose for remaining upon it. When the moon was at its highest, and the night half way finished, I would steal away to my step-mother's castle, and bed her until just before the sun rose. The only one who was ever aware of our liaisons was Aurial the slave girl, and she was like a piece of furniture. You could always trust a sofa to keep your secrets.

(Except maybe from you, oh god? Can you speak to a sofa? Do they speak a language you can decipher? Do sofas have an awareness? A storage of memories in their cushions that only you can access? Do our walls spy on us while you're away? Do our clothes follow us when we leave the house? Do you parlay with our socks to see where we've been?)

After my visits with Julia, I would return to a rented basement room in town, and sleep for an hour or two before waking and doing it all over again. I was perpetually sleepy, but determined, and god forgive me, deliriously happy.

Looking back on this absurd puppet theater now, oh my Lord, I can see the part I willingly played. I was a marionette to Julia Domna, yes, but it was I who tied the strings to my own wrists and ankles. I think of those nights with her, and for all my passionate blindness, I saw even then, the truth. In fact, she was not a very good actress. I was experienced with women. I knew when I had pleased them and when I hadn't. There was an air that would fill the bed after a woman was satisfied. I never once breathed this air with my step-mother. With her I breathed only cold distances. Her soul, if she had one, was always elsewhere, and her body was hurried to be away from me. When I was with Julia there was a persistent nag in my heart that whined, she is faking this. She despises you more than ever. This is temporary. She will come to her senses and she will ruin you, ruin you, ruin you. Yet, as you know god, there was an equally persistent nagging in another part of me, to suck every bit of nectar I could from a lovely flower that this forsaken winged bug felt blessed just to flutter near.

Despite my quixotic stupor, I never trusted Julia Domna with a full heart. And to my defense, oh Lord, I did take steps to protect myself against her. Without admitting it to myself, I knew that in order for our affair to continue, I needed to be the only access she had to power. I was her man, but as soon as an alternative to me appeared, she'd trade me in without a second thought. To this end, there were two requests that my mistress made of me repeatedly through our time together, that I repeatedly refused. At least until I didn't refuse anymore. That was, I would not allow her to make contact with her husband or sons in Briton, and I would not do any direct harm to my beloved uncle Gaius Fulvius. His assassination was out of the question. That is, until it wasn't anymore.

On the great bulk of our evenings together, the routine was standard. Aurial would greet me at the back service gate, I would be brought to greet my mistress Julia Domna in her bed chamber, where I would make a race of fucking her, finishing in minutes. Then I would brief her on my work yesterday, and on what new political routes would be open to her tomorrow. She would ask a thousand questions, give a thousand orders, and then fuck my brains out till just before morning, when I would be coldly dismissed. That was it. Except for the nights we ate together. There were ten of these nights, oh my Lord, and I counted them as precious jewels. Nights when the sun set unexpectedly early, and the moon was a dim fingernail. I could arrive at the palace earlier than usual, and Aurial would prepare for us a late night snack of raw lamb and olives.

These late night snacks, oh god, these late night snacks with my step-mother. Are they enough for me to forgive this horrible woman all the evils she thrust upon me? No, I think not. But what else could come close to a redemption for that bitch, if not her simple goodness during these late night snacks? She listened to me while we ate. She thought about what I said, she considered me, and she responded. Sure, we spoke of trifling matters. An impressive gladiator we had both seen, a new construction project in town that was a nuisance, the weather, and what it was like yesterday, and what we thought it would be like tomorrow. I made jokes about Gaius's weak bowels, and she would laugh with her mouth full of food, so you just knew it was a genuine laugh. She liked to tell old jokes, from her childhood.

One joke she told that I can't seem to forget, oh god, was about a party crasher. When the host of the party asked the interloper, "Did I say you could come?" He responded, "Did you say I couldn't?" And when the host then yelled, "But you were not invited!" The unwelcome guest replied, "Which was painful enough. But could you imagine the double agony of not being invited and not coming?"

Julia thought this was hilarious. "The idiot!" She cackled, "The unwanted fool!"

XIII.

Gaius Fulvius was increasingly on the toilet. A crew of masons and plumbers spent weeks building him a personal bath house on the grounds of his estate, so he could crap in full comfort at home. At his offices he began taking the bulk of his meetings while sitting on the shitter. Walls that connected his meeting chamber to his privy were knocked down, and a desk was set before the toilet seat. Gaius would cover his lap with a heavy blanket, and scented oils were constantly burned. Most visitors never had a clue that Gaius was moving his bowels in their presence.

I knew better, and on the day he called me before him to scold me about my recent lack of dedication, I could tell he was struggling to relieve himself. Struggling to do what healthy men do daily without thinking much of it. We take our bowels for granted, dear god. When all's well, they're a splinter of our thinking, but when something goes wrong, we've no mind for anything else. It was the distraction of his intestinal sickness, above anything else, that kept my secret plotting with Julia Domna from his gaze. Gaius had it set in his mind that Julia was my most hated enemy, a fact so built into what Gaius thought of me that it would have taken a great leap of mental creativity to picture me as a turncoat for her. And with his mind occupied by his bowels as it was, he simply lacked the imaginative space to see me for the incestuous bastard that I was.

"Where's your head gone, my boy?" Gaius said through gritted teeth. "You were my-" He ceased talking to strain, and adjust his stomach. "You were my best man. The only one whose information I could-" He groaned, and bit down tightly, his jaw quivering as he pushed to no avail. He exhaled with defeat. "And now look at you. False leads, phony snitches, holes in your pockets. What am I to do with you?"

I shrugged. I could care less. Gaius had no more sway over me. He was a disgusting, shitting, old man, and in a few more months, I would be emperor and have his head on a pike. "Sorry." I said cheaply.

Gaius fixed his gaze on me. "What are you up to, my boy? What has changed in you?"

"Nothing." I said.

Keeping his eyes on mine, Gaius began again to groan, and strain, and push, this time with all of his might. Secretaries looked up from their paper work. The praetorians pinched their noses shut. The whole room was watching him there, in his office, at his desk, squeezing out a turd, which from the sounds of it, was as hard as a rock. And the whole time he was heaving and hoeing, and giving that turd his worst, he was staring at me, right in the eye. I didn't look away. I smiled, I didn't know what else to do, so I smiled, oh god. Finally there was a gust of wind from beneath the Consul of the Roman empire, and then a splash from further below him, and then a great sigh of relief from his lips. Relieved themselves, the office bureaucrats and guardsmen went back to their business.

Gaius was out of breath, but he spoke firmly to me. "Rome is mine. There are men out there... there are women out there... who would have Rome for themselves. But we're not going to let them. Are we, my boy?"

"No, sir." I said. "I'm sorry." I said.

"Don't be sorry. Just stop fucking up." Said Gaius, and he waved me away dismissively. I saluted him and turned to leave. As I walked away, he added, "And if that step-mother of yours is trying to contact you, you know that's something you should tell your Uncle Gaius, yes?"

I stopped walking. I turned, and gave Gaius my best what-the-fuck-are-you-talking-about face. "My step-mother? Trying to contact me? About what?"

"To see about you, perhaps. She is your mother, after all. But she's also a dangerous woman. You understand this, yes, my boy?"

Did he know? Oh god, did he know what I had been up to? My heart took off, and I was sure Gaius could see it pounding from across the room. I was worried that he could hear it.

"I understand." I said, too afraid to risk anything more than that.

"Good." Said Gaius, already straining and groaning, and pushing anew.

XIV.

I spent the rest of the day worried about what Gaius knew and didn't know. I hadn't been discreet enough, and if he hadn't sniffed me out, sooner or later one of his smarter agents would, and I'd be dead. Maybe they already had discovered my betrayal, and were waiting for me to step blindly into some set trap. I was full of worry and fear, oh god, but the sun had set, and I was happily changing into my cleanest tunic, getting ready to see Julia. I was looking forward to spending some time with her, hoping she'd relieve me of all my unfounded fears. Instead, Julia Domna arrived unexpectedly at the door of my apartment, and confirmed every last one of them.

She was dressed like a beggar, with rags strewn around her shoulders and over her head, covering her forehead and her mouth, so that only her eyes were visible. I was shocked to see her. "What's happened?" I gasped. She shoved me into the apartment and closed and bolted the door.

"What's happened?" I repeated, like an idiot. Julia threw off her rags, and revealed a torn silk gown, bruised arms and legs, and a face damp with tears.

"Gaius has struck. There was an attack on the palace, the guards were slaughtered." She was in a panic, I put an arm around her and led her to my bed. I sat her down. Her hands were trembling. I sat down next to her and took her hands in mine, and she was immediately stilled. "The guards, the servants, the slaves. He killed every last one of them."

There had been an attack, just like the one I had orchestrated against the windows in the streets, oh god. Only this time the attack had been at the imperial palace. I remember being jealous, oh god, and wondered who had Gaius sent on such a bold mission in my place?

"He killed every last one of them." Julia repeated. "Every last one, except for young Aurial."

I was confused. "Aurial? Why was she spared?"

"They have taken her, don't you see? They have taken the slave girl, Aurial. Gaius Fulvius has taken her." That girlish voice of hers was gone, and would never return, at least never to my ear. Here was a woman. Frantic, but focused. "Do you see what this means?" She said.

I didn't at first. "So?" I said. "She slipped away during the slaughter. What does that mean? She'll turn up, and I'd wager-"

"No." Julia interrupted, and pulled her steady hands out of mine. "No, you damned idiot, don't you see? Everyone was killed but Aurial. She was targeted by the assassins during the killing, and she was specifically taken."

"It doesn't make sense. What does Gaius want with some slave girl?" I was slow to connect the pieces, oh god, as I always am when speedy deduction matters most. Julia's briskness had stunted me in a way. I couldn't think of anything more than to ask myself, why was she being so mean to me, when I was so happy to see her?

"The only thing stopping Gaius from murdering me is my husband." Julia explained. "If Gaius can disgrace me in Septimius's eyes, he thinks that protection will be gone, and he can finally eliminate me. That slave girl, poor loyal Aurial, is in some military jail right now, being tortured so she'll give a full confession of what I've been up to. And what I've been up to with my step-son. And she's in a unique position to tell Gaius, and to tell Gaius details. By morning, he'll have the information he needs to finish me off, once and for all. He'll parade her around the city, telling her story of my adultery in a lecture series. My husband may allow me to choose a relatively painless suicide as my exit, there's a chance of that. I couldn't say as much for you, my little bastard." Julia stood. "There's no other way. You've simply run out of options. Kill Gaius Fulvius tonight, and be done with it."

Julia collected her rags from the floor, and began to wrap herself up again. I stayed sitting on the edge of my bed. Not thinking. Not planning, or scheming, or plotting, oh god, just sitting. I took a deep breath, closed my eyes for a second, and when I opened them, my brain had reset itself, and fresh ideas came in. "It's just the word of a slave. A tortured slave, at that. Her confession won't be worth shit. It'll be our word against hers."

"We'll cry slander, yes." Said Julia. "And maybe that will be enough to spare my life. But will it be enough to spare yours? And tell me, what will become of our reputations? What will your brother Lucius think of this filthy rumor?"

"How did Gaius know to take Aurial? How could he know what she knows?" I asked, skeptically.

"However he knows, he knows." Julia wrapped the last of her rags around her mouth, and opened the door.

I stood up. "Where will you go tonight?" I asked.

"To Senator Sullius. He can help me to locate where they've hidden away poor Aurial. We'll set our agents about quieting her. But you're the only assassin in Rome with skill enough to silence Gaius Fulvius."

"Julia, please. I can't." I began to cry. I'm ashamed of my tears now, oh Lord, but at the time I didn't wipe them away. I wanted her to see.

"Do as you will." Said Julia, from under her hood of rags. "But know that if you don't act, your father will receive word within the fortnight that you've been fucking his wife." And then she was gone.

Almost immediately after the door closed behind her, I went to my belt to get my sword.

XV.

I went directly to the doma of Gaius Fulvius, on the Palatine hill, just north of the temple to Apollo. My plan was to find the closest entrance to the sewer, crawl through the muck of the tunnels until I found the one that lead to Gaius's ass, yank him down his toilet, cut off his head, cut his corpse into pieces, and make him disappear for ever and ever. Yeah, that would do the trick.

Though he held all the power in Rome, Gaius had maintained residence in a rather modest, two level mansion, built using only local stone. No marble. It was done this way so he would appear to be a man of the people, oh god, but you know the truth. Along with the deceptively simple looking doma, Gaius was also the owner of the massive rear gardens, and both insula across the way, which he used to house his elite guard. I kept a long, shadowy distance from the house and its conglomeration of praetorians, looking for a hole, and my way in. I had to walk for at least a mile past the gardens until I got nearer to the banks of the river, and found the closest entrance to the cloaca.

I kept to the wooded hills, and off the road, and was well hidden when I first saw the opening to the sewer. It was a large, welcoming, arch of limestone, but was blocked by a shiny metal gate, and a brand new lock. And in front of this gate, causing my heart to drop into my boot, were four legionnaires, with their spears and swords, sitting in the dirt around a small fire they had made. They had obviously been stationed there. They were guarding the sewers. And that meant only one thing, dear god. They were waiting for me. There are few sensations more terrifying than discovering your enemy is a step ahead of you.

I couldn't kill four legionaries by myself. And I couldn't hire someone to do it alongside me. Tell them the purpose of the killings? Tell them why I wanted into the sewers so badly? Not a chance. I considered walking another mile or so up the river, and looking for another way in, but thought again. At the distance I was already at, and with it being the pitch black middle of the night, it was going to be hard enough for me to find my way around down there. Adding another mile made the task nearly impossible. And there may have been guards at the next tunnel as well, and the next after that.

What was I to do, oh god? I couldn't give up. I couldn't very well have given up, could I have? Yes, I see now that I very well should have. I should have gone back to my lowly basement apartment, put my sword under my bed, and gone to sleep. I did no such thing, oh god. I pressed on.

With all of my faults, I guess I'm just that type of a man, oh delicate creator. I'm a scrounger, a survivor. A man who looks at an impossible situation, and from the thin air of his thinking pulls a solution. Sure, sometimes I go a little overboard, and people get hurt. I don't always come up with the most subtle of solutions. But you got to admit, Lord, you couldn't call them anything but that. Solutions.

So, this impossible situation presented itself, and I invented a solution. It may have cost big dumb Felix his life, but since his brother died, he was looking to spend it anyway. And, a solution is a solution, right god?

106

I felt I was short on time, and so was terribly out of breath from running when I arrived at Felix's apartment in town. My winded appearance no doubt helped my performance, not that Felix was ever a critical audience. When I found him that night he was still awake and still drunk from the evening before. His apartment was decorated with sleepy whores, spilled wine, and the smell of sweat. At first I thought he would be too dazed to be of any help to me, but as soon as I mentioned the name of his brother, Faustus, his eyes turned alert and ready. Or as alert and ready as the eyes of stupid Felix ever could turn, oh god. I told him that I had finally discovered his brother's murderers. They were legionnaires in the command of Gaius Fulvius, this is why their aim was noble enough to strike down the great Faustus. They had been trained to be the best, and to prove their stature they had killed the supreme Faustus, whom everyone knew was as powerful as Hercules.

Felix dressed, grabbed his heaviest hardwood cudgel, and I led him to the Palatine hill. We past the temple of Apollo, the mansion of Gaius Fulvius, and his gardens, to the limestone archway that led to the sewers below. We hid in the trees, and I pointed out the circle of legionnaires sitting around the fire. I invented names for each of them, and told him what part they had played in the conspiracy to murder his twin brother, Faustus. This one was named Virgil, and had kicked sand in Faustus's eyes. That one was named Virgilio, and had fired the arrow. The other two were Virgilium and Virgilius, who had laughed and pissed on Faustus until he was dead.

"These four there? They did that to my brother?" Asked Felix with a growing rage, and a tightening grip on his hardwood cudgel. "They pissed on him? These four there? They killed my brother, and pissed on him?" Between words he was crying, and biting his bottom lip so hard he was drawing blood.

"Yes." I whispered. "Those are the four who killed your Faustus."

Felix left my side like a gust of wind, and marched to the small encampment of legionnaires, his cudgel held with both hands, and raised high. I drew my sword and approached a short distance behind.

They didn't know what hit them, oh god. They were laughing and chatting and passing around the wine flask, and out of the darkness comes this bear of a retard, carrying a tree trunk of a club over his head.

Virgil wasn't wearing his helmet, and he took the first crack of the cudgel, and lost the top of his head and his life to the night air. Next, Felix kicked the small campfire, launching flaming embers into the face of Virgilio, who rolled over backwards, screaming in shock, and then in burning pain. Felix swung his cudgel again, and this time whacked Virgilium, who was wearing his helmet, and so survived. I stepped up to change that, and stuck my sword deep between his shoulder blades before he could stand up.

Felix loomed over the crying Virgilio, who was clutching his badly burned face. Felix kicked him with merciless strength in his dick. Vrigilio screamed out, and moved his hands to his crotch, stretching a streamer of melted flesh off his face with them.

"That the same dick you used to piss on my brother?" Asked Felix. Virgilio did not answer, and so Felix raised his cudgel, and brought it slamming down, breaking Virgilio's hands, and then his pelvis, and then his skull.

We had missed all but the fourth, oh god. We had forgotten to kill Virgilius, or rather, we didn't remember to do so until it was too late. I don't think he was the smartest of the group, necessarily, though he may have been. He was simply sitting furthest away, and so was the last to be attacked, and so had the most time to get a grip on the situation, to do anything about it. And he did. He picked up his spear, and he stuck it through the bear's heart. I don't blame him for doing it from behind the poor animal, oh Lord, though it is a coward who stabs his enemy in the back. I don't think anyone could blame him for it, though. It may have been four against two, but we did have the element of surprise, and with Felix, the element of insanity. You can't blame a man for stabbing a bear in the back while that bear is killing his friends. At the time however, oh Lord, I was a less understanding person, and when Virgilius killed Felix, I killed him in turn.

Felix looked at the steal tip of the spear sticking out of his chest, and then over his shoulder at the long handle coming out of his back. He reached for the handle, and finding it just too far, he began turning in circles trying to grab for it, like a dog chasing its tail. He eventually got dizzy, stopped spinning, and collapsed. I kneeled by his side.

"Did I kill them all?" Asked Felix.

"Well, I killed a couple, but not without your help." I said.

"But they're all dead? The ones that killed Faustus? And pissed on him after?"

I looked around at the miniature killing field we had made there by the entrance to the sewer. Not a bad bit of work for two men in what felt like less than ten seconds, oh god. "All dead, Felix. You did quite a job."

"I'd like to finish the job, but I can't seem to get on my feet." Said Felix. He was muttering. He was dying. "Yes, something's most definitely gone wrong with my chest, and it's taken all of the pep out of me." He coughed up some blood. "No, I don't feel very well at all. Will you do me a favor? Will you piss on these dead fellows for me?"

"Yes. Yes, of course, I will."

"Good." Said Felix, and then died, smiling with his eyes open.

I didn't piss on them, oh god. I didn't have time, and I didn't have to go. Should I have pissed on them? It was my dying friend's last wish. No, I think I did the right thing by not pissing on anybody.

I searched the slain legionnaires, and on Virgil found a key that opened the lock on the gate. There was a long, narrow, and extremely steep staircase that led down to the totally dark main tunnel of the sewer proper. I was blind. I knew generally where the doma was, so I laid my hands on the wall, and started to walk along it, moving in that direction. When I would come upon a tunnel that moved me closer to where I thought I wanted to be, I took it. As I moved from tunnel to tunnel, things got more wet, and more smelly and more cramped, until I was eventually on my hands and knees, crawling through shitty water up to my chin. I choked, and coughed, and I puked. I puked a few times. It was awful, and I was nervous that I'd get lost and die down there, but when I touched the first slab of what I could tell was brand new limestone, I knew I was close. Gaius had work done on the sewers when he had his new bathhouse installed, and I had found where it started.

Moving forward, into a wider tunnel, I saw light again. It was coming from above. Two full circles of orange torch light, and one crescent. It was three toilet holes, two were vacant, and one was occupied. I delighted at the discovery, oh god. I was so relieved I almost laughed, but lost the sensation quickly when I noticed those steel metal bars. There were three of them, they were driven right into the limestone, and ran along the underside of all three toilet holes. They allowed small shits to pass down from above, but stopped any larger creatures that may have wanted to crawl up from below.

I was hurt to see those bars, dear god. Not because they had thwarted me, but because they meant Gaius had never really trusted me. He had so distrusted me, in fact, that he took special measures to protect himself from me. When he had this new bath built, he must have given specific instructions to install the bars. The masons must have thought he was mad, and paranoid by power. But Gaius knew the nature of that rat bastard he had working for him, and damn it all if he was gonna be dragged down his toilet one night. Though Gaius may have been proven correct about me, it doesn't sting my feelings any less. Worst of all, oh god, is that he thought enough of my faults to know I would betray him, but didn't think enough of my strengths to know that it would take a hell of a lot more than four legionnaires and three metal bars to stop me.

I wasn't going to be able to climb up and ambush Gaius. I wasn't going to be able to haul his corpse down the toilet to disappear it. But I was going to kill him. That was for sure. I was more sure of that than ever now.

I moved beneath the occupied toilet hole, and turned an ear up to it. Groaning, moaning, pushing, and straining. It was most definitely Gaius Fulvius. Nothing was coming out of the bottom of him, solid or gas, and so I knew I had time. Knowing Gaius, he'd be sitting there till the sun came up.

I considered my sword, but it was far too short to reach him. I considered and quickly rejected the fantastic idea of unleashing a venomous snake, or a scorpion, or a horde of spiders. I thought about a poisonous dart, and a blow gun, but if I missed, or he didn't die quickly enough, I would be discovered and killed. Same problem with a bow and arrow. In the end I settled on the simple, but effective, idea of a legionnaires spear up his consul ass.

On my return trip to dead Felix and the Virgils, to retrieve the spear, I took my time and made sure I didn't get lost. I also made a map in my mind of what the area felt like, so I would be able to return to Gaius's toilet in half the time. When I got back, Gaius was still up there, still pushing, still moaning. I slipped the spear between the bars without a sound, and slid it all the way up the center of the toilet hole, until it was just inches below Gaius's asshole, which was open and in full bloom. I held my aim with one hand, and I put a sturdy palm under the end of the spear. I closed my eyes, I smiled, and I pushed.

(God. Oh, god. Please forgive me. What did I do? What did I do to that poor man? I stuck a spear up his ass? Did I really do that? God, forgive me, forgive me, forgive me. His cries, I will never forget his cries of supplice. His yelp, dear god, his yelp. That odious yelp he unleashed when I first entered him. God, take that yelp from my memory. Poor Uncle Gaius. Poor, poor Uncle Gaius. When I die, will I forget the sounds he made as I killed him? If you do forgive me, oh merciful father, will you take that accursed yelp from my memory?)

I thrust the spear as far up into him as I could. I think if I had been a little bit taller I could have gotten the spike to pop out the top of his head. Once he was skewered, I wiggled the spear violently to and fro, and then pulled it down and out with a spin like a corkscrew. This was followed by a whooshing waterfall of blood and shit, that I only narrowly dodged.

At last, Gaius Fulvius was able to fully release his bowels.

Sorry, god.

XVI.

After washing in the river, I returned briefly to my basement apartment, to dress in clean clothes and ready for my visit with Julia Domna. The sun was almost up, and I was practically mad with hope for the future. Was this it? Were my years of powerlessness over? Was I the next emperor of Rome?

No. Obviously, not.

Julia never revealed her deception to me directly, oh god. In fact, I never really spoke to her again after that night she came to me in beggars rags, and said she was going to kill the slave girl Aurial, and that I should kill my uncle Gaius. There was no dramatic final scene between us lovers, oh god. No revelatory argument, where we screamed, and tore at each other's clothes, and made passionate love one last time before saying goodbye forever.

When I arrived at the usual entrance, at the rear of the palace, at the usual time, the gate was latched and locked. I pounded, and pounded. No one came to let me in. I thought that perhaps since Aurial was dead, Julia had forgotten to unlock it for me, and was now fast asleep. I considered going back to town, getting a ladder, and climbing the wall. I should have. I fucking should have, oh god.

Forgive me my evil thought, oh Lord. I know I claimed to be rid of them, but this one is too delicious to not chew over, for just a moment. That night, oh god, when all that stood between me and the queen was a climbable wall, I should have rid the earth of her. There were no guards in there with her. There were no servants, no slaves, nobody. Julia Domna was one little lady, alone in one big castle, and I was an expert at getting into places I was locked out of. I should have gone in there, dragged that bitch out of bed, hauled her to the forum, and at sunrise, cut her head off for all of Rome to witness. I could have announced to the crowds that the night before, I had disemboweled the fascist, Gaius Fulvius. I could have made a case for myself as a hero of the republic, and give myself over to the will of the people. If they wanted to hang me? So be it. If they wanted to elect me their king, recruit me an army, and have me march against my own father and brothers in the west? Well, that would be just fine, too. Either way, I would have been a legend, and I would have been remembered.

Instead, I decided I should be patient, and a gentleman, and return to Julia Domna, and my reward, the following night.

I went back into town. My basement apartment was cold, and dark. I couldn't stop thinking about Gaius, and that yelp of his. I felt uncomfortable, alone with my own thoughts, oh god. The sun was coming up, I was sleepless, and terribly lonely. So, I paid a whore to stay with me, get drunk all morning, and sleep through the day. I woke up just before sundown, fucked the whore with my step-mother on my mind, and sent her on her way with a generous tip.

I dressed to make my visit to Julia Domna. On my way to the palace I stopped off at my old building, and had a word with my old lena. She was still soft on me, even though she had a new employer now, who treated her like crap. She let me in on what the city knew of my actions the previous night. As for Gaius, word had gotten out that he was dead, first from house slaves, then servants, and finally confidants of the family. Now, either the Fulvius family was confounded by the cause of its patriarch's death, or they were afraid of what might happen to them, or they were just plain old embarrassed, but for whatever reason, they were claiming that Gaius had died peacefully in his sleep. There was no mention of the toilet, or the spear.

As for Felix, and the dead legionnaires, it had hardly been mentioned in the day's gossiping. It was taken as another one of Felix's insane outbursts. "Such a shame, such a shame," people said, but that was the end of it.

As for Julia Domna, the people were convinced that whether natural or contrived, she was somehow responsible for the death of Gaius. They had taken her reclaimed power as proof of this. Indeed, Julia had wasted no time. In the morning she had gone to the quaestor, and demanded her accounts be unfrozen. In the afternoon she wrote large bills of honorary payment to the best praetorian guards in the city. Gaius was dead, and these men knew that the power vacuum would have to be filled by someone, and this bitch was paying the most. In the evening she marched her new elite guard on the Senate, and read a letter from her husband, giving her new special powers of authority, so that she may clean up the mess left behind by the two faced Gaius. The letter was most definitely written by Julia herself, and my father's signature forged, but no one dared to doubt that when Julia Domna spoke, she now spoke unequivocally for her husband. Now that Gaius was dead, this was as certain as nightfall, oh my Lord.

My old lena was happy for me. "You'll be a big man now, won't you? I know you sneak off to that palace every night. You and the queen cooked this up together, didn't ya?"

Grinning, I winked at her, and left for the palace.

When I got there, the rear gate was wide open, but four praetorians stood guard in front of it, and another six were nearby, patrolling the wall with torches. I wasn't surprised by them, but still, the sight unnerved me. I filled my chest, straightened my back, and with a confident strut, I walked right up to entrance, acting like I owned the place.

The guards recognized me almost immediately, and held their hands up while I was still some twenty feet away. "Hold your ass right there!"

I stopped walking, and my false good posture faded at the soldier's powerful voice. I cleared my throat and called out to the guards. I yelled, "It is I,-"

"We know who you are, you damn bastard!" Interrupted one of them. "Been expecting your bastard ass!" Said another.

Two of the patrolling guards were suddenly behind me with their torches. I hadn't even sensed them approaching. They had their swords drawn. "Toss the dagger." One of them snarled at me. I pulled the dagger out of my belt and threw it in the dirt. Another guard came over with his torch, suffocated the flame, and put it down. He took a length of rope from his tunic. "Give me your hands."

"You don't understand." I pleaded. "I'm expected. The queen-"

"No, you don't understand. If you don't give me your hands, these men are gonna put their swords through your heart, and kill you. The queen's given us special orders to do you in if you so much as disobey us once. So, give me your hands."

I refused. I wouldn't do it. I'm not a total idiot, oh god. The way they were talking, the way they were threatening, you'd really have to be a total fucking idiot to let them tie you up. I don't care what they say they're going to do to you if you put up a fight, they'll do it to you anyway if you give up, and at least with a fight, you've got a chance.

I told them to just go ahead and kill me if that's what they wanted to do, but there was no way I was volunteering to be tied up. Annoyed with me, but apparently less free to murder me than they let on, two more guards came over, broke my nose, and right cheek, with a few punches, wrestled me to the ground, tied me up like a hog, gagged me with my own tunic, and dragged me through the back gate of the palace.

Once inside the walls, I was plopped down in the dirt. Some of the guards went back to patrolling, some kept a lazy watch on me, sitting on big barrels of newly delivered wines. Gifts from Senators making amends with their renewed mistress.

The apparent leader of the outfit walked across the courtyard to the royal suites. After ten minutes or so, he emerged again. At his side was a woman in a black gown, her face was covered by a black veil. I knew it was Julia. I could tell by the curves of her body. Emerging from behind Julia, holding the train of her dress, was Aurial, the slave girl. And she was very much not dead, oh god.

As we both know by now, oh maker of me, I am slow on the uptake. I'm a fucking tortoise when it comes to any sort of up taking. So, when I saw Aurial, my first thought wasn't that it was all a rouse. I didn't see her and immediately know that my step-mother had seduced me, used me, and then pretended Aurial had been kidnapped in order to drive me to murder my beloved Uncle. This did not rush to my mind when I saw Aurial. Being the slow thinking fool that I so unrelentingly am, my first thought upon seeing Aurial was something like, "that's very nice of Julia, to give Aurial her position back after squealing to Gaius about us. I guess she decided not to kill her after all."

But, of course, oh god, Aurial's life was never in danger. Not from Julia Domna, not from Gaius Fulvius. She never squealed, and she never would have. She was never even interrogated, because no one ever knew that she knew anything of value. Gaius died concerned with his next shit, not with my affair with Julia Domna, of which I'm now certain he never even had an inkling of.

The guards stood up from the barrels and at attention as Julia and Aurial approached me.

Julia stood right above me, and lifted her veil. She was smiling. Her feet were right in front of my face, and under her gown I could see that she was wearing black caligae. Why was she wearing men's military boots? I wondered.

No one was saying anything. She was just standing over me, smiling. I tried to mumble something to her, but I couldn't speak because of the gag. I mumbled that she should let me go, that I loved her, that if we could just talk it over, she would see my point of view. But not a word of it came out as anything but incoherent mumbling.

Julia started to laugh at my attempts to talk, and then Aurial started to laugh along with her, and then the guards were laughing. What the fuck were they laughing at, oh god? Is it funny to see a man tied, and gagged, and worried for his life? All the times I put men in that position, I never once laughed at them. Oh, well, there was the badly crucified rabbi, but he laughed too, so it wasn't really laughing at him, so much as it was laughing with him, which makes it okay. Right, god?

Anyway, they were laughing at me, and then out of nowhere Julia rears back her right leg, and kicks me in the stomach. I no longer wondered why she was wearing boots. She reared back again, and kicked me in the chest. I heard the rib crack, and I lost my breath so grievously that it was like I had never had any to begin with. I gasped, and sucked for air, and got none. She kicked me in the stomach again, but I didn't feel that one as much. I was starting to pass out, and everything felt like pins and needles. She kicked me again, this time in my crotch, and that one I felt. My balls turned into gigantic ringing bells of agony. I felt the pain in my feet, I felt it in my teeth, I felt it in my eyelids, and in my fingernails. My hair hurt for my poor kicked balls.

I looked up at Julia with all the affection I could muster through the pain. With my eyes, I asked her, "why are you doing this to me?" And with her boots, she answered, "Because I hate you. I have hated you since the day you were born. I hated you when you were a boy. I hate you as a man. When you speak, my hate doubles. When you make love to me, my hate triples. I have hated you forever, and I will hate you forever more."

Julia kicked, and kicked, and kicked, and eventually a black cloud formed over my vision, and I passed out.

XVII.

I awoke in bed, and in the care of my sweet old lena. I had been dumped in the streets, and some beggars had dragged me to her for a reward, which my lena had given. She wrapped my chest, and bandaged my nose, and brought ice from the tabarnae for my balls. I was completely swollen with throbbing pain, and had there existed a lever to end my life, I'd have pulled it then, oh merciful god, and been glad to. There being no such lever, I just lay there, and allowed my lena to nurse me.

It took me several weeks before I was feeling healthy and myself again. And months more before I was able to walk and breath without suffering. During my convalescence I thought over the beating Julia had given me, with her loyal conspirator, Aurial, standing by her side and laughing. The whole scheme became obvious, and I was depressed by the revelation of my great stupidity.

I thought that I had been penetrating Julia Domna, that I had broken inside, that I had finally gained entrance. I was more wrong than wrong. No one penetrates Julia Domna. One is enveloped by her. One is surrounded by her. One is strangled by her. But one is never inside her. Like the snake, the only way in for the mouse, is to be eaten. When you made Julia Domna, oh creator of even the worst of us, you used hot metal. One thinks they've so easily glided into and through it, until it cools and hardens itself, ensnaring, and crushing.

But, Julia had let me live. Why? It made no sense, but now, oh god, knowing more than I did then, I know exactly why she was reluctant to kill me. She was afraid of the emperor. Not my father, him she could deal with. She was afraid of the next emperor. She was afraid of her son, Lucius. Julia envisioned a grand role for herself in her son's future administration, and that role relied on remaining in his good graces. If Lucius were to find me dead, and his mother rumored as the killer, it would not go unpunished. He would not let my death pass without consequence, even if it meant reaping vengeance on his own mother. I was unaware of this strength I had, because at the time I was unaware of something Julia, who knew her son better than anyone, was well aware of. That I was the only person Lucius truly cared for, and to hurt me would be to hurt him.

Also, as you well knew, oh keeper of our juiciest secrets, there was one other piece of information that Julia Domna was privileged to, that I wasn't. A piece of information that no one in Rome was privileged to, and its timing is likely what saved my life. In Briton, Septimius Severus was on his deathbed, and Lucius would be returning to Rome as the new emperor within the month.

CHAPTER SIX

I.

You know, so called god, so called Lord, so called father of us all, the more I talk to you, the less I believe you exist. Or, maybe you existed at one point, but now you're either dead or gone deaf. Do you really have nothing to say to me? This being my first prayer, I'm not exactly sure of how it works, but shouldn't you have responded in some way, by now?

I've told you of killing after vicious killing. I've told you how I enabled others to kill, and let my friends be killed when it suited my purposes. I've told you of my affair with my own step-mother. I've told you how I brutally murdered my beloved uncle. Still, you say nothing? Not a voice in my head to comfort or chastise me? Not a thunderclap to terrify me at your impending judgment? Not a sparrow in my window with a message of forgiveness in its song? Not even an untrustworthy vision? Not even a hallucination in my mind's eye, of your angels and their trumpets, aloft in their clouds? Not even that? You've got nothing for me?

Maybe you aren't listening. Maybe I've lost your attention, and you couldn't care less what I have to say. I don't blame you.

Or, maybe you're as patient as Brother Wojslaw and Sister Lousada would have me believe, and you're politely waiting for me to finish my story before you respond in kind. Very well. I shall continue with my prayer, willfully risking that I am going unheard by anyone but myself.

I am again exhausted and sickly with all this lonely talk of my own badness. It causes me tense frustration to recall the sins of my life with the mixture of sweet wistfulness and bitter regret, that I do. I know he was up to terrible wrong doing, oh god, but I can't help but feel warmth for the me of my past. He seems a frightened, wild animal. He seems a mess of reactions, a tangle of nerves, an exposed wound. I am, for now at least, weary of thinking on this stranger of a beast.

Fortunately, oh my Lord, I can now have a brief rest from self analysis, as the next portion of my confession deals mainly with the sins of another. Those of my brother, Lucius.

Give me a moment, Lord, while I go through some of my old things. Ah, yes, here they are beneath these winter robes, in the neat pile I left them in. Every letter Lucius ever wrote to me. Every word he ever put on paper for me to read. They are few, and they are precious to me.

I wrote Lucius dozens of letters while he was away with Geta and our father, killing Caldeonians in northern Briton. In the entire year that he was gone, he only wrote back once. It was a month before our father succumbed to gout, and died, and the whole mission was called off. I hold the letter before me now.

Shall I read it to you, oh Lord?

"To my dearest brother, Emperor of the toilets.

Apologies at my late reply.   Fucking wild Caledonian women into the ground can occupy a good portion of a young man's time. With such fun so readily available to me, my correspondences have been, needless to say, neglected. So much pillaging to do, so few hours in the day, you understand.

Before leaving the continent proper I had only ever killed three or maybe four children. I am now responsible for killing well over five thousand. So, you can imagine how busy I've been.

So plentiful are these woods with gangly limbed gingers, it has become a mundane routine to slaughter them. They are like communities of insects beneath my heavy boots. Only this morning I sacked four villages before breakfast. The men are killed, whether they fight or surrender. The huts are burned. The farms are destroyed. The women and children who run are captured, raped, and killed. The ones who do not run are captured, raped, and killed. And so on, and so on.

While I have been on expedition, engaging the civilian population with great ease, our foul little brother, Geta, has been leading his own contingent against the army of this backwards country, with far more difficulty. At first I thought this division of authority by our father to be an insult, and it's true, Geta has won every full scale battle against the enemies military, and much glory back home in Rome as result, I'm sure.   But, I promise you, he has suffered twenty terrible defeats for every one victory, and has become weak with hourly burden and anxiety. His battalions are under constant terrorist assault from the Caldeonians. They attack at night, while he sleeps. They attack in the morning, while he eats cold polenta. They ambush his supply lines, and burn ration deliveries. They send renegades on suicidal raids of his outposts, drunk to insanity off some local mushroom brew.

(Dear brother, I myself sampled this fungi brew, and found it to rival even the mead of our own hometown witchery. Under its sway I sat on a rocky shore and watched the ocean for an entire evening, until the waves seemed to freeze and then roar anew, all at my minds command.   As if I were master of time itself. Maddeningly fun stuff, oh my brother. I have enclosed with this letter enough dried mushroom powder for you to see for yourself. Just add wine.)

The Caledonians use any and every filthy barbarian trick, but refuse to engage Geta's armies in open battle. His legions have become tense, and wracked by a nervous spirit. The lush brown curls of our once lovely little brother, have turned thin and gray at the temples.

I'm sure you've heard rumors of our father's illness, and I can tell you, they are true and likely worse than told.   He's going to die soon, I would bet on weeks, not months. He's currently hold up at our fort at Eborocum, with military doctors tending to him at all hours.

Shortly after arriving in Briton, the emperor was complaining of joint stiffness. One evening a discomfort in his big toe spread into an excruciating throbbing of his legs, and eventually a total loss of movement. I saw him the morning after this first episode. He looked as fat as a fed tick, and red as a strawberry.

In the summer Father got a little better, and then this fall he got a lot worse. Now he has these grotesque lumps growing around his joints, and they've begun to spill white chalky material. He is struck with unbearable pain when he is covered with even the lightest of linens. You should see the awful fun I've been having with him. "You look chilly, dear father." I say, and cover him with my heavy fur coat, and he yelps like a small puppy whose tail I've trampled. On rainy or snowy days, when the illness has him in its tightest grip, he is sent into agony by the slightest vibrations of someone walking across the room. It causes me such tickled delight, oh brother, while sitting by our dying father, to gently rap my boot against the leg of his bed, and send him off into a fit of despair. I have laughed myself to sleep many nights this year, thinking of how pathetic he has become. After all his big talk, of being the big man on the battlefield, to be carried around by tiny nurses, helping him to piss and shit? It's hilarious.

With our father's decrepit sickness, and Geta's loathsome attrition, it turns out that I'm the true warrior in this family. I always knew I was Geta's superior, and I always knew that I would eventually surpass my father's greatness, but I must humbly admit, it is shocking to be so undeniably more glorious then them, at such a young age. My mother knew. She has always sensed my supreme glory. I must credit her with that. And every day, with every murder, my glory grows.

The great philosopher, Erasumus Grigio, has written that a murdered soul must serve his murderer for all of eternity, into the afterlife. This has given me the seeds of a cunning plan to hold power indefinitely. One day soon I will be the king of Rome, and so king of earth. With this power I will make myself the most terrible murderer this earth has ever seen. More terrible than the Athenians when they took Melos. More terrible than Hanibal Mago when he took Sicily. I'll kill more Jews on day one of my administration than the great Titus did in an entire career.

In the name of my own glory, I will organize the slaughtering of every frivolous and barbaric race on earth. In this way I will collect for myself, millions and millions of souls. Every soul will be a recruit in my army of the after life. When I die, surely hundreds of years from now, I will have a force large enough to march on the gods themselves, and then too shall I be the king of the heavens. As is my destiny. Just sort of a gut feeling I've always had. My mom too. She says so.

Stick with me, brother, you shall go far by my side. You shall see wonderful heights.

Before I end this letter, I must tell you, that despite my lack of correspondence, I have missed you. I have missed you terribly, in fact. I have made friends of my lieutenants, and of the more intelligent enlisted men, but none compare to your comradery. They are blind to my deepest truths. No one knows me as you do. I am a Caesar, and so above base emotions of love and devotion, but I can recognize them in others, oh dearest brother. I have sensed them in your unique way of gazing upon me when we are together. Away from you this year, I have felt, in an odd way, unseen.

Hope to have you see me again soon, oh my brother.

Emperor Caesar Bassianus Severus Marcus Antoninus Augustus,

Or,

Yours,

Lucius."

III.

Because of the rush to deify Septimius Severus, I did not get an opportunity to greet my brothers home personally, and the first I saw of them in Rome was at the very public funeral for our father. I watched from a nearby crowd of Senators and other high born citizens.

The state spared no expense, and the lavish ceremony to turn the emperor's corpse into ash, rivaled his glorious departure to war. A four story tower was constructed outside the city, in the wide open field of Mars. It was decorated with gold and ivory, and filled with perfumes, and incense, and an entire harvest of fruits and vegetables. What a damned waste, oh god. The emperor's body was placed within the tower, and then his two legitimate sons and heirs, holding together a single torch, set the beginnings of a blaze that would burn the whole thing to the ground.

I remember thinking how strange it looked, Lucius and Geta holding that one single torch. I even noticed that both brothers adjusted their hand placements on the torch, again and again, so to be holding the higher spot. By the time they reached the base of the tower, they were near holding the torch by its flame. It was meant to be a symbol of their unity, but only revealed their rivalry.

Rumors had proceeded the brothers into the city. Talk that each had already hatched failed plots to kill the other, but that Lucius had been the first to act in ill faith. On the very night our father died, Lucius ordered the murders of a number of top ministers to the emperor, the ones he knew had a preference for Geta. There were a lot of them. Good men, powerful men, who had been around for decades and were beloved and well respected in Rome. It was a great shock to the upper classes that such a turn of fate could have befallen these men so quickly, and they became fearful of their own positions. The poorer in the city heard the news with great relish, and there was an air of excitement at what other changes these new emperor brothers could bring about.

Being unsure of how much influence Julia Domna was going to have over her son, I stayed away from the palace until I was summoned by Lucius via messenger. I saved the brief note, and hold it here, oh god, with the other letters.

"Brother. I have returned, and long to be reunited. Why do you stay away? Answer immediately and in person at the palace."

Like all true friends, despite long distances, despite long times apart and away from one another's daily routines, our bond was rekindled at first sight. Lucius and I were reunited in early evening, and we did not stop talking until the following afternoon, when we were both exhausted from chatter, and passed out on the couches of his bedchamber. I told him about all that had happened in Rome, leaving out the part where I fucked his mother. He told me all about Briton, and had me try on some gaelic cloaks that he had brought back with him, which he hoped to make fashionable. He would try, oh god, and he would fail, accomplishing nothing more than garnering the detestable agnomen that would follow him to the grave, caracalla.

Lucius had dreams for his empire, and hearing of how useful I had been to Gaius Fulvius before his mysterious death, he knew that I would be a crucial tool in their realization. He gave me a cohort of elite praetorians to command, and set us to the tasks of his glorious visions. Needless to say, oh most delicate of directors, Lucius's plans never amounted to more than killing everyone who disagreed with him, and then having a party to celebrate the slaughter. So, it wasn't very hard to be useful to him, I just had to be willing to use my sword, and use it often. I was good at that, and well practiced too, god forgive me.

Working for Lucius was even easier than working for Gaius. The more powerful the target was, the more adamant Lucius was that he be killed out in the open, in front of as many plebeians as possible. I no longer used the sewers. I no longer covered my crimes at all. Lucius was proud of what he termed an "imperial use of shock-horror", and wanted everyone to know the depths of violence he was capable of. One of his first acts was ordering the strangulation of his cuckolding wife, Gaius Fulvius's daughter, Plautilla. Then he ordered her brother and mother killed. To round out the story, Lucius also began taking credit for ordering Gaius Fulvius killed, having been aware all the time of his treacherous ambition.

Lucius was bent on creating for himself a reputation as a historic blood letter, and an unapologetic decimator. He liked to know at the end of the day exactly how many had been cleared away by political action, and he was never satisfied with the number. His lists, dear god, his endless lists. Names he handed down to us to see to. Names he half remembered from his past; a market clerk who had looked at him funny when he was a boy, the entire family of a cook who served him tough oysters once, gamblers who won money betting against his favored charioteers, and naturally, anyone who he thought liked Geta more than him.

From Senators to slaves, if Lucius had a whiff of your preference for his brother, you were as good as dead. Not that Geta wasn't doing the same. He killed his share of politicians and military men that were in Lucius's pocket. Though, I must say, dear god, that Geta kept his assassinations targeted on those directly involved in the game of power. He never ordered, as Lucius continually did, the killings of artisans who sculpted his brother, or sold him a robe, or performed for him in a play, or cut his hair.

Of course, both brothers kept at trying to kill the other, but neither with any success. Both had become extremely guarded and paranoid. For the sake of appearances, they shared the palace, but a militarized border was set up right down the middle. Blockades were raised in the royal halls, and praetorian was pit against praetorian as loyalties divided. At first, Geta was at an advantage in regards to recruitment, him being so popular with the soldiers, but Julia Domna had the most gold, and she was for Lucius, and so what he lacked in leadership ability, she made up for with competitive salaries.

Why was Julia for her son Lucius, and not her son Geta? I never will know for certain, oh god, and you haven't answered me on major points, so I doubt you'll speak up on this more minor one. It couldn't have simply been about age. Lucius was older, and so was more entitled to sole rule. No, I don't think that was it. I think, like everything with Julia, it was about control. With his ego, his predictable selfishness, and his boredom for governance, Lucius was the easier boy to control. Geta had been his father's favorite, and so hadn't been coddled by his mother. In this way Geta had become an independent, self sufficient man, who looked upon the scenario of his little old mother whispering political advice in his ear as comedy. If Geta had been the victor, Julia Domna would have lost her empire, and been relegated to the role of the matriarchal figurehead. Important at ceremonies and pageants of state, but in any real sense, utterly powerless. Only with Lucius as emperor could Julia Domna be assured of her rule, and so that's how she would have it.

History tells its story, as is its job to do. But sometimes, oh god, that story is a fucking lie. And in the case of how the murder of Geta went down, history is full of shit.

(That must be terribly frustrating for you, oh my Lord. Like a playwright whose work goes misunderstood, and misinterpreted for generation after generation. Things happen one way, by your design, and yet the world imagines them happening differently, wrongly, and are never corrected. How many times must we have misread your intended history? Countless and countless. The world chokes with fools being mistaken for wise men, cowards becoming accidental heroes, and the invention of convenient motivations to stick where only chaos exists.)

The story of Geta's demise is a popular one, and everyone in Rome knows how it goes. I'm sure you've heard it, oh my Lord. The story goes that Julia Domna, wanting nothing more than for her sons to be at peace, arranged a meeting at her apartment, a safely neutral environment. Feeling secure under the protection of their mother's gaze, both sons agreed to the meeting. The story goes that once Geta was with Julia, Lucius called for his guard to storm the apartment, and cut the junior emperor down. The story goes that they did just that, and in the process of trying to defend Geta, Julia Domna was cut on her hand. The story goes that she held Geta in her arms as he died, and wept, and cared not for her wound, though it was deep. The story goes that Lucius abandoned his mother to this gruesome scene, so he could make haste to the praetorian camps, and tell them lies of Geta striking first, and his murder being an act of self defense. The story goes that the loving mother Julia Domna had her heart broken by her dog of a son that day. The story should go up its own ass, because its nothing but shit. I know, and you know, oh god, that the day Julia Domna witnessed her youngest son stabbed to death by her eldest, her heart, far from being broken, was full and aglow.

Lucius was hurt terribly by the world's ignorance to the truth surrounding Geta's murder. So hurt was he by his own mother's convoluting of the facts one night, that he did a most imprudent thing for an emperor, and committed to paper a detailed account of his fratricide. It was in a letter that he wrote to me while away on a short vacation to his estate in Capri. It arrived by messenger in the middle of the night.

Dear god, I pray that my reading of this letter will count as Lucius's own confession to you, and help in some way to give my poor brother's damned soul a measure of relief.

IV.

"Brother, I write you urgently to order the death of our mother, Julia Domna, and to appoint you her executioner.

I mean it, this time. No changing my mind, this time. My heart is hardened, once and for all. I've finally had enough of the masquerading bitch. Let's kill the old thing, and be done with all of her poisonous lying. I know I've said this before, and then recanted and back stepped, and given reprieve. She is my only mother, after all. She does love me, in her way. But this is the end of it. I have no more sympathy left for this weasel that calls itself my mother, and worse, the mother of Rome.

Julia Domna will be leaving my side at Capri for home shortly. This letter will leave just before her, with the fastest rider I have with me, and should arrive in your hands with plenty of time for you to assemble your cohort, and set a trap. Arrest Julia Domna, bring her somewhere private, and strangle her until she is dead. Be rid of her discreetly. Her body to the fire, her ashes to the river.

You'll no doubt be curious what sparked this sudden flame of vengeance in me. I am King of all the world, and you a mere mechanism in my divine turning of it, still I am compelled to tell you how the greater contraption functions. Since my return from Briton, my pleasure at your existence has grown a hundred fold. You are still the noble and gentle boy of our childhood, and yet now also an assassin of such sangfroid I am often left breathless by the lovely massacres you make. The world can misunderstand me, the fool historians can remain willful fucking idiots, and see if I care. However, I do desire that the true story of my life be as known to you as it is to my own heart, oh my brother.

My anger at our mother is again stirred by her outrageous show of grief for the dead traitor, Geta. It's been a year, and she still goes on and on about the squashed rat that she called her youngest son. She has become determined to instill on the upper classes of the city, and therefore on the history of man, an image of herself as a saintly mater familias, who was tormented by the rift between her two sons, and how it was so widened and opened by her evil offspring, Lucius, that it swallowed up her goodly and martyred, Geta.

The truth is that despite how willing I was to have seen Geta fall to his death in whatever abyss existed between us, it was Julia Domna who placed him at the edge of it, and urged me, push, damn you! Push!

I invited three of the most delightfully debauched young men about town to join me at my estate on Capri for a week of pleasures. A son of a great merchant, a son of a powerful Senator, a son of an influential general. And a sadistic son of a bitch, every one of them. I was so looking forward to a romp alongside some friends with similar interests to my own, away from the smoke and noise of the city. I had the estate filled with thirty of the finest looking slave girls from the region for us to fuck and maim. I was going to drown a dozen of them in the shallow waves of the beach. It was going to be a fucking blast! Apologies for not inviting you along, brother, but it was hastily arranged, and you were out of reach, and other such excuses.

And what did we four princes discover upon our arrival at the estate? My mother awaiting us, having proceeded our journey to Capri with her own army of servants. She greeted us, all hugs and kisses, and a big fake smile. She told us that she had heard of our plans, and decided to arrive before us, to inspect and clean the whores we planned to fuck. She said that many of them were diseased, and so she sent them to be drowned early. Then she chose the prettiest girls, and had them perfumed and sent to our chambers, all ready to greet us. She had the idea that she would serve as supervisor and facilitator for our sexual festivities!

I tell you, brother, and you know well, I have seen men and women laid bare and stripped of all humility, without so much as a nervous curling of my brow. But this shit? To hear my mother speak so liberally and approvingly of my lustful thirsts? I turned red. My friends laughed. And who could blame them for it? A mother presiding over her son's orgy? Making herself available as its referee? What disgusting hilarity!

Despite my humiliation, I knew immediately she was not here for anything to do with my fucking, she was here to play her own games. There is always a game to be played with this bitch. It had nothing to do with me, really. She was ingratiating herself with my young friends. Their fathers, all three of them, were important to Julia Domna in ways so boring to me I shutter to recount them. She was playing politics with my vacation time. She was playing politics on top of my precious orgy of shock-horror!

I could not contain myself, and I lost my anger in her face. I screamed and spit. I told her she was a foul minded, old bitch. In front of everyone, my friends, the servants, the slaves, I told her that her unwanted presence made me want to vomit. I told her that no queen I had ever heard of made herself welcomed where she was not invited. I told her that her behavior resembled a snake far more than it did a queen-mother. I told her that it made sense, because she was as ugly as a snake. I really let her have it, brother. You'd have been so proud of me. You'd have relished her crushed expression.

Ever the actor, Julia Domna had to win back her audience, and so turned to what every desperate woman turns to, emotional hysterics. She fell on her knees, weeping and howling, "My only son is a murderer! My only son is a murderer! He killed my beautiful boy, Geta! I fear for my life! I fear everyday that he will cut me down like he did my precious and wonderful, Geta! I humiliate myself to please a murderer! Gods forgive me! Gods forgive me!" She went on with such a believable performance of grief that she not only won back the crowd, but even my debauched friends, who had been laughing at her a moment earlier, were now by her side, consoling her, holding and petting her hands, and sweetly kissing her wet cheeks. And, oh, the filthy looks I began to receive. The outrage, the utter fucking outrage!

I lost my cool, I pulled my sword, I killed a slave, maybe two. I don't know, I was blind with rage. I screamed to the crowd that if they hadn't evacuated the queen back to Rome in the next hour that all of their lives would be forfeit. I stormed off into the estate, and barricaded myself in my chambers. When I heard the horses being mounted, and the carriage being prepared for Julia Domna's departure, I began writing this letter to you, to order her long deserved culling.

Despite my rush to have this letter delivered to you, and have you set about organizing the task given within it, there is one more story I would write, and have you read. I would have you read it, memorize it, and put to flame the paper it is written upon. It is the story of how Julia Domna killed her son Geta with a burning dagger.

She didn't stick the burning dagger into his gut, or his chest, or his back. The burning dagger never cut my brother, Geta. My dagger, a very cool one, is the one that sliced into him, and drew his blood in puddles. But there was another dagger present at his killing. A burning dagger. And it was just as responsible for killing Geta as I was. More so.

The start of the story does go the way most people tell it. With Julia Domna inviting both Geta and I to her royal suite for a meeting on neutral territory. Where the story goes wrong is the assumption that I went to this meeting with the intention of double crossing and killing my brother. This is not true. You are well positioned to know that this is not true.

You remember the arrangement of this meeting well, don't you, my brother? We discussed the possibility of sneaking a blade in, or hiding assassins on the rooftop, or under the floors. We decided that the meeting would be too well publicized and too well guarded. We decided it was impossible to get a weapon in, and the best course of action would be to hear Geta out at the meeting, and try to ambush his party on horseback as they left the complex afterwards. Once he was stabbed and dead, I told you that I had had a sudden change of heart, and secretly ordered the dagger hidden in my mother's suite, without her knowing, the night before our meeting. This is not true. The truth is that I never made the decision to kill Geta, and never hid any weapon to do so. This was a decision made for me by my mother, who also provided the dagger.

When we arrived at her apartment, Geta and I were greeted curtly by our mother, and shown quickly to a tiny table that she had set up at the center of the room. It was a table that I had never seen there before. It was covered in a heavy white linen. She put her hands on our shoulders and without a word she stood us across from one another, the tiny, linen covered, table between us. Once we were positioned as she would have us, she gave a short speech.

She said that there was only going to be one emperor. This is how it had always been. This is how the gods wanted it. And this is how it would always have to be. She said that our father had been weak, and in his weakness he had not chosen between the two of us. She said that there could only be one Romulus, and that the other was most certainly Remus, and had to be put down.

I tell you truly, we pleaded against her. We agreed that it didn't have to be that way. That we could divide the empire quite amicably. We were both open to the idea of Geta setting up a new eastern empire, with a capital in Antioch. I swear to you, my brother, and it even surprised me, but Geta and I were closer to a compromise than ever then, just moments before I stuck a dagger into his heart.

At all of our shocking new offers of reconciliation, our mother simply closed her eyes shut, and shook her head, no. She said that a compromise would not do, and to split the empire in half would be to split her very body in half. She said again, even calmer this time, that one of us was Romulus, and one of us was Remus, and only the crossing of daggers could tell us for sure which was which.

She said the words, be quick about it, and then she grabbed a hold of the linen covering the tiny table between us, and with one tug, pulled it away.

On the table, oh my brother, lay two identical, steel daggers. One with its handle before me, and its blade pointed at Geta. The other with its handle before Geta, and its blade pointed at me.

Our mother stepped away from us, and it was immediately clear what she wanted. We both hesitated for exactly the same flicker of time. Our eyes were locked for that second of delay, oh my brother, and it was almost as though we mutually agreed with our gazes that there was no other way but to go through with it. This was our moment of destiny, and how right that it should be our mother who prompted us to it. I wish it truly had been a fair fight, and left to the will of the gods, and the speed of our reflexes.

We both reached for our daggers at the exact same instant. Both of our hands picked them up at the exact same instant. Honest! And both of our arms raised them at the exact same instant. I swear it! But then something uneven happened. When it came time to lower the dagger, and make the first downward stab, Geta faltered catastrophically. Instead of holding tight to his dagger's metal handle, he simply let it go. He just opened his fist, widened his fingers, and dropped his dagger to the floor.

I saw him drop it, and I saw him wince in pain as he did so, but I did not stop. I did not pause. I did not think. I lowered my dagger, and I stabbed him right in the center of his chest. It made a nice thunk. He wrapped his hands around mine. I kicked the table out from between us and stepped towards him. I pulled the dagger out, stuck it in again, pulled it out, stuck it in again, and again, and again. I tumbled down on top of him, and didn't stop stabbing. I don't know for sure, but when I dream about it now, my mother was laughing through it all.

The next piece you know well, my brother. You were there. Geta screamed in agony, and my mother in fake grief, and I called out politely for some assistance. You and your cohort rushed into the room, and were met by Geta's elite guard. It was a wonderful sword fight, one of your finer shows, dear brother.

The next piece you know nothing of, my brother. No one does, but me, Geta, and our murderess of a mother. In the chaos of the skirmish, I threw myself to the ground by Geta. I made certain that he was dead, and then I went for his dagger. The one my mother had given him, and the one he had dropped at the crucial moment. I grabbed its metal handle and immediately dropped it myself. For it was burning hot. So burning hot was this metal dagger, that it must have been sitting on a stove for hours before being placed under that cloth. Geta never had a chance. She cooked the dagger! She damned her own son to death by cooking his dagger!

So, brother, now you know the truth. And I'm glad someone finally does. You can understand why I keep this embarrassing story a secret. If it were not for the scheming of an old woman, I would not be King. Without my mother I would have likely never had a chance at killing Geta, and would likely have agreed to dividing the empire in two.

She set up the final game, and rigged it for the son of her choosing. As glad as I am not to go unchosen, it fills me with such a devastating anger to think that I am who I am because of the will of some other, not my own. You know what I mean?

I refuse to live this way any longer.

It is my will that you murder Julia Domna. Do it as soon as possible.

Yours,

Lucius."

A second, shorter, letter from Lucius arrived an hour after the first, oh god.

"Dear brother. I have made an error in judgment. Cancel all plans to murder my mother. I wrote in haste. We will talk when I am back in Rome. I repeat myself: do not kill my mother."

An hour later, a third letter arrived.

"Brother. After continued deep thought I have concluded once more that Julia Domna has no place in this world. She must be killed. I officially order you to kill Julia Domna."

And finally, a fourth.

"Forget it. Let her live. Do not kill Julia Domna. Do not kill Julia Domna. Repeating again for utmost clarity: DO NOT KILL JULIA DOMNA."

V.

After this falling out, oh god, there was a sort of falling together between mother and son. Perhaps it took Lucius being brought to the edge of getting rid of his mother forever for him to realize how he could never live without her. Without her, or her vast and ever growing fortune. As Lucius's appetites grew harder to satiate, so too did his expenses, and only his mother could keep up the payments.

Lucius reached the bottom of his public funds very rapidly, and plans had to be devised to bring in new tax streams. In the classic tradition of leaders doing noble things for less than noble reasons, Lucius extended citizenship to millions of barbarians living in and around Roman borders. Hardly the honor it once was, still it was taken in stride by many, and easily forced upon the others. It brought in money, but not enough.

Lucius was not a prophetic wordsmith. Lucius was not a man of the people. Lucius was not a champion of the nobility. Lucius was not a shrewd gamesman. He lacked all qualities that usually rose a man to power and leadership. What he had was a rich family, with access to giant pools of private wealth, which he used to pay his soldiers.

There's a story that's become popular, oh my Lord. About my father, on his death bed, instructing his son Lucius, honor the military, forsake all other men. Whether or not this singular and dramatic scene ever took place doesn't matter, when you look at how Lucius ruled, you know it's true, oh god. High wages for the men in Rome most willing to use violence. That was the extent of his managerial style.

Without Julia Domna, there was no silver. Without silver, there were no wages. Without wages, there were no soldiers. Without soldiers, there was no empire. Without an empire, Lucius couldn't spend his days inventing new ways to get himself off at the expense of another's misery. You see, god? You see the way it works? Must I explain to you that no matter how much my brother may have loved me, he would always need his mother? Must I explain to you, oh god, how often need makes a gullible ass of love?

I proved myself ever useful during the purge of the city following the death of Geta. Lucius had the Senate officially condemn his brother's memory, and proceeded to have him erased from history altogether. Statues of him were torn down, and murals repainted. Coins with his face on it were collected and melted down. His name was removed from all imperial records. And, of course, we killed a lot of people. I've heard some call it thirty thousand. I've heard some call it fifty. It was probably no more than ten or fifteen, but still, that did feel like quite a lot of work while I was doing it.

At the risk of sounding both repetitive, and flippant, oh god, please forgive me for killing all those folks during the Geta purge. It was a terrible time, heavy with guilt. I gloss over my wrong doings during this time not because they aren't worthy of contemplation, but because I carried them out with such haste, sterility, and frequency, that I cannot recall them with enough detail to repent in any meaningful way.

Anyway, time passed, and the purge ended, and suddenly a pile of silver was more important to Lucius than a pile of corpses, and one morning a messenger delivered me this.

"My brother, I am ordering you to Antioch. In truth, I am ordering you to a community of desert villages just one day and one night east of Antioch.

Do not hate me. I demand that you not hate me. An order is an order, and you shall go where I please, and not hate me for sending you there.

The cause of your deportation is our mother, of course. She can be very persuasive. She would have me either in financial ruins, or you dead. Don't worry, brother. Instead, I offered her your exile from Rome, and thankfully she accepted. I am sending you with a near elite cohort, ten servants, ten slaves, ten whores, and enough gold to last you for two years comfortably in the east. That should be enough time for me to figure out a way to remove my mother from power without disturbing the precious economy of the empire. We must, after all, always be diligently watching after the economy of the empire.

It won't be so bad, I don't think. Like my time in Briton, you'll find much shock-horror to keep you occupied. I've had some experience, and let me tell you, brother, nobody takes a killing quite like these new christians. An entire religion of would be martyrs! You're in for a real treat!

You'll be leaving at the end of the week, joining an expedition already organized by Prefect Kaeso Rutilus. I'm told he's an extremely capable unit commander, if not a bit of a bore. Please report to him at the Praetorian Barracks in the morning.

It feels impolite to mention this, yet dangerous not to. As part of my arrangement with Julia Domna, she has reserved the right to kill you, should you be seen in the city at the end of a week's time. We could fight her on this point, yes, but I've chosen, in my wisdom, not to shake the boat. She is our mother, after all. And in addition, I have the economy to think about.

Eat, and drink, and fuck, and get yourself a nice tan. Please, brother, make a vacation of this exile. Calm yourself with the knowing that your emperor is grateful for everything you have done for him in the past, and is working tirelessly to find a place for you in the future. Two years is not such a long time. Get yourself a barbarian girl, or two, or ten, and the days shall fly. Trust me.

This is not goodbye, my brother. It's only, later.

Also, there seems to be a genuine uprising in the area I am sending you. Followers in the cult of the man-christ have been attacking our sentry outposts, and taking our tax collectors as hostages. I'm told it's a nasty little revolt. Have a bit of fun and squash it for me, would you?

Later,

Lucius."

CHAPTER VII

I.

Dexius Januarius, the pink-wolf, murderous brute that he most certainly was, when I knew him, was also a great romantic. Though he never elaborated on its origin, he was fond of quoting the rule, that every man on earth was given by the gods three great loves in his lifetime. For every man, three women. According to Dexius Januarius, if you were to ask even the grandest conqueror, Julius Caesar, what was the story of your life? His answer would be, Cornelia, Calpurnia, and Cleopatra.

Dexius believed, for he loved both sexes equally, that naturally he would be granted six great loves by the gods. Three female, three male. During our time of youthful shock-horror on the streets of Rome, Dexius was at a count of five loves, and on the lookout for the final one.

As a little boy on a farm, as little boys on farms do, Dexius had fallen in love with two little girls. One blonde, one brunette, both devilish. Dexius spoke of them with great pain, as if the wounds had never healed. I remember him saying, god, "I had them and lost them both in a single summer. Still, those two girls made a life long poet of me." I don't think the pink-wolf ever learned to read, let alone write a verse, but I knew what he meant, and if you've ever been in love, I'm sure you do too, oh god.

When he joined the army, Dexius forgot about the love of his first two girls, by finding that of his first two boys. He had been older than both of them, had trained them, had killed for them, and they for him. I remember him saying, god, "we faced death side by side together, everyday, for years at a time. How could we not hold each other at night?" The pink-wolf lost these two boys in battle with Germans, and he didn't like to talk about the details, oh god, except to say that he couldn't help but blame himself.

There was a third woman, a slave who worked for a commanding officer. When they returned home from an extended expedition, Dexius used his bonus to buy the slave woman's freedom. He retired from the military, and set to making a family with her, somewhere in the south, on the coast, where she was from. I remember him saying, god, "I tried, but she was good, and simple, and I'm just not. Losing the land, kicking the straight life, the baby that died in her, all of it was my fault. I didn't say a word when she told me she was leaving." After his wife miscarried and left him, the pink-wolf returned to Rome, and to soldiering.

The night my father announced the military campaign in Briton, Dexius Januarius was at my brother Lucius's side. He disappeared halfway through the party, though, leaving only a steaming puddle of piss behind. You remember the piss, my Lord? That was the last time I saw the pink-wolf for several years. He didn't go to Briton, and I didn't see him in Rome the whole time Lucius was away, nor when he returned. The pink-wolf seemed to have vanished. You knew where he was, oh god. Not heaven, but perhaps as close as a man can get while still breathing.

It was halfway through my journey to my point of exile, in the city of Byzantium, where I saw the pink-wolf again and likely for the last time.

I was having a terrible journey, oh god. I was furious with Lucius for sending me away. I felt worthless, and the only remedy I could come up with involved abandoning my cohort, returning to Rome, finding Julia Domna, and cutting her fucking throat open, like I should have done when I had the chance. This was impossible in reality, and would have most definitely cost me my life.

I remained silent for days at a time while we traveled. Kaeso, the expedition's bore of a Prefect, would pressure me to discuss strategy for dealing with the rebellion when we arrived in the desert, and I would give him a cold stare, turn away wordlessly, and go hide in my carriage, or my tent. My mind was elsewhere. It was obsessed, as you perhaps recall, oh knower of my deepest thinking, with all of the opportunities I had had to kill Julia Domna, which I had let slip by. All of those nights that she lay beside me, totally naked, totally vulnerable, I could have killed her without even putting gloves on. I could have killed her with the heal of my bare foot, oh god, I could have killed her with my teeth. But I hadn't, and now here I was, crossing from the western world, to the eastern, at a distance so far from my beloved brother, that I may as well have been headed to the stars.

We were stopped in Byzantium, oh my Lord, and while the slaves and servants tended to the horses and carriages, and the men were filling up the whore houses, and Kaeso was at the library, studying strategy or whatever. I was wandering the markets, alone, like a ghost. I was stopped at a merchant's stand, looking at a collection of Socratic scrolls I was going to buy, when I saw him pass. The pink-wolf.

He was in a fantastic disguise. He was holding the hands of two little boys, one on each side, and an adorable little girl was sitting atop his gigantic shoulders. There were other children about him, too, a little bit older than the ones right beside, but equally innocent looking. He was covered in children, oh god. As the wolf and his entourage of kiddies past by, I thought, it couldn't be him. But as they got closer, I saw his scarred face, and his unmistakable hulk of a frame. It was Dexius Januarius, no doubt, and had he become a father eight times over in less than four years? It certainly seemed that way.

I watched them as they strolled from stand to stand, looking at the goods and laughing and playing. And all the while there was the pink-wolf, acting like the pink-hen, keeping them in line, and in sight. He was even clucking at them when they got too far away from him. He was saying things like, "back where I can see you, sweetheart," and, "that's too expensive, my darling, maybe for your birthday." I was flabbergasted, my Lord.

When Dexius put down the little girl from off his shoulders, and let go of the boys hands so they could get a closer look at a street puppet show, I walked over to him. Still in a haze brought on by weeks and weeks of feeling sorry for myself, I numbly tapped the pink-wolf on his shoulder.

"Pink?" I asked.

Dexius turned around slowly, not looking happy to be called by that old color of his. But when he saw that it was me, he smiled, oh god. I smiled. I hadn't smiled in a month. My face muscles were out of practice, and I couldn't hold it for long. I asked him what gives with all the children?

"My sixth." Dexius said proudly. "I met my sixth love, old friend. These are his little brothers and sisters. His mother died early, the father ran off, and the children are his, and so the children are mine." The wolf explained, oh god, "Do you remember that night at the Coliseum? That fighting at that orgy, when poor Faustus was killed? Do you recall the wild boy who was with me? The beautiful boy with the scar across the bridge of his nose?"

(I didn't remember the boy, oh god, but Dexius described him to me in detail, and now when I dream of that orgy at the coliseum, the beautiful boy, with scar across the bridge of his nose, is always there.)

The scarred-nosed boy was the eldest in a family of orphans. He had gone to Rome to learn a trade from an uncle, and make his fortune. He had done well for himself, making and selling furniture to wealthy families. His work had even become fashionable, and when he planned on returning to his many younger brothers and sisters, to open up a factory in his hometown, he asked his beloved pink-wolf to go with him. Dexius wasn't going to miss out on his sixth and final chance at love. So, off he went to Byzantium, for a life of blissful domesticity.

While the young man with the scar across the bridge of his nose is busy all day at his carpentry works, Dexius Januarius stays with the children, bringing them to their lessons, making sure they're fed, and most nights, tucking them in to bed with a story. This, the pink-wolf said, had become the great joy of his life. The years of war and killing, the years of wine and mead, they seemed to him the memories of a stranger.

Dexius couldn't talk long, oh god, the puppet show was ending, and his adopted family needed his attention once more. But I told him about my exile, and my frustration at Lucius. He seemed to feel for me, oh god, in a genuine kind of way. In a compassionate way that only a man truly happy in his new life could afford to feel for an old friend.

Dexius told me that when he was at war, and felt lonely or homesick, it helped him to pray. I told him that I didn't believe in the gods. He told me that I didn't have to pray to the gods, that I could pray to a person, and it would almost be like talking to them. I told him that I would feel silly speaking to voices in my head, and joked that I was close enough to mad as it was. He told me that some of the more educated soldiers would write letters to the ones they loved, and when the lines were surrounded, and no messages could get out, they would continue writing the letters, regardless.

"Who would they address these unsent letters to?" I asked him.

"The paper." Said the pink-wolf.

I bought some ink and expensive papyrus at the market that very day, and began keeping a journal of my exile. I have those old pages here, with me now, in my very hands. They account my latter and most terrible sins, and I will use parts of them to aid in my confession, oh Lord.

II.

8 Aprilis, 969 ab urbe condita.

Lucius is a fucking liar. After the nightmarish journey to Nicomedia, our slog south through the miserable wasteland of a country, Cilicia, and a trip on a leaky boat across the gulf of Issus, we finally arrived in Antioch. Lucius told me no more than a day outside of the city, and I'd be at my final destination. Lies. It's taken nearly four days, following the Orontes river west, and then south, and we're still a day from arrival at the imperial stronghold.

Talk about the middle of fucking nowhere. Who the fuck thought it would be a good idea to build an outpost here? The valleys near the river are flush with green grass, but beyond that is nothing but rock and sand. The land is too hard to grow anything you could make any coin from. The people seem to live off their sheep, which they herd up and down the river. And the locals are all ugly, brown old women, with skin like leather. Where are all the young women? Where are the men? Did they all run off together? It seems to be a population of nothing but abandoned fucking grandmas. What is our interest in this country? What Roman could possibly care about anything that ever happens out here, in the asshole of the empire?

...

9 Aprilis, 969 ab rube condita.

We arrived on the outskirts of the christian village earlier this evening. I heard its name spoken many times, but I still can't quite pronounce it, and have no clue about how to spell it. This pleases me. I don't want to know the name of this awful place. I want to keep myself as unknowing of its parts as I am of the moon's.

Well, except for one part I wouldn't mind getting to know. There is a girl I saw today, who I would like to remember, and perhaps make the acquaintance of before my time here is up.

When the Roman fortress came into the view of our caravan, so too did the small town across the valley from it, and so too did yet another group of local bitches, herding their flock of sheep along the river. They were made up of the broken old widows I'd become accustomed to seeing from aloft my horse, but this time there was a crystal amongst these boulders. A hazel eyed herder girl, of seventeen or so. When my impressive entourage of horsemen and military carriages passed, these old women all broke their attention from the sheep to look up at us. To look up at me. Some cursed and spit, some preened and mocked youthful flirtation. Both performances were disgusting, and the men all turned, or fixed their views on the fortress ahead. But as if by an extra sense that had never called to me before in my life, I knew not to look away. I knew that she was there.

I saw her before any of the other men. I saw her first. She was looking down at one of her black sheep. Every other woman around her had her eyes fixed on me, they even shaded the sun form their eyes to get a better look, but she was only concerned with her tiny, black sheep. Even the black runt was looking at me. Truly, he was. He was looking right at me. And then, as if prompted by this little black sheep's gaze, the herder girl finally looked up at me, and I saw her eyes, and the green birch of them seemed to blossom from the brown dirt of my own.

Where does this shrill poetry come from? Is Dexius Januarius right about the effect of love? Is it ridiculous to call what I feel for this stranger, love? I do not know her name.

I have not heard her voice. I know not her character, or her ways. Yet, a definite sensation, that she is all that I want. Yes, it can be put in only those terms. I want that hazel eyed herder girl more than my next breath.

Luckily, these pages are, as the pink-wolf prescribed, unaddressed and unsent. The content is already humiliating. On to more important, less foolish matters.

The commander of the fortress outpost is Rufus Balbus, a disgraced prefect who was given the job of overseeing this rebellious village as punishment for fucking some politician's daughters. All five daughters, as the rumor goes, but probably no more than two, in fact. Maybe the story is true, and they were just some grievously ugly daughters, and he had his way with all five of them for a song and a dance. Who knows? I'll have to ask him about this one night. Either way, he's here against his will until the problem is solved, and wants to get back to Antioch, and civilization, rather desperately. This urge led him to a bit of independent thinking.

I'm not sure yet how I feel about it, he may have overstepped his authority, but this ambitious hound, Rufus Balbus, has taken it upon himself to essentially put an end to the entire uprising before I ever arrived.

I was greeted warmly at the fortress. I was fed, and washed, and then we sat down by a fire. Rufus, my second in command, Kaeso, and me.

Rufus explained, over goblets of wine, that the uprising began as no more than twenty or so radical christian men. They had formed a committee of judges from the leaders of their community. They received and deliberated local disputes which Rome saw as falling under their purview. When taxes started being collected by this committee, Rufus ordered their churches closed, and when that was resisted, burned.

The christians militarized, and attacked the fortress. Rufus sent soldiers into the village, and killed as many christians as he could. But many of them weren't involved with the committee in the first place, and local resentment grew, and more village christians turned radical, and the fortress was repelling attacks, again and again, day after day. Rufus knew that he had only enough troops to fan the flames, not blow them out. He begged for reinforcements, but the politician in Antioch, whose daughters he'd fucked, kept him in need. Until, quite out of the blue, the Emperor himself became interested in far off escapades to get his bastard of a brother entangled in. Fucking, Lucius.

Anyway, Rufus had word that Kaeso, the soldiers, and I, were on our way, but there had been a particularly nasty attack recently, and he couldn't wait for us any longer. He got a loan from some wealthy local Jews, who were sick of the christians stirring up trouble, and he hired a cadre of Syrian mercenaries. Using information obtained from the Jews, Rufus and his Syrians swept through the village with utter thoroughness, and killed every christian male, men and boys alike. The leaders of the committee, the most important men from the village, were spared. They were arrested, and are being held in the fortress dungeon, awaiting my arrival, and instructions.

I've decided to crucify these christian committee members, nineteen in all, tomorrow morning, on the high hill to the west of the village.

So, that settles that. All's well that ends well, I suppose. Though, it's going to be awful boring around here without any more problems left to solve.

...

10 Aprilis, 969 ab rube condita.

This morning I freed every christian prisoner I held in captivity. I had a "change of heart", as they say.

I awoke this morning to a breakfast of eggs, a mug of ale, and the expectations of a show of mass crucifixions. Rufus joined me, and seemed to be in the same good spirits as me. I asked him about the politician's daughters, and he claimed it wasn't five, but six! I pressed him on it, but he was adamant. Six sisters in the same family. Six daughters of the same father. Outrageous! It proved to me that I could not trust him.

After we ate, Kaeso joined us. He disagreed with Rufus and I over what to do with the prisoners. Kaeso believed that since the christians were so well decimated, and a new leader had arrived, there was an opportunity for reconciliation. Only this, Kaeso insisted, was a sustainable path forward.

Interrupting our jovial, kill-morning moods, Kaeso came to inform me, soberly, that the wives and daughters of the prisoners had assembled at the front gates of the fortress, and had kept a candle light vigil through the night.

Rufus barked at Kaeso, he should have told us sooner. He was about to order the guard to clear the women, or cut them down where they stand. I put a hand up, and quieted him.

I was thinking very rapidly. The hazel eyed herder girl could be with those women. What would she think of me if I killed her father, or her brother? What would my chances of ever possessing her be, if her first impression of me was as the murderous bastard that I am? I could just grab her, and rape her, but then that would be the end of it. And the thought of making her do something she didn't want to do made me feel a discomfort in my chest and stomach that I have never experienced before in my life.

"Bring the women before me." I said.

"You really shouldn't see them, sir." Advised Kaeso. "That is, unless you plan on freeing the men."

"I do." I told him with casualness, and sipped my ale. "I've slept on it, and I've had what people call, a change of heart."

Rufus was outraged, and let me know it. Kaeso was all, "wise choice, sir. Wise and magnanimous."

Truth is, I just really want to take that herder girl to bed. If she was with the group of women, I would play the newly arrived, and eminently merciful, savior. There, I would begin my seduction of her. If she was not with the group of women, and only bitter old grandmas were brought before me, I'd have no qualms with killing the lot of them, and then crucifying their men folk, as planned. As luck would have it, she was with them.

We met in the courtyard of the fortress. I shaved my beard before meeting her, something I hadn't done since leaving Rome. I stood tall and straight to greet her, my finest soldiers lined up behind me, their armor polished and shining. I was in my uniform, but I did not wear my helmet. I wanted her to see my face, and my hair, which I also had freshly cut, and greased with raw egg whites.

The women sent their leadership to speak to me. Five grandmas, and at the center of them, the lovely hazel eyed girl. Only she spoke, the others kept their flabby arms folded over their sagging tits, and nodded in agreement with every word their little princess said. The fact that her elders deferred so completely to her, was a mystical thing to witness.

Her plea was angered, but respectful. She spoke of compassion and forgiveness, and all that stuff. But she also spoke of politics, and compromise. She told me that Rufus Balbus had been cruel, and unfair, and she hoped that with me, she could find a partner, not an enemy. She hoped that with me, her people could find peace. She could have asked me for my tongue, and I'd have cut it off, right then and there.

I played it cool, or as cool as I could. I told her that the men held in captivity were rebels against the Emperor, my brother, and justice must be satisfied. But, I added cautiously, perhaps it already has been. Perhaps the thing that needs satisfying now, is peace.

She smiled. I saw her smile for the first time. She smiled while she was looking at me in the eyes. Best moment of my life? Arguably.

I released the christian men in the afternoon. Kaeso and I even went down to the dungeon together to unlock the chains ourselves. I played the role of savior once more, and was all, "I'm so sorry for what you've had to endure. That Rufus is a spiteful monster. You won't have him to worry about anymore. Let's be friends."

I fed them, I washed them, I listened to them talk about their man-christ over wine, and I made some allies. All with the hopes that they would go home to their women, and the hazel eyed girl would heard word of my kindness, and start feeling for me what I am for her.

Perhaps she already is feeling it? She did smile at me. No two ways about that. She smiled at me.

After the men were freed, and the christians all returned to their village, I had Kaeso, and a few guards, arrest Rufus and bring him before me. I asked him once more, how many of that Antiochene politician's daughters did you screw? "Be honest", I warned him. He insisted that the number was six, so I had his head chopped off.

What a wonderful day it's been. A change of heart is damnable thing.

I realize now, as I sit in my lodgings, preparing for sleep, that I do not know the name of my hazel eyed christian girl. More than that, I do not know what specific man she was here to save. And more to the point, what is the nature of her relationship with this man?

It will be difficult to sleep tonight with these questions. Yet, I feel good. It must be admitted, for the first time since our parting, I do not miss Lucius.

...

30 Quintilis, 969 ab rube condita.

I return from dinner in town. I think I shall give in to the wishes of my new friends, and be baptized at the end of this week. Not to satisfy myself, of course, and not to satisfy the community, whose stupidity I tolerate to serve a greater purpose. I will let them dunk me in the river, for the sake of my Margaret. My Margaret, my Margaret, my Margaret. I like to say her name. It calms my nerves to say her name. It calms my nerves to write her name. Margaret, Margaret, Margaret.

I drank at dinner. I drank a lot. These christians know how to drink. They pray, then they get totally shit faced drunk, then they pray, then they stuff themselves with lamb and figs, then they pray, then they drink some more, then they dance. When the dancing is done, the less faithful shuffle off for home to pass out. The true believers remain in the town square until sunrise, lost in enthusiastic discussions of the teachings of their beloved man-christ, Jesus, a wood working fellow who made a stink in Jerusalem a bunch of years ago.

It's these late evening, early morning times, when the music has stopped, and the crickets have taken over, when my love, the hazel eyed herder girl, my Margaret, comes to me.

I wait for her on the stone bench, by the dried up fountain dedicated to Livia. I pretend I don't see her, as she leaves her crowd of friends and family, and walks slowly over to me. "Oh, hello there, didn't expect to see you out tonight." I say, and she sits beside me, and we talk, and we talk, and we talk. I let her do most of the talking. Everything she says is interesting. I am content to smile and nod to the rhythm of her voice for all of eternity.

She knows nothing of my past. She does not know what I am capable of. I think of telling her. Why? What would telling her accomplish? She would never speak to me again. Yet, I want more than anything to be honest with her, and to give her a full accounting of who I am, and how I've lived.

Ridiculous. Ridiculous. I address myself now: you are a ridiculous, drunk, idiot. This girl is nothing but a pretty stranger. Forget about being baptized by these lunatics. Have your wits about you. They may very well drown you in that river. What you, and millions of tired old poets who came before you, call love, is no more than a sexual, animal impulse. Do yourself a favor, jerk off, and go to sleep.

...

5 Sextilis, 969 ab rube condita.

I have been baptized. I know, I know, I feel like an idiot. I couldn't help it.

Margaret said that it would refresh my soul, and I'd be able to feel its newness immediately. She said it would be like nothing I had ever experienced before. She said that when she was baptized, she had seen god, or at least sensed him, anyway. She guaranteed that I most certainly would have this sense of god. She claimed it was unmistakable. I got a lot of foul river water up my nose, I sensed that shit. I fear sinus infection.

After it was done, Margaret came to me, she seemed nervous. Unsure if I had had the divine experience she had foretold I would. I was so pleased to see her want for a reaction in me.

"How do you feel?" Margaret asked me. It seems an utter miracle to me that this beautiful girl could care at all how I feel about anything.

I lied to her, naturally. As if touched by the serenity of the kingdom of heaven, I told her, "I feel love."

...

3 December, 969 ab rube condita.

After spending nearly every evening of the last few months with Margaret, I went to her home tonight to find her out, with another man.

I nearly killed her mother and father in their own doorway when they informed me. Margaret must have forgotten that we had plans to eat dinner together, they told me, she had gone to the market with Giles. They said his name as though I must know this Giles, and as if they were on very familiar terms with him. Good old, Giles. The boy from next door, of course. Everybody knew Giles. Margaret had grown up with Giles. A good boy, grown into a handsome young man, didn't I know?

No, I didn't know. Who the fuck is this Giles, a piece of dog shit?

My first impulse was that the mother and father had invented him, and were using him as a way of keeping me from their daughter. I put my hand on my sword, and was ready to open up their stupid guts on the threshold.

I took a breath. I thought of Margaret. Who ever this Giles was, real or imaginary, if I killed Margaret's parents, she wouldn't want to talk to me ever again.

I smiled, and said, "Oh, well. Nevermind. You give Margaret my regards, and tell her I'll pay her a visit again some time soon."

They invited me in for some wine, and a bite to eat, but I politely excused myself, said I was late for another engagement. It was beyond obvious that I was lying, but I didn't even try to come up with a plausible excuse. I was so hurt that Margaret had abandoned me to spend time with some man, some Giles, all I cared about was getting away from there.

I do not know what will come of this Giles. I hope tonight is the first and last I hear of his sickening name.

...

7 December, 969 ab rube condita.

The worst has occurred. After being avoided by her for five days, I finally caught Margaret at home. She apologized for not seeing me, she said that she had been neglecting all of her friends as of late. She refereed to me as her friend. This girl, this little sheep herding nothing, referred to me, the second most powerful man in Rome, as her measly friend. She said that she had been spending time with a suitor, his name was Giles, and had I ever met him? He's the handsome, athletic boy, who grew up next door, she told me. And he is one of the most devoted christians in town. And she was beside herself with happiness. I could smell it on her.

"Do you know him?" She asked me. "Do you know my Giles?"

Her Giles? Her Giles? My Margaret's Giles? I'd have killed her, but then I'd have to kill myself.

I'm too depressed to write. I wish I had the nerve to walk out into the desert, lay down, and die of thirst.

...

Mercedonius 2, 970 ab rube condita.

She loves me! She couldn't come right out and say it, but I know it to be true. My Margaret loves me.

It was a terrible struggle, but I did it. I stayed away from her for over two months. I haven't been down to the village even to have dinner, or visit my new, and fraudulently made, church friends. She sent messages, I ignored them. When members of the council came over for meetings with Kaeso, they told me how Margaret had asked for me. I told them that she was a nice girl, but I was a very busy man. Finally, tonight, she came to the fortress herself to ask after me.

I nearly bounced off the walls when I heard she arrived, and wanted to talk. My heart was exploding to see her again, to be around her, to hear her voice, and smell her. I can still smell her now, only moments after she left.

I wanted to kiss her more than ever, tonight. I wanted to run my tongue across her lips, and stick it in her mouth. She wanted me to, I know it, I could sense it. It's in the way she smiles. It's in the way she breaths. I sense it.

Margaret told me that she understood why I had stayed away from her. She told me that I needed to understand that even though she was being courted by Giles, it did not mean she didn't care for me. She said that I had been doing so well in my journey on the path to true christianity, and that it meant the world to her that I keep at it, with her as a partner. She told me that she knew what I wanted, but I had to look at things clearly. I was a Roman, and I would be heading back to Rome in a year and a half. It was not meant to be.

I told her I understood. I told her I was happy for her and Giles. She kissed me on the cheek, and told me to come visit her tomorrow night, and we would restart our studies of the man-christ.

She wants me. I know it. Why else would she have come over here tonight? Oh, I'm practically bursting. Another few months of close, intimate, friendship, and then she'll be mine!

...

October 19, 970 ab rube condita.

Margaret and Giles have announced their engagement.

I don't feel angry. I don't feel vengeful. I am not raging with jealousy. I think of the man-christ, Jesus. I think of his suffering, and I know that my heartaches are nothing by comparison.

I will never get to kiss my Margaret, I will never get to run my tongue across her lovely cheeks. I will never know what her body feels like against mine. Still, I am blessed to know other things about her. I know her deepest thoughts on god. I know how her heart feels about most topics of philosophy and the history of man.

In such a short time, we have become what everyone in the community recognizes as the best of friends. No one thinks it's strange that we are not romantic, except for me.

There seems to be no controversy. No one, including her fiancee, Giles, could ever imagine that a girl as honest and chaste as Margaret could have any intentions other than the ones she claimed. The redemption of my soul, and the protection of her community. If good relations with me meant good relations with Rome, all the better.

She still has no idea what kind of a soul she's contending with in me. More and more often, I wish that she did. I wake up in the middle of the night, and am desperate to confess my many sins to her. Not because she has become the religious guide that she wants so badly to be in my eyes, but because she is kind to me. Because she is sweet to me. Because I love her for pure reasons, that I have never known before. She laughs at my silly jokes. Real laughter, I can tell. And she has some funny jokes of her own. The more we spend time together, the more I realize that that's all I ever want to do with my life. It doesn't matter if we're kissing when we do it. It doesn't matter if I never know how her body feels. I have felt her soul, and that is enough.

And, who knows? They won't be getting married for another few months. There's still time.

...

Februarius 12, 971 ab rube condita.

Tomorrow, Margaret and Giles will be married. Tomorrow, my Margaret will be another man's wife.

I have professed my love for her, and she has told me in clear terms to move on with my life and forget about her. I plan on doing of what she instructs. I will leave for Antioch in the morning, and stay there for the remainder of my exile. What I will never do, is forget her.

I haven't been sleeping. I lay awake thinking of Margaret, and how she would judge my wicked existence. What would she think of me, if she was there that night in the horse stables, when I killed the gooseneck boy? Would she think I was justified in killing the bully, Marcus Gallus? Was I right to cut out his heart while he was still alive? What would my Margaret think of me, if she knew what I did to old Rabbi Ben? What would my Margaret make of the soul who helped destroy a family, on an artichoke farm, where a man was forced to witness his own son butchered and deformed, and his daughter raped and murdered?

If Dexius Januarius was right, Margaret is one of the three great loves of my life. No doubt about it. Maybe the first? Maybe the last? Am I to count my brother, Lucius? Am I to count my step-mother, Julia Domna? I am loathed to, but I fear that if I am to be honest, than I must.

Is Margaret the last great love of my life?

Can't be! I will not, and must not accept this! I'm only twenty eight years old! I have many years ahead of me, and many loves. One of the things I've got to get better at, is seeing the bigger picture. Margaret is a bump in the road. As my carriage wheels crash over her, I am shaken, but the road continues.

Yes, here is the truest and deepest effect of my friendship with the christian girl, Margaret: a sunnier disposition. I see the brighter side of things, as she does. She sees god in everything, and so sees the good in everything.

"Even in bird shit?" I once asked her. "Especially in bird shit." She answered.

Yes. I will be an adult. I will let her go her way, and I will go mine.

What a relief it is to finally be freed from the impulsively murderous mind of a bastard, that I once called home.

Praise, Jesus.

III.

That was the last entry ever made in the journal, oh god.

The day after I wrote it, I slept late, awoke well after sunset, collected a cohort of my best men, ambushed the wedding party, killed every guest, and crucified the last great love of my life on a hill to the west of the village she was born in.

IV.

I want to stop. I don't want to remember anymore. Where are my killers? Should they not be here by now? The moon is gone. The sky is dark blue. The sun returns again, oh god, and let it be the last time I'm around to greet it.

I must continue. I have arrived at what was perhaps the most important hour of my life, dear god. It will cause me terrible pain to relive it. It will again break my heart, which has been mended and remended so many times that the patchwork has made a shoddy rag of it.

God, forgive me, I will now detail to you the murder of the christian girl.

The wedding tent was raised at the foot of the hill, on the other side of the river. The music could be heard from a mile away. The smell of cooking lamb filled my nostrils, and made me sick. As we rode over that night, our horses never moving faster than a trot, my mind just sort of slipped away, oh god.

What happened to me, on that horse, trotting out to kill the woman I loved? Where did I go? What new land had I found myself in? I had seen this country of the mind before. I had been on its outskirts, on its borderlands. It was a dark country. A country that I passed near, and around, but never through. But on this night, oh god, in that hour, once and for all, I became lost in its heartland.

I did not enter the tent, oh god. I stayed on my horse, watching as my men rushed into the wedding, spears and swords drawn. The tent was echoing laughter and singing. Happiness was seeping from its moonlit canvases. Drunken conversations, and bellowing laughter.

There was one woman I could hear, in particular, and above the others. It may have been the christian girl's mother, but I'll never be sure. She was singing in a high falsetto, in a language I could not understand. As my soldiers breached the tent, and surrounded the reveling christians on all sides, her falsetto voice shifted. Without ceasing or even quivering, it turned from a cry of joy, to one of shock-horror. She didn't even stop to take a breath. It was one long, continuous note, that turned from pleasure to pain. And following her lead, the other party guests joined in, screaming out in communal agony.

I don't know what it was about that scream, but it somehow dragged me outside myself, for the first time ever. I started to laugh. I saw myself, sitting up there, on my horse, in full legionary regalia, listening to this woman's scream turn so drastically. She was in that tent, being killed, and I was out here, listening. I cannot tell why now, oh god, but at the time, this seemed very funny. I had ordered this massacre. Me. And this had not been the first time. I had done this before. I was responsible for the death of thousands of people. Thousands! That made me laugh even harder. There had been so many, I couldn't remember a third of them. I laughed harder and harder, and then suddenly, all at once, I stopped laughing, and never would again for the rest of my life.

Two soldiers had the christian girl, each clutching an arm. They were dragging her out of the tent, parts of which were now in flames. She had been dressed in white, but was now covered in the maroon insides of her relatives. She was kicking. She was wailing, and crying. When she saw me there, looking over the scene from a distance, she went absolutely mad with rage. Her grief turned to anger, and she cursed my name, and damned my soul to hell. To hear her call my name with such hate, oh god, it pushed my mind further into that dark country. Away, away, away I went.

Or, god, was it you who took leave? Was that the moment you finally turned your back on me? I never felt such a numbness, as the instant when that odd laughter broke, and ended, and I saw the christian girl dragged through the dirt at my will. Did you see me, cackling, and smiling, sitting on my nag, and decide that enough was enough? Yes, I think that is exactly what happened.

Through all my horrible sinning, through every vicious murder, still you had remained by me. Weeping, yes, but watching, always watching, always hoping I would change. Always hoping that I would sense you, or at the very least, sense the spark you placed in my fellow human beings. You longed for me to hear your many sirens on this earth, and when, time and again, I proved myself deaf or unlistening, you would wait for the next chance, and the next, and the next. Everyone has their breaking point, oh my Lord, even you. And you reached that point with me, that night, when I killed my love.

The numbness, the blankness, the emptiness, they continued to spread within the deepest parts of me. And as my men prepared the wood for a cross, and as my christian girl reeled and prayed in the mud, tied like a hog, I had such strange thoughts, oh god. I had a terrible sense that I would live forever. A sense that thoughts, the tick tick ticking of thoughts in my head, would go on forever and ever, without rest. I had an insane sense that the hill, the river below, the sand and rocks of the desert in the distance, were all figments of my imagination.

I remember staring for a long time, at the suffering of the christian girl about to die, and then at the desert in the distance, and feeling the same for them both. They were paint on a canvass, nothing more. I looked down at the last love of my life, and up at the night sky, and had the thought that, in very much the same way astronomers invented constellations, so too did I invent this christian girl. Assembled her from parts I did not understand, into a whole that I wished to see. In this way, I had invented her. So too, I sensed, did I invent the nails which would be hammered through her hands, and feet. So too did I invent the wood.

She was put on her cross, and raised up high. The soldiers I had brought with me were seasoned, this was a professional crucifixion. She was up, and she was staying up until she bled out. She went the same way they all do. She would cry, and scream, then pass out, then wake up, and cry and scream some more. It made her seem so average to me. So run of the mill, human, and most of all, real.

The soldiers were hanging about, some had returned to the massacred wedding tent, to put out the fires and pick through the corpses for treasures. The ones that stayed to watch the christian girl be tortured on a piece of wood, were sharing a flask of wine, and jokes. When the wine was passed to me, I chugged it, hoping that I would get a little drunk, and maybe feel a little sad for what I had done. The sadness would be vastly preferably to the numbness.

This numbness was not agreeing with me at all, oh god. I wanted desperately to escape my own skin, which no longer felt like my own. I passed forward the flask, and caught a glimpse of my right hand which held it. Whose hand is this? I thought. I raised it before my eyes, and looked at it like a foreign artifact. I held it up next to the christian girl, who was exhausted, and now mumbling to herself quietly.

Side by side, I viewed my hand, and a young woman on a cross. Neither looked like the thing it was. Both seemed to be more a collection of shapes, than anything with solid meaning. I couldn't even tell which one was closer to me, the mess of fingers or the tangle of limbs and wood? My vision, oh god, and perhaps my soul, were playing tricks on me. I could not decipher whether the crucifixion was being staged on a grassy hill, or the at the tip of my nose.

The soldiers saw my strangeness, I could feel their eyes focusing to me. I was staring at my hand in the most peculiar of ways, my mouth was agape, and my tongue was hanging out. I all at once became aware of my tongue. It wasn't just hanging out, it was sticking it. It was pointing out. It was aimed at the christian girl.

I was suddenly struck by a memory of my journal. How often I had written in it about wanting to kiss the christian girl, about wanting to lick her. How badly I wanted to kiss her with my lips, and taste her lips, and her body. I had written that it was more important to me than anything. I would have given my life, just to love any part of her with my tongue. I didn't feel that desire then, oh god. I felt no desire at that moment, whatsoever. I had no desire to take a sip of water, to blink my eyes, to breath air, let alone be romantic. But the numbness was turning to a sickness, and I was rapidly becoming desperate for a cure. I thought, maybe if I kissed her, licked her, I would feel something.

With the soldiers watching me, and guided by the compass of my pointed tongue, I walked over to the base of the cross. I looked up at her head, it was hung completely slack. If she wasn't dead yet, she was close. I looked down her neck, and at her breasts, and her stomach, and thighs, and knees and ankles and her feet. Her feet, the black steel nail sticking through them, were directly before my face. They had turned pink from the blood that had spilled over them, but had now dried up to an occasional drip.

I licked her toes. I still felt nothing. I licked the wound around the nail. I felt nothing. I showered her feet with kisses. My lips were becoming wet with blood, and I could taste the metal. I put my lips over the wound, and sucked, and drank. I felt nothing.

I knew that the soldiers were becoming outraged. They were calling out in disgust, demanding that I stop. I would not stop. I did not stop until I heard the hissing.

The soldiers heard it too, and saw what produced it, and they all at once turned silent. The hissing was coming from above me. I pulled my face away from the bloody feet. I put my tongue back in my mouth. I looked up. Coiled around the wooden peg at the top of the cross, slithering its way down, was a black serpent. I stumbled backwards at the sight of it, and fell hard onto my ass. I did not take my eyes off the snake, and neither did the men.

The black serpent was sticking out its tongue and shaking it at us, and hissing louder than I'd ever heard a snake capable. It moved its head over the christian girl's head, and then slithered right down her face, licking her cheek and lip as it went. It passed down her breasts, wrapped around her back, circled her waist, and then pulled itself between her crotch, around her thigh, then around her left leg, and to her feet. All the time, its tongue out, licking and hissing. Finally it reached the base of the cross, uncoiled itself onto the ground, and slithered off into the dark grass.

I looked at the christian girl. Her chest was motionless. She was dead, and gone forever. God, forgive me.

CHAPTER EIGHT

I.

Some wonderful news, thank god! Wojslaw just came to visit me in my room. Nervous with worry for me, he couldn't sleep last night. He decided to go into town, and find out what he could about my assassins, and see if there wasn't a way that he could put a stop to it all.

Wojslaw went to the tavern beneath the only inn that would possibly house foreigners. The barmaid was still awake, and Wojslaw sat down to chat with her. She was tipsy from the evening, and Wojslaw didn't have to pry much to get her to tell him about the two new guests at the inn. They had arrived just after sunset, a father and son, and they had many questions about the monastery, and who was staying there. Wojslaw asked her who in particular the father and son were asking after? Of course, oh god, she told him, the monk who came from Rome. The monk without a tongue.

The father and son had rented a room, and requested not to be disturbed until sunrise, when they were to be given a loud knocking on their door to wake them. Wojslaw had the information he was looking for, and he returned to the monastery to warn me. My assassins, a father and son, would be here shortly after sunrise. It is now shortly after sunrise.

There were two other pieces of information that Wojslaw collected from the barmaid. This is the wonderful news I mentioned, oh god. First, the father and son have brought with them two strong posts of wood, one longer than the other, and a sack of tools. Likely nails, and a good hammer. They mean to crucify me, oh god. How wonderfully appropriate. These two know what they're doing.

The second piece of information was even more delightful to me. The father and son at the inn, the father and son who mean to kill me within the hour, are missing an arm a piece. When Wojslaw told me this, I knew immediately who my assassins were, and this was even more wonderfully appropriate than the cross.

Wojslaw begged me to run. I wanted to tell him that it was I who caused the father and son to be disfigured so. I wanted to tell him that I had done that, and much worse, to them and their family, on an artichoke farm in Italy, years ago. Instead I just gave him a hug, pat him on the back, and closed the door on him.

So, I may as well finish up here, with you, oh god. Only one more sin left to confess, and then I will walk out front, and wait near the road for my executioners to arrive.

II.

After the massacre of the wedding party, and the crucifixion of the christian girl, I returned to my fortress, and paced the halls. I could not shake the numbness. It would not release me. I was stuck in the same state of detachment. I was above myself. I was behind myself. I could not get back inside. I was covered with a sort of panic that I would never return to my normal way of being. I never did, oh god, but thankfully the panic did eventually cease.

I couldn't sleep, and not for lack of being tired. It was just that, with this new frosty perception, I was hyper aware of my body, and how it functioned. Its mechanisms, in all their simplicity, were laid bare before me. I would get close to entering the haze of sleep, and my conscious mind would see its own demise on the horizon, and rebel, and wake me with a chill and a pounding heart.

When the sun rose, I went to see Kaeso. I told him I was eager to leave. He was clearly disgusted with my behavior the night before, and was eager to see me leave. He said he would arrange an entourage to escort me to Antioch. I told him that I wasn't going to Antioch. I had made the decision to return to Rome immediately, to see my brother. I needed to see Lucius. I needed to see him. I thought, oh god, that in his presence, I would most certainly feel again.

Kaeso told me that if I wanted to see Lucius, I wouldn't have to go as far as Rome. I didn't even have to go west, but east. Lucius and his court had been traveling, and were now in the city of Edessa, not a week away. I had become so wrapped up with the christian girl that I hadn't been paying any attention to the outside world.

Lucius had passed right by me. He had come to the far east to manage a new war he had started with Parthia. He had passed through Antioch, and not contacted me. He had avoided me. I should have been hurt, oh god. I knew that I should have been hurt. I felt nothing.

I told Kaeso to forget the entourage, to prepare me a horse, and provisions to make the journey to Edessa by myself.

III.

I took the eastward road, toward Nisibis, until I reached the imperial camp outside of Edessa. It was a hellish ride, oh god. I road the horse to death by nonstop travel through the desert. I walked the final two days, eating nothing but bread, and stopping to sleep for only an hour or so each night.

I was recognized immediately upon my arrival at the barracks. A guard informed me that Lucius was no longer in Edessa. He had taken his personal guard even farther east, to Harran, to visit the temple of Luna, and a whore house of world renowned, which was on the way.

I asked to be given a new horse, so I could begin the ride to Harran immediately. But I was told that the ranking officer in Edessa wanted a word with me before I moved on. It was Marcus Macrinus, Prefect of the Praetorian Guard, and as you and I know, oh god, the next Emperor of Rome.

Macrinus was a bundle of nerves when I met with him. He seemed nearly as off put as I was. We had a relationship back in Rome, and worked together during the purge of Geta, and even earlier than that, when Fulvius was still running things. I wouldn't say we were ever friends, oh god, but he knew me enough to know my character, and that he may be able to put it to use.

I told Macrinus that it was good to see him again, but that I was terribly eager to see my brother, and wanted to be on my way. He told me that he would give me the horse I wanted, and whatever else I thought I would need, if only I would just sit and listen to him for a few moments first. I curtly agreed, and asked him what was on his mind?

Macrinus told me first of his own recent troubles. They involved a popular soothsayer in Rome. A witch who was well respected, and whose visions were given much credence by many powerful people in the city. One morning she decided to up and have a vision of Macrinus, well known as a top member of Lucius's staff, as a newly crowned emperor, sitting in a cloud, dressed in flowing purple robes. She announced to any who would listen that Prefect Macrinus was destined to depose the Emperor, and take his place. Whatever the details of the vision were, and whatever the soothsayers motivations, it didn't matter, Romans were chatting about it as though it were fact. Word of the prophecy reached Edessa, and would in another day or so, reach Lucius. Macrinus was worried for his life.

"You'll tell him, won't you? You'll explain that what this witch says is utter nonsense, yes? Anyone who listens is a fool. I have no plans on the throne, and would never dare to. I am as loyal to your brother as you are." Macrinus said that he saw my arrival in Edessa as an opportunity for the empire. "Finally, the return of the only sane voice remaining that the Emperor will listen to."

I had been sent away by Lucius, but apparently I still had the reputation of being his closest, most trusted, advisor. "What of his mother?" I asked. "Does Julia Domna not keep him on a leash?"

"Not anymore." Answered Macrinus. "That poor old woman has been through so much. She's not fit to rule anymore. It's only appropriate that your brother has softened her powers. She was getting on his last nerve, and so now she's been retired to an estate outside of the city."

I should have been pleased. I should have been thrilled, oh god. I knew that I should have been thrilled. I felt nothing.

Macrinus continued, "But solitary thinking is dangerous in a leader. The emperor has changed since your exile. No one knows his mind. One is never sure who he will turn on next. He has made many enemies, at home and abroad."

Macrinus was studying my reaction closely. He knew me well enough, oh god, to know how bad of a gaming face I had. In the past, before this numbness, I would have surely fallen decisively on one side or the other. Either I would have chastised Macrinus for even thinking to question Lucius's methods, and he would still be able to back peddle from his boldness. Or, otherwise, I would have allowed my jealousies, and resentments towards Lucius, to stir me into collusion with Macrinus, and we could begin plans for a change of regimes. Either way, my opinions would have been obvious, and Macrinus would have known where I stood. He'd have been able to read my thoughts as plainly as if they were words written across my face. As I was, though, with that disease of emptiness still festering in me, their was nothing to decipher. I was a blank sheet of papyrus.

Macrinus tried another tactic to get a reaction out of me. "When we were in Antioch, so near to where you were stationed, in that christian village, I must tell you, I asked the Emperor if he would like me to send messengers. I asked him if he wanted to see you. Do you know what he said?"

I answered coolly, "I don't."

"He said that he couldn't bare for you to see him this way."

I asked curiously, but uncaring of the answer, "What way?"

Macrinus turned coy, and thought for a brief moment, then asked, "Have you heard about what happened in Alexandria?"

I told him, "I haven't."

"They put on a play. A popular group of actors, in the city. It made comedy of the Emperors gaelic way of dress, and lumbering way of carrying himself. They mocked his claims of self defense, as the cause for killing Geta. Outrageous, yes. A vicious lie, yes. But the Emperor's reaction was, let's say, disproportionate. We knew who the actors were, knew who was responsible for the play, but your brother wouldn't hear their names. He said the whole city was to blame, and so too, be punished. He brought nearly his entire eastern army to Alexandria. He invited dignitaries to greet him at the walls. He killed them all, and unleashed his army in the city for days to plunder it as we liked. That weepy fool, Cassius Dio, is claiming we killed twenty thousand in three days!"

I stared at him blankly.

Unable to gauge me, Macrinus teased, "Someone will have to intercede. For the sake of the empire, someone will have to do something."

I aloofly told Macrinus that he shouldn't worry. Lucius was not a superstitious man. He did not believe in the prophecies of soothsayers. He only believed in himself. I stood to leave, but I added something before I did. I regret adding this, oh god, for I believe the words I said kept me alive for longer than I would have liked to be.

Before I parted with Macrinus, I said to him, "Leave it to me. I will take care of my brother."

I believe now that Macrinus took these words as meaning I had planned to do what I did, all along. You may not know this, dear god, or believe it, but I did not plan on it. I did what I did quite off the top of my head.

IV.

It's not a hard thing to track and follow an imperial entourage. Especially one as raucous as my brother's. I spoke with some peddlers, and easily discovered what route they were on. I caught up with them on a road near Carrhae.

The guards noticed me approaching, and two scouts were sent back to intercept me. One of them recognized me, and had served under me during the purge. The caravan was called to a halt, and I was escorted by the scouts to the emperor's carriage.

When Lucius climbed out, I hardly recognized him. Not that he looked very much different, oh my Lord. A little heavier, and a little worn out around the eyes, his hair a little thinner, but he looked much the same. Regardless, it was like I had never seen the man before in my life. He looked at me and smiled. I thought, who is this stranger?

I got off my horse, and he hopped down off the carriage. We stood there, looking at one another. Him smiling, me staring blankly, waiting to feel something, anything. The guards all around were watching, and I think because of this pressure, Lucius finally took the first steps. He walked to me, embraced me, and kissed both of my cheeks. The guards applauded. Lucius wrapped an arm around my shoulder and presented me to them.

"My long lost brother!" Announced Lucius, and the guards hoorayed loudly.

I felt nothing.

Lucius ordered the caravan to dismount, and prepare lunch, while he and I went for a walk together into the rocky fields by the road. This was the spot where the great battle of Carrhae had taken place, hundreds of years earlier. Rome lost twenty thousand men in a day, oh god, and only killed a hundred Parthians. This land was bad luck for Romans. Only a fool of an emperor would have stopped his entourage here for a picnic.

We had been walking for ten minutes or so, and were far out of view of the guards. This would have never been allowed for just any visitor, but after all, I was the emperor's beloved brother. Who on earth was he safer with?

We spoke of how hot it was in the east, and he apologized hurriedly for not seeing me when he was in Antioch. Very busy time, he said. He asked how things had worked out with the christian uprising. I told him it had been squashed. He told me he knew that I could be counted on. Then he had to piss, and so we stopped walking.

He turned his back to me, pulled his dick out of his tunic, and started to pee on some rocks.

I looked at him. I looked at his shoulders, I looked at the back of his head. I hadn't noticed it earlier, the light hadn't been right, but he had a bald spot. Right at the very top of his head, he was loosing his hair. Could this be my brother? The one I spent so many years obsessed with? The one I lived for? Was that him there? That balding killer, taking a piss? I wanted to cry, but I couldn't. I felt nothing.

I asked him, "Why did you send me away?"

"What?" He pretended not to hear me over the splash of his piss.

"I asked, why did you send me away? Didn't you want me around? Didn't you love me?"

Lucius finished peeing. He stood silently for a while, his back to me, his dick in the wind.

"Yeah." He said finally, "I loved you. But no, I didn't want you around." He shook the last drops of piss from his cock, and laughed. "Love like yours is a drag to have around."

Lucius put his dick back in his tunic and began to turn, but I already had my dagger out, and before he could do anything, I stuck it in the center of his back. He looked at me over his shoulder with pain, and, god forgive the use of Lucius's own term, shock-horror. He finally got to taste his own cooking.

I pulled the dagger out of him. Lucius gasped, turned to me, and fell forward into my arms. I pushed him back onto his heels, and stuck the dagger down into his breast. I pulled it out, he stumbled back a step, and I stuck it in again. He fell away from me, and the dagger came out of his chest with a splash of blood as he did.

There were no words between us. I had pulverized his lungs, and he couldn't breath, let alone talk. He squirmed in the dirt, grabbing aimlessly at my boots, and suffocated to death, drowning in his own blood.

Still, god, I was no closer to feeling anything. In fact, the numbness had worsened. I looked at Lucius's pathetic body on the ground. I looked up at the clouds. I sighed, and knelt down beside my dead brother. I kissed him on both cheeks.

I reached into my mouth, pinched my tongue, and pulled it out as far as it would go. I picked up the dagger, and with one smooth motion, I cut my tongue off.

I felt something. Praise, god. I felt something.

The pain was atrocious, like boiling hot water filling my mouth. I screamed out uncontrollably, and it seemed like the screaming was the only relief I would be granted. But then, by way of miracle, or a handy mechanism of the body, I was freed from my anguish. I suddenly couldn't hear myself screaming. My vision turned gray, and then black. Even the throbbing pain was on the retreat. Then, like falling asleep all at once, my mind just slipped away.

V.

I remember once, oh god, when Lucius and I were still little boys, running around his room like two wild animals, jumping up and down on his bed. First we ran in a circle, around the edges of the room, leaping over furniture, me chasing him. When I'd get close enough to smack him in the back of his head, we'd change direction, and circle the room the other way, Lucius chasing after me.

As Lucius gained on me, and was a hands reach away from smacking me on the head, I came upon a small foot stool in my way, and I tripped over it. I took flight, and then crash landed, head first, into a hardwood chest of drawers.

I remember, oh god, laying on the floor, looking at my brother, looking up at Lucius, and him saying, "Go on, let it out. You'll feel better if you cry."

But I couldn't do it, oh god. I couldn't cry, I couldn't speak, I couldn't breath.

Lucius took my hand, and held it tight. "Cry, brother. Breath. You've got to breath."

I did not breath, and soon I was asleep.

VI.

When I awoke in the military hospital, Macrinus was waiting for me, sitting by my bed, sleeping, and snoring.

My mouth was stuffed with linens. I couldn't taste anything, oh god. I noticed that before I noticed that the tongue itself was gone. I must have lost a lot of blood, I was exhausted to the point that I couldn't lift a finger. The pain was there, too, and with every beat of my heart, I felt the grievous absence of flesh in my mouth.

I wanted to scream, but didn't have the energy, so I began to moan. The moaning felt very good, indeed, and I began to do it louder and louder. Soon Macrinus was awakened, and seemed happy to see my eyes open, and my gullet making noise.

Macrinus was a different man from the one I had met, not a day before. Gone from him was any sort of worry. He looked delighted to be alive. He looked like a man who just became Emperor.

Macrinus told me that he was very busy, much to do, but that he wanted to be the first to see me when I woke up. He explained that the guards had come upon me and Lucius, him dead, me nearly. The guards were unsure of what had happened, whether I had killed Lucius, or we had both been attacked by some hidden and now escaped assassin. In a panic they collected the two of us, and made haste for Edessa, and Macrinus's camp.

"I don't know how you gained the courage to cut off your own tongue, but I tell you, boy, it may have saved your damn life!" Macrinus chuckled, and pat my stomach. "Those guards would have killed you on sight, if they hadn't have found you a bleeding, disfigured mess. What man in his right mind could do that to himself? Truly genius, I give you a lot of credit. Quite the sacrifice you've made for Rome, young man, quite the sacrifice."

If I could have spoken, oh god, I would have told him how full of shit he was, and politely asked that he kill me.

"You saved your life in the field, and I shall preserve it at home. Tonight, I will choose from your brother's guard a man of little value. On this man, I will pin the blame of assassination. You will be remembered as a great hero, who lost his own tongue in loyal defense of his old Emperor. And as your new Emperor, I shall build statues to your honor." He never built me shit, oh god.

Macrinus stood, patted me on my stomach again, and said, "You rest. My doctors are the best in the eastern world. They've sewn your wound, and now all that's left is to heal."

Macrinus left me alone. In the silence of the room, the pain in my mouth gripped me twice as tightly. I began to moan. I felt a little bit of relief.

VII.

I lay in that bed, moaning and suffering, for the next three months, oh god. The wound became infected, and some disease caught hold of me. I was near death, day after day, until one morning I felt a little better, and the next morning, completely better.

Being sick for that long gave me plenty of time to practice not thinking. I focused on nothing but my body for the entirety of my illness. What have I been able to eat, what have I been able to hold in my stomach, what have I shit out, what have I vomited, how hot is my fever, how cold are my bones? This is all I thought of. I did not think of Julia Domna, I did not think of Lucius, I did not think of the christian girl, I did not think of the bastard that I was. I most certainly did not think of you, oh god. Not once, not even for an instant.

When I was healthy again, I got an apartment in Antioch, and lived off the more than generous pension that Macrinus had set up for me. Having no want or need to work, and being on the outs with my mind, I began to build my body. I spent another year in the east, doing nothing but exercising my body, day in and day out. I spoke to no one, out of choice as much as out of lack of a tongue. I visited prostitutes, I got into tavern brawls for the sport of it, and to feel something, and to be touched by another person in emotion. I'm sorry for this year of malingering, oh god.

I was disconnected from humanity in almost every way, and so was never informed of political news from Rome. Once though, while laying in bed with a whore, after services rendered, she was going on and on about some great woman who had come to Antioch. A fine woman, a woman of the old world, a woman of great beauty, and dignity, and compassion. She was a role model to every girl in Rome. She was the example of the goodness in the feminine spirit, and its strength. Of course, dear god, this whore was talking about the legendary, Julia Domna.

Julia had played the devastated mother after the assassination. Stories of her grief had become part of our canon as a people. This great empress, Julia Domna, who served Rome, and her husband, as an equal to any man, only to be rewarded by the gods with the brutal slaying of both sons. She was adored by the people, and among them her name became the very synonym of the word, mother.

But time had passed, and Julia Domna was hungry again for real power, not the mythical kind. She was in Antioch to conspire with her allies against the new Emperor, Macrinus.

An excitement struck me, oh god, like I hadn't felt in a long while. From the whore, I found out where in town Julia Domna and her entourage were staying. It was in a sprawling compound, under the protection of Julia Domna's sister, the equally cunning, wicked witch of the east, Julia Maesa.

I walked the perimeter of the compound that very night. It was heavily guarded, sure, but I was still who I was, and this was what I did. There were sewers, I could swim through shit. There were hypocausts, I could crawl through fire.

Once inside, it didn't matter if I made it out alive. All I wanted, oh god, was to see the look on Julia Domna's face when I got my sword through her heart. At last, I thought, I will truly penetrate her. There seemed a symmetry to it. Julia was simply next on my list. Three loves, three murders.

Thinking of love, oh god, made me think of the christian girl, and then, for the first time, I thought of you.

I returned to my apartment, and got my sword. I put it in a sack, along with the journal of my time with the christian girl, as much bread as I had, and an extra pair of boots.

I tightly tied the boots I had on, threw the sack over my shoulder, and began the two thousand mile walk to Rome.

VIII.

The walk took forty five days. On it, my mind was clearer than ever in my life. I found peace in it, oh god, putting one foot in front of the other. My body was strong from all of the work I had put into it in Antioch, and I was well prepared for the hardships of the road. In my darker moments, I lamented this, and in a way was wishing, all along, that the walk would kill me. It did not.

When it rained, I kept walking. When it stormed, I kept walking. I walked through open fields, miles wide, during violent thunder storms, and not once was I struck by lightening.

I swam across rushing rivers, and never came close to drowning. I swam across infested swamps, drinking stomachs full of stinking water, and I never grew ill. I swam through frigid lakes, and walked for entire nights in wet clothes, through freezing weather, and I did not become sick.

I stopped to buy a new pair of boots once, and bread and wine at several different times. Whenever I did this, I would make a big show in the market of getting the gold coin from my purse. I made sure that any scoundrels around were able to see just how much gold was in that little purse, and how easily they could get it from me, if only they were willing to shed a bit of blood. Namely, mine. Sadly, god, no one ever took me up on the bargain.

On one of my stops, the market was aghast with news that was rippling through all of Europe. Julia Domna was dead. Unable to ask anyone to give me the full story, I had to listen in on at least a dozen conversations before I had an idea of what had happened to her.

Macrinus had discovered her plotting against him in Antioch, and she was ordered back to Rome, where he could keep a close eye on her. Despite the protests of Julia's sister, who was becoming a very powerful woman in the empire, she was kept there, under constant supervision, essentially a prisoner.

It was under this house arrest, that Julia first began feeling ill. A full examination of her body discovered a lump of tissue on her breast. It was removed, and another was discovered. It was was removed, and another was discovered. Eventually they had to cut both of her tits off. After that she began refusing to eat, and then drink, and soon enough she was dead.

I took no joy in the news, god. Quite the contrary, it pained me terribly. I thought of Julia, that strong and horrible woman. That hurricane of a woman. I thought of her, old and wrinkled, butchered of her femininity, starving to death in her own stink. I thought of the life she had lived, and what she must have reflected on in her last hours, alone, wracked with suffering.

I found a quiet alley of the market, curled up in a shadow, and wept, and wept.

IX.

When I reached the outskirts of Rome, my thoughtless walkabout nearing an end, I realized all at once that I had no reason to be there. Why had I returned?

I ducked into a country public house, and sat down for a drink, and then another, and then another, until I was drunk. Rome was no longer home. I had no home. I began to weep, which was becoming a favorite pastime of mine.

Brother Wojslaw was there, oh god. He was in town on one of his missions, and was in that very bar, flirting with the barmaid. He saw my tears, and in them saw a chance to be the evangelist of god. He strolled over, with his drink and his pot belly, and sat down beside me.

"There, there, brother." He said, and put an arm around my shoulder. "It can't be all that bad."

I stopped crying. I sniffled, and looked up at Wojslaw with wet eyes. He smiled so warmly at me, that I began to weep again. He laughed at this, and pat me on the back. "Come now, son. What's your name?" He asked.

I opened my mouth wide, and showed him my stump of a tongue. His face became very serious. "I see." He squeezed my shoulder and said, "You have suffered terribly, haven't you?"

I stopped crying, for good this time, and wiped my tears away, and cleared my throat. I shrugged at Wojslaw, as if to say, "what did it matter if I had suffered?"

I chugged what was left of my beer. Wojslaw gave me the rest of his. "It matters." He said. "It matters to god."

What he said next wasn't important, oh my Lord. Yes, I think I realize this now. He could have said anything to me at that point, and I'd have believed him. If Wojslaw said he worshipped Jason, I may have started calling myself an Argonaut. As it was, he worshipped the man-christ, and so I became a Christian.

What affected me, was that Wojslaw was kind. He was kind at the exact right moment, and without knowing me, and without caring to know me. He saw that I was a human being, and that I was suffering, and that was enough for him to deem me as worthy of whatever comfort he could give.

In the kindness of this monk, I sensed the christian girl. And in the kindness of the christian girl, I had sensed you, oh god. This, in the end, is how I came to believe. Through others.

(Does anyone believe in you on their own, oh god? Is that why you made so many of us?)

X.

I have gone outside into the fresh air of the morning, dear Lord.

I have walked to the top of the monastery's western hill, where the road in from town ends. I can see that down the hill, at the edge of the valley, two men approach. They are on horseback. It's hard to tell for certain from such a distance, but the riders both appear to be one armed men.

This is it then, oh my Lord and savior. The end of my life. I'd list through all of my sins again, and apologize for each of them once more, but you've heard enough of that now, haven't you?

If I am afraid, it is only because I know that I am to die painfully. I know that it is justice that I die this way, and I will not ask that you spare me its torture, just that, you show me as much mercy as you did when I cut my tongue off. Or when I hit my head as a boy, playing with Lucius. Let the pain come, yes, and I will accept it, oh Lord. But let me go away from it quickly. That is all that I ask.

The riders are closer now, and as they make their way up the western hill to meet me, I can see that they are most definitely missing an arm each. Though they don't look exactly as they do in my dreams or memories, I have no doubt that this is the father and son from the artichoke farm. They are moments away, oh god. I pray that their vengeance is sweet.

The birds are singing. I used to listen to the birds, chirping with the morning sun, and my ears would hear the cries of suffering beasts. Starving, and urgently on the hunt for worms to eat. Desperate just to survive. They chirped, and I heard them fighting off predators, eager to ransack their nests and eat their eggs. But today, oh god, on this final morning of my life, to my ear, they are singing.

Amen.

THE END.

Made in the USA
Coppell, TX
17 September 2021

62541938R00090